"Wow."

Luanne whirled around to the source of the compliment, only to feel her heart about to explode out of her chest at the sight of Alek in a white dinner jacket and black bow tie, looking like something out of a James Bond movie.

Then she swallowed, wishing she had something to grab on to. Like her sanity. She watched as Alek came up to her and said, "I come bearing gifts."

She froze. "Alek. I—"

"—*would be honored to wear your mother's necklace tonight,*" he murmured as he lifted a strand of perfectly matched pearls spaced with small, brilliant diamonds, which he smoothly draped around her neck.

"Alek, I can't accept this."

"You're the mother of my child," he whispered against her temple. "If I want to give you an occasional gift, that's my prerogative."

She shook her head. "I can't be bought, Alek."

His smile didn't even waver as he leaned over, placed a soft kiss on her forehead. "Which makes the challenge all the sweeter," he whispered.

Dear Reader,

Happy (almost) New Year! The year is indeed ending, but here at Intimate Moments it's going out with just the kind of bang you'd expect from a line where excitement is the order of the day. Maggie Shayne continues her newest miniseries, THE OKLAHOMA ALL-GIRL BRANDS, with *Brand-New Heartache.* This is prodigal daughter Edie's story. She's home from L.A. with a stalker on her trail, and only local one-time bad boy Wade Armstrong can keep her safe. Except for her heart, which is definitely at risk in his presence.

Our wonderful FIRSTBORN SONS continuity concludes with *Born Royal.* This is a sheik story from Alexandra Sellers, who's made quite a name for herself writing about desert heroes, and this book will show you why. It's a terrific marriage-of-convenience story, and it's also a springboard for our twelve-book ROMANCING THE CROWN continuity, which starts next month. Kylie Brant's *Hard To Resist* is the next in her CHARMED AND DANGEROUS miniseries, and this steamy writer never disappoints with her tales of irresistible attraction. *Honky-Tonk Cinderella* is the second in Karen Templeton's HOW TO MARRY A MONARCH miniseries, and it's enough to make any woman want to run away and be a waitress, seeing as this waitress gets to serve a real live prince. Finish the month with Mary McBride's newest, *Baby, Baby, Baby,* a "No way am I letting my ex-wife go to a sperm bank" book, and reader favorite Lorna Michaels's first Intimate Moments novel, *The Truth About Elyssa.*

See you again next year!

Leslie J. Wainger
Executive Senior Editor

Please address questions and book requests to:
Silhouette Reader Service
U.S.: 3010 Walden Ave., P.O. Box 1325, Buffalo, NY 14269
Canadian: P.O. Box 609, Fort Erie, Ont. L2A 5X3

Honky-Tonk Cinderella
KAREN TEMPLETON

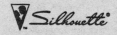

INTIMATE MOMENTS™

Published by Silhouette Books

America's Publisher of Contemporary Romance

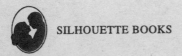

SILHOUETTE BOOKS

ISBN 0-373-27190-5

HONKY-TONK CINDERELLA

Copyright © 2001 by Karen Templeton-Berger

Visit Silhouette at www.eHarlequin.com

Printed in U.S.A.

Books by Karen Templeton

Silhouette Intimate Moments

Anything for His Children #978
Anything for Her Marriage #1006
Everything But a Husband #1050
Runaway Bridesmaid #1066
†*Plain-Jane Princess* #1096
†*Honky-Tonk Cinderella* #1120

Silhouette Yours Truly

*Wedding Daze
*Wedding Belle
*Wedding? Impossible!

†How To Marry a Monarch
*Weddings, Inc.

KAREN TEMPLETON,

a Waldenbooks bestselling author, is the mother of five sons and living proof that romance and dirty diapers are not mutually exclusive terms. An Easterner transplanted to Albuquerque, New Mexico, she spends far too much time trying to coax her garden to yield roses and produce something resembling a lawn, all the while fantasizing about a weekend alone with her husband. Or at least an uninterrupted conversation.

She loves to hear from readers, who may reach her by writing c/o Silhouette Books, 300 E. 42nd St., New York, NY 10017, or online at www.karentempleton.com.

To our own little Chase,
who was clearly a royal child in some other life,
and to his four nearly grown big brothers,
of whom we couldn't be more proud if they had been.

Chapter 1

He felt like an insect being scorched under a magnifying glass.

Barely nine in the morning, and already the west-Texas sun seared through Alek's knit shirt as he walked down the dust-filmed, airless street. Even on shaded porches, petunias drooped in their baskets, commiserating with the patches of bleached grass infecting otherwise tidy lawns, while dogs sprawled like dead things under whatever shelter they could find, dreaming, not of steak or rabbits, Alek imagined, but of cooling breezes.

Hottest August on record, according to the woman at the quaint little bed and breakfast where he was staying. *Just might be something to this global warmin' business after all,* she'd said, then told him the street he was looking for wasn't but four blocks away, he couldn't miss it. He walked slowly, squinting up through his sunglasses at hazed house numbers, uncomfortably aware of his loafers scuffing against the root-buckled pavement.

No one had recognized him. Thank God. True, he was more filled out, his hair both darker and shorter than it had been during his twenty-four-hour sojourn in Sandy Springs more than eleven years before. But unlike his hitherto reclusive sister, Sophie, Prince Aleksander Vlastos of Carpathia wasn't exactly unknown to the press. Not these days, at any rate. And Jeff Henderson had been the town's fair-haired boy, especially with his string of Grand Prix wins last year—

Up the street, a screen door slapped open. He stilled as a very pregnant woman, her dark, curly hair clipped up off her neck, came out onto the porch of a modest yellow-and-white two-story house huddled underneath a pair of ungainly mulberry trees. She paused to let out a half-grown, straw-colored pup too young to know how hot it was, then made her cumbersome, barefoot way down the gray steps. The dog tumbled down in front of her, nearly tripping her as she crossed to a hose neatly coiled by the outside spigot.

He said her name, softly. Prayed for the strength to get through this.

A sandwich of some sort clamped in one hand, she twisted on the water, then dragged the hose across the yard to a small flower bed, bending awkwardly to lay it among the wilted plants. Alek was still far enough away, his presence apparently camouflaged by the comfortless shade of a struggling cottonwood, that she hadn't noticed him. His wrist, only recently sprung from a cast, complained; absently, he rubbed it.

And watched.

Too-thin arms protruded from a sleeveless white T-shirt underneath a pair of baggy, thigh-length overalls tenting over her bulging middle. Scraps of hair floated around her jaw; she impatiently shoved one of them behind her ear, her wedding rings flashing in the sunlight. He was pressing an unfair advantage, he knew, but he needed these few minutes to observe, to adjust. To prepare.

To face his memories, one at a time.

She slowly straightened, absently kneading the muscles in her lower back, turning just enough for him to glimpse her face. His breathing damn near stopped altogether: she was far too pale and frighteningly gaunt, despite the obvious weight gain from the pregnancy. Yet, oddly, her limbs seem weighted, burdened with a deep, soul-weary sadness that tore at his heart.

He'd bet his life she wouldn't take his sudden appearance well. But he had his reasons for finding her, some of which would be readily apparent, even as others, still undefined, would perhaps become clear to them both with the passage of time. One reason, however, he would keep to himself. He'd hurt her once, albeit unintentionally; damned if he'd do it again.

Grief and regret clawed at the door to his consciousness, demanding an audience he refused to grant. Not now, at least. Now it was all he could do to make himself cross the street and face his past.

Not to mention a future that, six weeks ago, he couldn't have dreamed of.

Luanne shoved her bangs off her already-sweaty forehead, allowing as how it was only marginally cooler out here than in the unair-conditioned house. God bless little boys who could sleep no matter what, she thought, then forced down another bite of the packaged cheeseburger she'd just microwaved, the only thing with protein in it she figured she could manage, just at the moment. The ketchup helped some. Funny how she'd always taken her hamburgers plain, until this pregnancy. Nowadays she pretty much only ate the hamburgers as an excuse for the ketchup.

She grimaced at the sorry-looking flowers, half of 'em all burned up and papery around the edges. Why was she even bothering? Wasn't like she'd planted them herself, since they were here already when she'd rented the house two weeks ago. Like as not, unless they got some decent rain sometime soon, they were all gonna die, anyway—

Icy fingers squeezed her heart until she just about couldn't breathe. She clamped shut her eyes, waiting it out, wondering why, instead of lessening, the pain only seemed to get worse with every passing day. After more than six weeks, it still made no sense, even though she'd reminded herself of Jeff's death a hundred, a thousand times in a desperate attempt to assimilate the truth. Since the race had only been a practice session, there'd been no tape made of it, which she'd at first thought a blessing. Now she wondered if maybe witnessing her husband's death might make it any more real.

Except she knew, deep down, that this was the good Lord's way of sparing her and Chase from even more sorrow. Intellectually she knew the raw agony of loss would fade, that grief would eventually yield to acceptance....

The flowers blurred, the last bite of burger turning to cardboard in her mouth. Deep in her womb the baby stirred, sweetly oblivious. Luanne skimmed her fingers over her belly, almost reverently. She loved this child, who had taken so many years to conceive, with all her heart.

And she'd never resented anything so much in her entire life as she did being pregnant right now.

Guilt swamped her as she lunged for the spewing hose, jerking it up and across the yard, praying Odella didn't get it into her head to come outside—

A movement out of the corner of her eye made her spin clumsily around, nearly tripping over the dog. She didn't recognize him at first, what with his hair being shorter and him being older and the way he'd caught her off guard like that. On a cry of alarm she hurled the remains of the cheeseburger at his chest, then turned the hose on him, those being her only means of defense at hand.

"Luanne!" Alek tried to dodge the spray, as well as the dog who had dived for the burger before anybody might notice. "What the hell are you *doing?*"

Jerked back to her senses, she jettisoned the writhing hose and took off for the house, wanting to hide, wanting to die, wishing, wishing, wishing the nightmare would end—

Except Alek cut off her flight before she even hit the steps, whipping her around to face him. She could see little rivulets of water meandering down his just-shaved cheeks, dripping off a sharply defined jaw rigid with anguish; she flinched, even as her hands balled into fists of their own accord and began pummeling his chest.

"Why are you here?" she cried, flailing and beating and sobbing like a dadburned fool, dimly aware this was the first time since Jeff's death she'd given her emotions their head. Ketchup streaked the drenched shirt, she noticed, sending a perverse trickle of satisfaction through her fury. "You are the *last* person I want to see right now!"

"You think I don't know that?" His clipped, not-quite-British accent sent a herd of unwanted memories stampeding through her already muddled brain. She let out another sob, of frustration mostly, then suddenly Alek was holding her, stilling her hysteria, one gentle hand stroking her hair. "I'm so sorry," he whispered, and she shut her eyes, realizing he smelled like ketchup and pricey cologne and, after all this time and much to her extreme annoyance, a lonely twenty-one-year-old girl's fantasies.

She wrenched out of his arms, scrubbing the tears from her face, not sure which of them she was more angry with. Shame ripped through her that she should let another man—*this* man— touch her like that when she hadn't been a widow but a few weeks. "Then why'd you come? And why now?"

Lord, but she sounded like a bitch. Which was not like her, not at all. Mama had always said there was little point in letting the bad stuff get you down, that a person's outlook on life went a long way toward shaping his or her experiences. And Luanne, who had had more than her fair share of opportunity to put that philosophy to the test, had found it a useful one, more times than not.

Until now.

It was ungodly hot, she was pregnant, and her husband had died less than two months ago, leaving her with a devastated child who looked to her for bolstering when she could barely keep from drowning in sorrow herself. And then this man, whom she didn't ever figure on seeing again, shows up without so much as a by-your-leave at eight-thirty in the morning and with her looking like…well, like someone without much reason for fixing herself up anymore.

Luanne swiped a stray hair out of her face, trying not to shake. "You could have at least given me some warning, instead of scaring me half to death like that."

"I didn't know where to find you at first," Alek said, which she had to admit was a valid excuse, since she'd gone into seclusion with Chase immediately after the accident. But then he added, "And after I found out where you were, I was afraid..."

Luanne narrowed her eyes at that, straining to catch his meaning. "Afraid of what?"

Alek swept a trembling hand through his damp hair, not looking at her at first. And when he did, his eyes begged forgiveness.

"I want to meet my son."

And Luanne marveled, in a stuttering, not-quite-focused kind of way, that there had been enough of her heart left intact to now be crumbling into a million pieces.

Even as short as she was, there was no avoiding the bitter, brittle heat of those impossibly blue eyes as Luanne backed away, her arms laced over her unborn child. The pup circled her feet, worried.

"Jeff swore to me he wouldn't tell you."

Alek swallowed down the acrid taste of guilt, hating this moment more than he'd ever hated anything in his life. "I haven't known for long."

He watched as her eyes squeezed shut, as she drew in a shuddering breath, opened them again. Resolve now flickered in their bright-blue depths, if not ameliorating the panic of moments before, at least fortifying it. "And I don't suppose you'd consider pretending you'd never found out, would you?"

It was as close to begging as he imagined she'd ever come, and it nearly broke his heart. He dragged an arm across his wet face, then shook his head. "I think it's time we all stopped pretending, don't you?"

The prick to his conscience came hard and fast. How ironic to reach a point in his life where integrity should suddenly become all-important, only to have circumstances laugh in his face. But, in those cases where kindness and honesty seem to be mutually exclusive, which one was the more noble choice?

However, as he watched the clearly distraught woman in front of him, his ambivalence vanished. As did, apparently, some of her reticence. Her emotions as transparent as he remembered, Luanne stared at him for several seconds, then banged back the screen door. "Inside," she said softly.

Alek and the pup both obeyed.

Once in the house, she headed down the short hallway toward the back, leaving a trail of damp footprints on the bare floor. She flapped her hand toward a sparsely furnished living room off to the left. "You may as well take a load off while I go to the little girl's room." The words were almost flippant, the tightness with which they were spoken, anything but.

"Luanne."

She turned, her gaze wary.

"I'm not here to take Chase away from you."

Purple smudges lurked underneath eyes now gone expressionless. "And I reckon I have your word on that?"

"Yes."

He hadn't expected her to laugh, although the sound was as dry and dusty as the air outside. "And just what've you ever done that would give me any reason to trust you, *Your Highness?*" she said, then disappeared down the hall.

Point to her.

Every muscle in his neck strung tight, Alek wandered into the bare-floored living room, the pup clicking at his heels. A quick swipe at his backside determined that he was dry enough to sit stiffly on the edge of a cushioned wicker chair; the pup wriggled over to him, flopping onto his back to get his stomach scratched. Alek complied, distractedly, glancing around the white-walled room, glaringly bright from the sunlight streaming in through the pair of curtainless windows. A large ceiling fan droned lazily overhead, barely stirring the thick, stifling air; dozens of boxes, like an oversize children's block set, were towered throughout the room. Even from here he could see the labels: Books—History or Books—Bio or Books—Novels A–D. He wondered, vaguely, why she'd moved back from Dallas.

Back to where their child had been conceived, eleven years ago.

Alek leaned back on his elbows in the bleachers, oblivious to the sun biting through his cotton shirt and jeans, oblivious to everything save the sassy little Chevy Corsica spitting dirt from its wheels as it sped around the makeshift track. He'd come to Sandy Springs as he had to a dozen other small American towns—for the racing. Not the major venues, but the dusty little amateur tracks where tomorrow's stars were earning their stripes, where dreams burned through a young man's—or, less frequently, a woman's—veins as hot and fierce as the souped-up stockcars burned rubber. He'd heard about the track from someone in another town, fifty miles to the east. And about twenty-two-year-old Jeff Henderson, who was gonna win one of the big ones one of these days, you just wait and see.

Prince Aleksander was hardly the first royal to be bitten by the racing bug. In fact, he could name at least a dozen blue-bloods who either drove or sponsored various teams, traveling from track to track to satisfy their lust. In Alek's case, however, it wasn't the thrill that had lured him into the sport as much as his discovery that racing was a terrific common denominator. Socioeconomic barriers simply vanished, leaving nothing except shared euphoria—or profound disappointment—in their place. And that camaraderie had gone a long way, in the past nine years since his parents' deaths, to stanch a despair so chronic, he barely felt the ache anymore.

Still, it lurked inside him, just waiting for an unguarded moment to assault him afresh. So he kept on the move, racing pretty little cars and dallying with equally pretty women who understood not to expect emotional commitment. Not now, certainly. Perhaps not ever.

His grandmother, Princess Ivana, didn't understand. And he knew she worried. Which worried him, in turn. To an extent. But not enough to date anyone for more than a few months. Or stay in Carpathia for more than a few days at a time.

Alek had been gone nearly six months this go-round, didn't plan on returning for several more, at least. For some time he'd had the odd thought about putting together his own racing team. He had both money and connections; he could certainly get the cars. Now all he needed were drivers.

New drivers. Hungry drivers. Drivers who handled a car as

sweetly as the cocky, loose-limbed kid he'd been honored to watch tear up a track this afternoon.

Not that he was anywhere near ready to make an offer, or even to reveal his true identity. In fact, he was using his father's name—Hastings—rather than Vlastos, the royal name handed down through his grandmother and mother, masquerading as just another bored, wealthy European bumming around the States. Watching, taking mental notes, planning—those were sufficient for the moment. Alek took risks, yes, but he wasn't impetuous. Or incautious. Still, a frisson of exquisite, almost sexual pleasure had hummed through his veins at the way Jeff Henderson seemed to effortlessly balance passion with precision. Like Alek, Jeff clearly only took chances he knew he could pull off.

The young man said as much, when Alek approached him after the practice session to compliment him on his style. Determination glittering in his golden-brown eyes, the freckled, mustached redhead with the ready smile soaked up the compliment, then went on to say that he intended to drive professionally one day. Just as soon as he found a sponsor.

Alek just smiled, then took Jeff up on his invitation to join him later on for a beer and a bite to eat at the local watering hole, if he had a mind.

The night had already cooled considerably when Alek pulled his rented Porsche convertible alongside a monster SUV in front of the post-and-rail fence edging someone's pasture. A light breeze stirring his shoulder-length hair, he sat and stared for several moments at the neon-drenched adobe box from which blasted the sounds of a live country-western combo, complete with female vocalist with a set of lungs to rival any opera diva he'd ever heard.

Well. He supposed he was about to pay his first visit to a *gen-u-wine* honky-tonk.

Alek got out of the car, imagining that, unless he opened his mouth, he'd fit right in. The soft, button-fly jeans hailed from his Oxford days, as did the worn denim shirt, the sleeves rolled to just below his elbows. Of course, his two-week-old custom-made boots—when in Rome and all that—did creak a bit as he crossed the dirt lot, nodding in silent response to assorted "howdys" and "heys" along the way. His self-consciousness vanished, however, the instant he stepped inside the dimly lit bar choked with noise and body heat, his nostrils flaring at the tangled smells of hops, barbecue sauce, cheap perfume.

He scrubbed a palm across a jaw hazed with three-day-old stubble, then grinned, the despair retreating just a bit further into the shadows.

Cigarette smoke ghosting around the stage lights, the microphone squawked as the sultry-voiced singer asked for requests. A slightly slurred voice shouted out something rude: The dubious-aged, big-haired blonde, a blur of sequins and six-inch-long satin fringe, laughed and lobbed a zinger of a rebuttal in the heckler's direction, just as a piercing whistle sliced through the din.

"Alek! Over here!"

Alek squinted through the haze and bodies, then chuckled at the sight of Jeff Henderson standing atop one of the tables, madly waving his arms and grinning with youthful exuberance.

"Sit, sit," Jeff ordered after Alek threaded his way through the crush, then dropped into his own chair, edging back the brim of a ball cap with his thumb. "Beer?" Jeff asked. "Or something stronger?"

"Beer's fine." The singer launched forth into her next number. Jeff nodded, signaling to the pretty, dark-haired waitress a few tables away. "And food," Alek added, snatching the laminated menu from the metal stand in front of him.

Jeff grabbed the menu from his hand, plopped it back into the stand. "Menus are for wimps. You come to Ed's, you eat the barbecued ribs. Period. Side of slaw, side of beans. Biscuits to sop it all up with. Hey, sugar—" With another of those ingenuous grins, he reached up, playfully tugged at the hem of the waitress's apron. "What took you so long?"

A quick laugh met Jeff's remark—along with a good-natured smack on the hand with her order pad. A bit of a thing in a white sleeveless blouse and jeans, her nearly black hair waves framing classic features, the young woman was one of those rare creatures who, while undoubtedly pretty enough without makeup, could knock a man's socks off with it. Smoky shadow and carefully applied eyeliner only served to accentuate huge, ice-blue eyes, while she had the kind of mouth just made for red lipstick. And Alek knew more than one European model who would kill for that flawless complexion.

"It's about all these other customers, Jeffrey Eugene?" she said in an accent thick as treacle, then turned that bright, sweet smile on Alek, and he was startled to feel his blood stir in a way it hadn't for a long, long time. Flirting with waitresses wasn't Alek's thing. Nor was he flirting now. Exactly. But that smile certainly snagged his attention. Not to mention a libido he'd been sorely neglecting of late.

"Luanne Evans, Alek Hastings." Jeff took a swig of his beer, then another tug of her apron. "Be nice to him," he said in a stage whisper. "He's from out of town."

"Oh, yeah?" Her voice was breathy and weightless, like a child's. She picked up Jeff's sweating bottle, then wiped off the already-clean table, which made her breasts move in a way Alek found more than a little distracting. "From whereabouts?"

His eyes jerked to her face. "Carpathia."

"No foolin'?"

Alek leaned back in his chair, a smile tickling his lips. "You've heard of it?"

"*Some* of us," she said, obviously for Jeff's benefit, "actually paid attention in geography class." Then she rattled off not only the location of the tiny principality nestled in central Europe, but the square mileage, Carpathia's capital and the fact that their monarchy—now constitutional—had gone unchallenged for more than four hundred years. And while Alek sat there, at once flummoxed and extraordinarily impressed, she stared at him for a long moment, ignoring repeated entreaties from the next table. Then she crossed her arms underneath that pair of truly lovely breasts. "One thing bothers me, though."

"And what might that be?"

"What in *tarnation* are you doin' here?"

Alex smiled. Slowly. *Now* he was flirting, no holds barred. Her directness, her intelligence, her spirit—and, all right, her physical attributes—positively inflamed him, body and soul. "I thought I knew, up until a few minutes ago." The smile broadened as he leaned forward, let their gazes tangle. "But now I wonder if perhaps I've been led here…for reasons I've yet to discover."

Although she kept her smile in place, not even the darkness could disguise her blush. Alek felt duly—and justifiably—chastised. But before he could apologize, he caught the look on Jeff's face, one that clearly said *I want that* as he gave Luanne their orders, then snatched her pencil out of her hand. Playful, still. And respectful—Alek, took note—despite an attraction that Alek surmised had more substance than his friend was letting on.

"So, darlin'—when you gonna put me out of my misery and marry me?"

Ah.

But, apparently recovered from Alek's gaffe, Luanne only laughed. Carefully arranged tendrils grazed her cheeks when she shook her head. "Now, you know as well as I do that marrying you would be like marrying my own brother." She recovered her pencil, then popped him lightly on the head with it. "Wouldn't be natural." Then she sashayed off, giving them both an enticing view of the way her jeans cupped that extremely nice, perfectly rounded bottom, how her hair waterfalled nearly to her waist.

On a sigh, Jeff lifted his bottle of beer, peered at it with one eye closed. "Kinda makes incest look a lot more attractive, don't it?"

Alek chuckled, counting his blessings the young man had apparently missed Alek's lame, and ill-considered, attempt at a pick-up line. "You've got a thing for her, I take it?"

Squinting, Jeff tipped back his chair. "Oh, we tease a lot, Lulabelle and me—shoot, we've known each other since we were in grade school—but I don't suppose it would seem natural, like she said. But I'm here to tell you—" he nodded his beer bottle in Alek's direction before he took a pull "—I'd do anything for that gal, I really would. No matter what my dang-fool family thinks."

Alek frowned at the edge to Jeff's voice. "Meaning?"

The chair thunked back to the floor as Jeff leaned forward again. "Meaning, some folks seem to think where you live or what you do for a living is more important than you who are. Never mind that Luanne was the smartest girl in school—fact, if it weren't for her, I never would have gotten my sorry butt through algebra—or that, after her mama got sick, she supported the two of them for three years without askin' for a lick of help from nobody." Jeff shook his head, disgust pulling his mouth taut. "Galls the life out of me, sometimes, the way people judge other people, y'know? Well, damn it, *I* know what she's worth. If anything, she's far too good for the likes of ninety percent of the men around here, and that's a fact."

Although Alek had to smile at the young man's pup-protecting-his-mistress loyalty, something—a vague disingenuousness, perhaps?—kicked up the odd hackle or two. Nothing he could define, just an odd feeling that a smart person would do well to not take Jeff's easygoing manner at face value. However, applause for the singer, followed by Luanne's appearance with their food, stanched further musings. The waitress had a smile and hair ruffle for Jeff…and a cool, cautious head-nod and "Hope you enjoy your dinner" for Alek. She didn't seem angry or hurt, though, as much as…disappointed.

She moved off to another table a few feet away, chatting and joking with the patrons as if she'd known them all her life. Which she undoubtedly had.

Alek suppressed a sigh. Granted, he was used to getting what he wanted. In fact, most people would probably consider him spoiled. With good reason. Even so, he found no pleasure in using people or in taking undue advantage of his position.

Or in hurting feelings, if he could help it. That a woman working in a bar should be more thick-skinned was beside the point. Perhaps she had little choice in her place of employment. Perhaps she dreaded coming to work, night after night, fearing that, just because she was pretty and friendly, some moron might misinterpret her natural ebullience as a come-on.

Well, the least this moron could do was to attempt to remedy the situation.

She jerked, a little, when he caught up to her at the bar a little later. Although her lips curved into a smile as she deftly loaded drinks onto her tray, a certain guardedness immediately settled into those bright blue eyes—eyes that, nevertheless, had no compunction about meeting his.

"Everything okay?" she asked over the barrage of conversation cocooning them. "C'n I get you boys anything else?"

"I just wanted to apologize," he said, and the eyes went saucer wide.

"For what?"

"For offending you earlier."

She stared at him for a long moment, clearly having no earthly idea what to do with his comment. Then she yanked the tray off the bar, averting her gaze. "No offense taken," she said softly.

Only she turned back, the beginnings of a smile tweaking at one corner of her mouth. "But I appreciate you taking the trouble to apologize. That was real sweet of you. Most men... Well, it was just real nice, is all. Thanks."

And that should have been that. Except, for the rest of the evening Alek found his attention straying to the vivacious young woman with a laugh or smile or friendly word for everyone. If life had been less than kind to her, she certainly didn't seem to be holding it against anyone. And he acknowledged to himself that, in those few seconds between his apology and her acceptance, something in Luanne Evans's honest blue eyes had shot straight through to the cynicism knotted inside him, loosening it just a bit.

Edging aside the despair just enough to let in the barest trickle of something he couldn't quite define. An alien feeling, to be sure, but pleasant enough to make him think, *More, please,* to inexplicably draw him to whatever it was that kept Luanne Evans's smile so naturally, so constantly, in place.

To make him take the kind of chance he rarely did.

Jeff and he left together, around eleven. But at one in the morning—closing time—Alek returned, the parking lot now empty save for three or four pickups and a motorcycle the size of Poland close to the building. A storm had begun to brew:

wind slapped at his hair and shirt as the tang of imminent rain filled his nostrils. Thunder trembled in the distance, accompanied by lightning that pounced across the relentlessly flat landscape in an eerily beautiful dance. He put up the top, then cut the engine and waited, realizing the odds of his making a complete ass of himself were about as high as they could get.

The first enormous drops began to pound the dirt when Luanne and another waitress emerged a few minutes later. He saw the other woman poke Luanne in the arm, point toward him; Luanne glanced over, enough light spilling from the bar for him to see her hesitate, then shake her head and swat in his direction, before the two of them took off in a blur of raindrops and giggles across the lot to their vehicles, their purses held over their heads. In an almost comical synchronization, two doors opened, two women jumped into their trucks, two doors slammed shut. The other woman took off first, tires spitting gravel as she gunned the truck out of the lot. Then, on a teeth-rattling bellow of thunder, the skies split open.

Well. Nothing ventured, nothing gained, Alek thought on a bemused sigh as he reached for the ignition....

He squinted through the deluge at the sight of a figure clumsily hauling itself out of another pickup some twenty feet from Luanne's. Obviously drunk and yelling something indecipherable, the man lurched unsteadily in her direction. Alek froze, barely having time to wonder why Luanne hadn't left yet before the man jerked open her door.

Alek shot from the Porsche, reaching the old Ford just as the huge man lunged inside, groping like a bear for the obviously terrified waitress now huddled against the passenger-side door. Between the din from the storm and the other waitress's departure, she must not have heard the man's approach.

The walrus might have bested him in sheer mass, but at six foot one and nearly solid muscle—not to mention having sobriety and adrenaline on his side—Alek had the clear advantage. Greasy ponytail viced in one hand, the other twisting a massive, flabby arm into a tight hammerlock, Alek yanked the sputtering, cursing oaf out of the truck, keeping his grip iron tight as torrents of surprisingly frigid, blinding rain pelted them both.

"I take it," Alek shouted to Luanne over the downpour, "this man's attentions were unwelcome?"

A crack of thunder made her jump, but in the yellow glow from her truck's ceiling light, he saw her wide-eyed nod.

"Just checking." Alek then spun the drunk around, fully intending to connect fist to flabby jaw. Except, before he got the chance, the cretin let out a truly hideous belch, then splatted into the mud like a harpooned whale.

"What the hell?"

Alek's gaze shot to another man in a white T-shirt and jeans—middle-aged, balding, big-bellied—bending over the fallen one. Hands on knees, completely oblivious to the rain, the man let out a short, pithy expletive before he glanced up— still bent over—and stuck out a hand. "Hey. Ed Torres. The owner."

Alek returned the shake, blinking against the rain slamming into his face. "Alek Hastings—"

"Yeah. I know." Ed grabbed the downed man's chin, torqued his face from side to side. "One of those damn Simmons boys, looks like. Probably here for Earl's third girl's wedding, figured a little celebratin' was in order. Worthless piece of..." Shaking his head in disgust, Ed straightened, pointlessly hitched up his jeans, then glanced into Luanne's truck, rain sluicing off a face folded into a frown of genuine, fatherly concern. "Luanne, honey? You okay?"

She nodded, even though she clearly was anything but.

"Thirty-two years I've had this bar, and this is the first time one of my waitresses has been out-and-out accosted. I was just coming out, y'know, saw dogturd here headed toward Luanne's truck. Lucky you got here when you did." Worn features perked up into a grin; Alek thought he might have heard a chuckle over the next roll of thunder. "Yeah. *Damn* lucky. Hey—you mind gettin' his feet, helping me drag his sorry ass inside? Last thing anybody needs is this idiot back behind the wheel. He can just wait inside until the sheriff shows up. So you might as well...you know..."

Ed nodded in Luanne's direction. Offered a sodden, conspiratorial wink.

Alek wasn't sure quite how to take that. However, he leaned into the truck where Luanne was still hunkered by the far door, still obviously shaken. His heart did a slow turn he decided he'd best not think too hard about. "Would it be too presumptuous to ask that you stay put until I get back?"

Her breasts rose rather prettily with the force of her enormous sigh, disseminating a hint—over the lethal dose of secondhand smoke trapped in her hair and clothes—of actually rather nice perfume. "Looks like I don't have a choice, seeings Miss High and Mighty here—" she slammed the heel of her hand against the dashboard "—won't start. Again. Otherwise I would've been gone long before..." She bit her lip, hauled in a short, steadying breath as she looked away. "Thank you," she said, before her gaze met his, albeit reluctantly. "I'm much obliged."

Alek shrugged. "Can't take much credit, I'm afraid. But I can give you a ride home."

She stiffened, looked away again. "I can get one from Ed."

One hand braced on the roof of Luanne's truck, Alek glanced around the lot. Other than the Porsche and Romeo's truck, the Harley was the only vehicle in sight. He leaned back inside, determined to exude patience and sensitivity when, in fact, he was soaked through to his briefs and beginning to shiver and the adrenaline that had fueled his macho performance a few minutes ago had long since petered out. "It's pouring."

"I know that."

He was reminded of the time when, as a child, he and the palace gamekeeper had come across a wounded wolf in the woods backing the estate. The poor thing was frightened out of its wits, but still fiercely wary of the humans who only wanted to help it.

"Luanne?" Ed's exasperated voice cut through the pounding rain. "I know you're shook up and all, but this ain't no time for prevaricatin'. And you and I both know, you don't want to be riding on the back of the Hawg in this weather."

"I am not prevaricatin'!" Luanne shot back, then swiped

back a stray hank of hair, obviously nearer to tears than she cared to admit. "I'm...weighin' my options."

Alek and Ed exchanged a weary, universally understood glance.

"Besides," Alek pressed, trying to keep his teeth from chattering, "Ed has to stay until the sheriff shows up. And who knows how long that could take?"

Luanne's mouth thinned, her arms tightening around her ribs.

"Tell you what, then," he said. "You 'weigh your options' while I help Ed get this creep—" who was beginning to groan ominously at Alek's feet "—inside. Then you can let me know what you decide when I return. Would that be acceptable?"

Very slowly one dark eyebrow slid up. And, if he wasn't mistaken—yes, there it went—a corner of her mouth twitched as she gave a nod.

But damned if she wasn't sitting in the Porsche when he got back....

Loud, irregular clomping in the hallway behind him jerked Alek to his feet. Instinctively he faced the door, almost immediately finding himself the recipient of a mutinous, ice-blue glare, a sharp contrast to the tinges of childish pink that still lingered in the high-boned, freckled cheeks, the flattened mouth.

Then the mouth opened and spat out, "Who the heck are *you?*"

Chapter 2

Drowning in a gray T-shirt, baggy shorts and a pair of heavily-tooled, well-worn cowboy boots that wouldn't fit him properly for at least another three or four years, the kid seemed tall for ten. And thin—his wide, serious eyes enormous in the narrow face. Red highlights glimmered in uncombed brown hair that straggled below tops of ears and eyebrows, the color not dissimilar to Alek's at that age. Luanne's eyes, absolutely; but to someone who didn't know otherwise, Jeff's build, Jeff's coloring.

That nose, however, could be seen in any number of portraits lining Carpathia's palace walls, a feature that had chosen, as it had done with both Alek and his sister, not to transform until the onset of puberty. Jeff had shown Alek innumerable pictures of Chase as a little boy, and not once had Alek even suspected that Jeff wasn't the child's father.

Until now. Now there was no doubt, even if he hadn't already known. Without thinking, Alek rubbed the telltale bump on the bridge of his own nose, then rose and extended his hand, swallowing down the nerves that threatened to make him dizzy. His sister, the one who'd set up the refugee children's home in Carpathia, the one who'd married a man with five kids, had a natural affinity for children. Not Alek. Children had always made Alek feel awkward, off-kilter.

Especially grief-stricken children who just happened to carry his genes.

Awe and anger, both, nearly rendered him speechless. Except he managed to get out, "I'm Alek, Chase. A friend of...Jeff's."

Recognition flared in the boy's eyes. "Why'd you come? It's all your fault! Why'd you have to come and make everything worse?"

The room fairly shook as the child stomped out of the room, the pup whimpering at his run-down heels.

Luanne had just about made it back to the living room when Chase nearly mowed her down. She grabbed him by the shoulders, her heart cramping all over again when she saw the tears. Even before Jeff's death, he'd always cried more than any boy she'd ever known, and he hated it. *Hated* it.

But there used to be a lot more giggles than tears. And almost never any anger. During the past weeks, however, it was almost like someone had taken away her bright, easygoing child, leaving in his place this pile of screaming, snarling emotions and Luanne at her wit's end. It wasn't like she didn't understand, or even thought Chase was overreacting and should be settling down a bit by now. After all, she was just as much torn up as he was. But it frustrated the very life out of her that she couldn't make her baby's hurt go away. In fact, more than once she'd been downright panicked that she might lose it herself.

However, since there was nobody else to pick up the pieces if she did fall apart, that was a luxury she simply could not allow herself.

"Hey, baby," she said over her own thudding heart, combing his hair back from his face. "What's going on—?"

"Why's he here? Why'd he have to come? If it wasn't for him, Daddy'd still be alive!"

Luanne flinched. "That's not true, Chase Eugene Henderson, and I don't want to hear you say that again, you hear me?"

"But if it hadn't've been for him and Daddy making that bet—"

"Then Daddy would've found somebody else to make it with! Now you listen to me..." Her grasp tightened, making him look her right in the eye. Not that they hadn't had this conversation a dozen or more times already, but you would've thought the edge might've at least begun to wear down some by now. Instead, the pain only seemed to get sharper, brighter, like the way the sun hurts your eyes when you walk out of a movie theater in the middle of the day. "Your daddy had the racing fever long before he met Prince Aleksander. *Long* before. Oh, shoot, honey—I know all you can think is, if he hadn't've been racing, he wouldn't've been killed. But your daddy could've no more stopped racing than he could've stopped breathing. Racing's what he lived for." *And what he died for,* she thought as she sucked in a sharp, dry breath. "Whether we understood it or not—"

"You could've asked him to stop! Bet he would've quit, if you'd've asked him!"

She looked over Chase's shoulder to see Alek standing in the living room doorway, frowning, looking like he didn't know what to do with his hands. Or the rest of him, for that matter. "Should I leave?" he mouthed. And if she'd thought he meant *really* leave—as in leave her house, the state, her life—she might've nodded. Since she doubted that was the case, she shook her head, pinning him with her gaze. *Stay,* her glare said. *See how much my baby needs his mama, the only constant in his life right now.*

Except, she hadn't expected to see her silent demand register on Alek's expression quite so clearly. She lowered her eyes quickly to her son's face, stumbling over her words. "Wh-which is why I n-never asked him to."

Chase swiped at his cheeks. "That don't make sense, Mama."

"*Doesn't* make sense, and no, I know it doesn't. But, see— your daddy always said he'd do anything for me. So how could

I ask him to quit doin' the one thing he loved most? That would've killed him, or just about, because it would've killed his soul.'' She cupped Chase's jaw in her hands, wishing she could kiss away the owie the way she used to when he was little. "I just couldn't do that to him, baby."

Her son just looked at her long and hard for several seconds, then asked, "When's it gonna stop hurting, Mama? When's the pain gonna go away?"

His plea echoed through the icy hollowness where her heart was supposed to be. She pulled him into a fierce hug, pressing kisses into his unkempt hair. He didn't return the embrace, which tore her up inside even more, but no way was she going to let go. "I don't know, baby. All I know is, it will. Eventually, it will."

It had to, or her heart was going to plumb crack right in two.

Alek cleared his throat. Chase jumped, whirled around, plastering his bony little body against Luanne's.

"I didn't mean to upset you." He lifted his gaze, briefly, to Luanne's. "Either of you." His crisp accent only added to the edginess crackling around them. "I would never have done anything to purposely hurt your father. Or you."

Luanne touched Chase's head. "Alek got hurt in that crash, too—"

"Yeah, but he's alive! Daddy's not!"

"Chase—!"

"It's all right," Alek said gently, if a little stiffly. But like he was making an effort, at least. "I understand what he's feeling—"

"No, you don't!" Chase's hands fisted at his sides; his thin frame feeling brittle underneath Luanne's hands. "You can't!"

The child's pain vibrated in the room like a living thing as Luanne watched compassion flood features more sharply defined than a decade before, features she hadn't really gotten a good look at until this point, what with the sheer shock of seeing him again combined with all these emotions and worries clawing at her. She'd seen photos, of course, during the past decade, photos she'd deliberately sought out, just to prove to herself…

About a hundred miles underneath her misery, memories stirred and stretched. She refused to pay them any mind.

Then she noticed that Alek had crouched down in front of the boy, his hands resting on his knees, not even blinking when Chase recoiled further against her. She could tell Alek was as much at a loss as she was. Maybe more so. That he was scared, too, and maybe more than a little confused. His attempt to comfort a strange child when it was obvious the whole situation made him highly uncomfortable impressed her in a way she would not have thought possible ten minutes before.

And if it was a bad thing to feel a little relief at having someone take the burden from her shoulders, even for a minute, well then, the world would just have to deal with that.

"I lost both my parents when I was sixteen, Chase," Alek said. "And for a very long time, I felt as if someone had poured acid into my gut, it hurt so badly. So, yes…I do know what you're feeling."

Luanne decided Chase's silence was better than his arguing. Alek straightened up, a slight shake of his head halting her apology for her son.

Well. Now what? She kneaded Chase's knobby shoulders through his T-shirt for an awkward second or two, then turned him around and handed him a tissue from the pocket of her overalls. "Here. Blow."

"I'm not a baby," he grumbled, swiping his hand across his cheek.

"Did I say that?"

Chase glowered at her, but took the tissue anyway and honked into it, after which Luanne suggested he go get himself some breakfast.

"I'm not hungry."

"You need to eat something, honey—"

"I *said,* I ain't hungry!"

Irritation flashed inside her, so hot and fierce it scared her half to death, adding a walloping dose of guilt to her emotions. She'd never once laid a hand on her child. Yet now, when she most needed to have control over herself, there were times when it was everything she could do not to smack him for what, in any other child, she would have called out-and-out insolence. He knew how much she detested that particular backwoods expression, one that wealth and success had never been able to eradicate from Jeff's speech, either.

But this was not the time to call him on it.

"Fine," Luanne said in a shaky voice, turning her attention to the dog and away from the pair of astute silver eyes that she wished would just take their astuteness and go away. "But Bo is. So go fill his dog dish, then go on outside and play ball with him for a little while, before it gets any hotter."

To her amazement—and immense relief—Chase did as he was told.

Minor crisis resolved for the moment, she turned to the much bigger one standing far too close for her comfort. She did not wish him to find her wanting, which she feared he would if he studied her hard enough and long enough. But, oh, she was so weary. Crossing her arms, she leaned heavily against the wall. "I think it's pretty obvious Chase can't take any more stress right now." She looked at him directly. "And, frankly, neither can I."

Alek's mouth went thin and tight. "I'm not turning my back on my son."

"But you said—"

"And I meant it. I'm not here to take him away."

The determined set to his features told another story, however. "Then what, exactly, *do* you have in mind?"

A pause, then he said, "There didn't seem much point in formulating a plan until we'd talked things through."

Luanne had nothing to say to that, which seemed to rattle Alek. Again, he swiped a hand through burnished dark-brown hair much shorter now, though still long enough to defy taming. Just like him, she imagined. He glanced away, then back, his brow pleated. "I'm flying completely blind here, Luanne. I know the timing couldn't be worse on this, but…" His mouth twisted in frustration. "Chase isn't just my son. He's my heir. Not just to a throne, but a sizable fortune as well."

"We don't need your money." Might as well get that point cleared up, right now. "Jeff left enough for us to live comfortably on for some time. I finally got my degree, too, a couple years ago. Once I get my certification, I can start teaching as soon as this one's old enough to go into daycare." Another stab to her heart: she'd opted to stay home for Chase, had fully intended to do the same with the new baby. Now, however... "We won't starve, Alek."

"That doesn't change anything," he said quietly, and that set her to trembling all over again.

Her lip stung. She hadn't realized she'd been biting down on it. "Jeff's name's on the birth certificate." At Alek's stunned expression, she added, "I couldn't very well put down yours, could I?"

Her grandmother's old cuckoo clock chimed the half hour before Alek said, "I know I've done precious little to earn your trust, but please believe me—I only want to work out whatever's best for all of us. Granted, I don't have the slightest idea how to go about that, but we have to start somewhere. And the sooner, the better."

Luanne swiped at her nose with the back of her hand, trying to convince herself she wasn't trapped. Oh, Lord...the last thing she wanted to do was deal with any of this. But she was in no condition, physically or mentally, to put up the kinds of walls now that would only give Alek a reason to use his power and influence down the road.

She frowned. If she lived to be a hundred and ten, she'd never understand why Jeff had told Alek about Chase when he'd been so all-fired intent on Chase's real father never getting the opportunity to mess things up.

The baby kicked, hard. Luanne tried not to react, but there Alek was, right in front of her with his arms outstretched, asking if she was all right.

"I'm fine." She stood up straight to show him she didn't need his help, either long- or short-term. "So tell me—if it hadn't've been for Chase, would you be here right now?"

She couldn't read his expression. "To be perfectly honest...I don't know. Oh, I would have made sure you were all right, I suppose, but..." He ended the sentence with a sad shrug.

Well. Since it was obvious none of this was going to go away and leave her be, she let out a long sigh, then turned and waddled down the hall toward the kitchen, feeling like somebody else had moved into her body until the rightful owner came to her senses. "You hungry? I could fix you some breakfast—"

"Luanne?"

She told herself it was only because she was so on edge that his voice sounded like a caress. That it was only because she was seven months pregnant and a new widow that anything of Alek Vlastos had any kind of power over her at all. But the fact was she'd never felt more alone in her life. Or more helpless. And right this very instant a large part of her wanted to walk smack into those big old strong arms and cry her eyes out.

However, since she had no earthly intention of letting that happen, she simply turned, one hand on the kitchen door frame, and said, "What?"

"I could be angry as well, you know."

Holding back the tears, she swiftly turned and headed on into the kitchen.

Holding back the memories of that night eleven years ago was something else again....

Sitting in the Porsche in the pouring rain, wondering if she'd truly gone and lost her mind, Luanne could just make out Alek's mad dash from Ed's to the car. Not that running did him any good, seeing as he was already soaked through. Unmindful of the wet leather seat—he'd left his door open—he scooted behind the steering wheel and slammed shut his door, shoving one hand through his dripping hair which, combined with his shadowed jaw, made him look almost...wild. For a brief moment she thought he might shake himself like a dog, finding herself mildly disappointed when he didn't. Her gaze then lingered on his body just long enough to determine that what the wet shirt and jeans had molded themselves to was lean and hard, and that this was having a profound and disturbing effect on her good sense.

She quickly looked away. Here her nerves had just settled down some, and then all that lean, male hardness had to go sending them haywire all over again.

Not, however, because he frightened, or even intimidated her, despite his being more refined and classier than any man she'd ever met, let alone ridden alone in a car with. Oh, no. What had gotten to her, from the moment they met—and what had, paradoxically, made her turn away when she'd seen his car in the lot—was what she'd seen in his eyes.

Working in a bar the way she did, Luanne had gotten real good at discerning, from a person's body language and the expression in his eyes, not just whether he was dealing with some trial or other, but what that trial might be. She wasn't sure whether this ability of hers was a gift or a burden, but her knack for pinpointing people's troubles had proved to be extremely useful on more than one occasion.

Maybe she was only twenty-one, but she'd already seen for herself any number of times that there was a lot of truth in what folks said about money not buying happiness. An adage she suspected held especially true in this case. Off and on throughout the evening she had found herself contemplating Alek Hastings, coming to the eventual conclusion that this was a man with great emptiness inside him, despite his surface cheerfulness. She had not, however, arrived at this diagnosis because she had any special powers to read a person's mind, as much as this was a general truth she'd learned about men with wanderlust.

Unfortunately, neither of those things stopped her from being powerfully attracted to the man, nor from thinking about things she shouldn't.

"All recovered now?" Alek now asked, interrupting her thoughts. She managed a nod, not trusting her voice. The rain had dropped the temperature considerably; even wearing the sweater she kept in the truck, she wrapped her arms around herself, only to realize how cold he must be, being wet and all.

"Where you staying?" she asked, only to feel her face immediately flame at how he might interpret her question. "What I mean is, you're gonna freeze to death if you don't get outta those wet clothes...."

That got a chuckle. Now even the roots of her hair felt hot, propelling her next words out on an exasperated rush. "I just meant maybe you might be more comfortable if you changed into dry clothes before you took me home. That's all."

"I know that's what you meant," he said, and she could hear the grin in his voice. "And yes, I think that's an excellent idea, since I don't much relish the thought of catching pneumonia. I'm staying at the Come On Inn."

She burst out laughing. "You have got to be kidding!"

In the glow from the dash, she saw another grin split the dark contours of his beard-hazed face. "So sue me. I'm a sucker for tacky motels."

"Well then, buddy, you are definitely staying at the right place. How on earth do you get any sleep, though, is what I want to know. I hear the walls are notoriously thin."

His resulting low laugh sent a whole swarm of warm, foolish thoughts spiraling through her. "Earplugs."

She found herself chuckling back, wondering at how she could feel so relaxed with her nerves all lit up the way they were. Then she allowed as how the Come On was on the way to her place, and off they purred in his fancy car, his headlights spearing the night as the windshield wipers whispered away the rain. He handled the car like it was part of him, with finesse and confidence, but no bravado, for which she and her twanging nerves were immensely grateful.

Alek popped a cassette into the player on the dash. A minute later, lush, glorious music filled the car.

"It sounds like Beethoven," she said deliberately, "but I don't recognize it."

She saw the flinch of surprise, his hands tighten, just barely, on the wheel. "It's the Choral Fantasy. He used this as a warm-up for the Ninth Symphony."

"Ah." Luanne sighed and let herself sink into the glove-soft leather, shutting her eyes, silently thanking her mother for sending away for one of those cassette sets of *The World's*

Best-Loved Melodies for $24.95 when Luanne wasn't but a little girl. "It's beautiful."

Which would have been the cue for most men to say, "So are you," but he didn't. Instead he said, "So tell me—when that jerk opened your car door, why didn't you pop out the passenger side and run back to Ed's?"

"Can't," she said on a shrug. "That door hasn't worked since probably 1976."

"Never mind the engine?"

"Oh, the engine's all right, usually." Then she laughed. "Hey, I bought her off of Fred Sellers for two hundred bucks, what did I expect? And Jeff keeps her tuned up for me for free. Ordinarily Flo and I get along just fine."

"Flo?"

"The truck. Which reminds me—don't let me forget to call Jeff when I get home, have him go over and see what's wrong with her."

She thought she saw Alek do one of those things with his jaw that men do when they want to ask you something that's none of their business, but they were pulling up in front of his room at the Come On, anyway, which Luanne figured was probably fortuitous.

He wasn't gone five minutes, during which time the storm pretty much played itself out. When he returned, he was wearing a serious bad-boy leather jacket over fresh jeans and a plain white shirt, open at the collar, that showed off his dark complexion quite nicely.

Luanne reminded herself that staring was impolite.

She also reminded herself, as she directed Alek onto the dirt road that led to her trailer on the Carlisles' property, where she lived rent free in exchange for her tutoring their kids during the school year—which was more of a challenge than she'd ever admit to the children's parents—that she was not in the habit of inviting strange men into her house in the wee hours of the morning, not even those who had come to her rescue. Heck, she didn't even invite men she *knew* inside her trailer. Bad enough fending them off in their trucks.

And if the rest of the ride from Alek's motel had passed in

silence, or been filled with dribs and drabs of stilted, boring conversation, she supposed she wouldn't be tormenting herself like this.

But it hadn't. And because it hadn't, it struck Luanne that she had been sorely neglecting herself of late. And then there was this out-and-out sexual attraction that was making her itchy all over and her blood purr like the Porsche's engine. So by the time they got to the trailer, and Blue, the shepherd mix who'd shown up on her doorstep last year, had made a mad dash out of his dog house for the car, barking his fool head off, she had just about twisted herself inside out with her ambivalence.

Then she looked up and saw her home for what it was—a tacky single-wide with fake wood paneling and fifteen-year-old gold shag carpeting besides.

Alek cut the engine. Luanne leaned out and told Blue to go on, git, which he did. Then she sat there, smelling Alek and listening to her heart stutter, reminding herself that she was not an impulsive person, and that expressing even a friendly interest in this man was very possibly the most impractical, illogical thing she could ever do. Except, right on the heels of that thought came the equally compelling argument that life was awfully short and unpredictable and here was an opportunity that, in all likelihood, would never come her way again. And that tacky though her place might be, it still beat the Come On all to heck.

Staring straight out the windshield—she somehow couldn't bring herself to look at him—she said, "I don't suppose you'd like to come in for a little while? For a glass of iced tea or something?"

Silence followed, and she thought, *Oh, Lord, I have gone and done it now,* except then Alek asked, very softly, "Are you sure?" and her heart bumped even harder in her chest as she replied, still not looking at him, "Yes."

Then Alek leaned over, his smooth, elegant fingers carefully bracketing her jaw, turning her to face him. And oh, my, how her insides went all liquidy and warm. The clouds having moved off, silvery moonlight flooded into the car, accentuating what was easily the most handsome male face she'd ever seen. A handsome male face that was now within easy kissing distance, she realized. His scent mingled with that of the cool, rain-washed air as his fingers grazed her face with more gentleness than she'd ever thought possible from a man. And she thought, *Oh, dear Lord—!* but that's as far as the thought got when Alek whispered, "It's very late."

Oh.

All she could do was nod, not having the wherewithal to know what else to do. He was giving her an out, she realized. So she should feel neither rejected nor disappointed, but grateful for his concern for her person and reputation.

Except he leaned just the tiniest bit closer, now clearly intent on kissing her, which both confused and delighted her. Then he hesitated, just as clearly waiting for her to give the go-ahead. So she edged a little closer, too, closing the gap between them, and then she heard herself sigh as his lips touched hers. It was a soft, sweet kiss, not at all what she might have expected from someone who she imagined had known more than a few women in his time, but all the more arousing for the tenderness of it.

There was a lot to be said for a man restraining himself, she thought as the first, tentative contact blossomed into something with a little zing to it. Never before had a man touched her as if she was something rare and precious and delicate, something to be cherished, not wrestled into submission. And when the kiss ended, instead of feeling her usual sense of relief that the ordeal was at last over, she felt a sense of wonder, as if something magical had happened. Oh, it was silly and girlish to feel such a thing, her practical self knew that, but magical moments were few and far between in her life, and she saw no reason not to clutch this one to her heart.

And while she was thinking on all this, she realized Alek had gotten out of the car and was standing by her open door. Slowly, as if in a dream, she gathered her wits and purse, sure by now he could hear her heart pounding in her chest. But then she got a good look at his face, which seemed to be filled with all manner of confusion, and it was only then that it occurred to her that he had yet to answer her question.

"If I accept your invitation," he said, all seriousness, "I would be no better than the man you thought I was earlier this evening."

Well now, that was certainly a good argument. Only she heard herself say, "It was only for a glass of tea...."

He snagged her chin in his fingers, his eyes blazing in the moonlight.

"Was it?" he asked, and she felt her skin go warm that he should have guessed her innermost thoughts when she herself hadn't even had a chance to take a good look at them yet. But it was true: crazy though it might be, this was the only man she'd ever met that she'd been the least bit inclined to let see her naked. To touch her in places she didn't normally like to be touched. That he was one step removed from being a complete stranger, that she'd had colds that had lasted longer than this relationship would, and that neither of those things particularly bothered her, made no sense.

"I guess it wasn't," she heard herself say, nearly stunning herself with her own boldness, only to turn and walk away, her palms cool and damp against her hot cheeks.

"That hardly seems fair to you."

She twisted around, her laugh sounding a little tinny to her ears in the breeze smelling of clean air and damp soil and the sage plants that grew wild around the trailer. "I stopped believing in *fair* when I was five years old. I do, however, believe in making the most of whatever opportunity life seems interested in tossing my way."

And there are times when I think I might die from the loneliness.

The thought had popped up like a jack-in-the-box, nearly making her flinch. Generally speaking, she liked living alone. Preferred it, in fact. Not once that she could recall had she ever felt lonely....

Until this very moment.

Alek was somehow standing in front of her—when had he closed the space between them?—his breath sweeping over her temple before he placed a soft kiss on her forehead. "And I'm not the sort of man," he whispered, "to take a woman up on an offer she'll undoubtedly regret."

A real prince, she thought as she backed up and looked him right in the eye, even though her insides were shaking as badly as Flo navigating a country road. People would say she'd plumb lost her mind, and they'd be right. Whether what she suddenly, desperately wanted was right or wrong, whether her desire—such a puny word for what she was feeling—stemmed from wanting to stanch the gaping hole of longing inside him or her, she had no idea. But whatever this was, it had taken on a life of its own, as palpable and uncontrollable and unstoppable as the rain or the wind or the moonlight. "If you didn't want to take me to bed, why'd you come back tonight?"

He studied her quite carefully for some time before he said, "I'm not sure, to tell you the truth. I just..." His breath left his lungs in an exasperated sigh. "I just know I don't want to hurt you."

Well, she thought on that for a bit, and what she decided was that a man who had that much trouble putting the make on a girl could probably be trusted. So she lay her hand on his rough cheek, just the feel of him enough to send prickles of longing skedaddling through her blood.

"I am twenty-one years old," Luanne said in a voice stronger than she felt. "I have lived on my own since I was seventeen. I survived my father's abandonment when I was five and I took care of my mama for three years when she was sick. I have received two marriage proposals, neither of which I was inclined to accept, nor do I plan on marrying until I have completed my college education and begun my career as a schoolteacher."

She lowered her hand to his chest, feeling his heartbeat pick up the tempo underneath her trembling fingertips. "I do not consider myself an impetuous person, Alek. And I do not pretend to understand why I am so attracted to you. But I am of the considered opinion that I am perfectly capable of not only deciding whether or not to enter into a relationship, even a temporary one, but of handling any consequences that may arise from my decision...."

"Luanne? Are you all right?"

Rudely yanked back to the present, she whipped around to meet Alek's gaze, eerily similar to what it had been that night in the past. Knotting her arms across her belly, she shook her head, as if trying to dislodge the memories.

It didn't work.

"Just got to thinking, is all," she said at last, offering a lame attempt at a smile. "My mind tends to wander these days."

When he looked like he might reach out, she quickly moved to the refrigerator, plucking a can of orange juice from the freezer and swallowing past the lump in her throat. Maybe she'd been able to tuck her memories away in the very back of the bottom drawer of her consciousness, where they'd lain, undisturbed and unmissed, for more than ten years. But try as she might, there was no way to hide them completely, to pretend that things had happened differently. The fact was, she had prodded Alek into the affair, knowing full well nothing permanent could come of it. She hadn't expected anything more. She hadn't *wanted* anything more, not then. She'd said she'd deal with the consequences, and she'd meant it.

So she'd best be about dealing with them, hadn't she?

Chapter 3

In a daze, Alek watched Luanne make up the frozen juice as he scanned the sunny, white kitchen, wondering again why she'd left Dallas. While the house was spotless—no surprise there—even a quick perusal revealed the chipped paint on the cabinets, the worn gold-flecked linoleum, the out-of-date appliances flanked by cookbooks and glass jars holding pasta and rice.

He self-consciously crossed to the aluminum-framed screen door to watch Chase half-heartedly toss a tennis ball for the dog in the weed-choked backyard. The scene he'd just witnessed between Luanne and Chase had nearly been his undoing, coagulating his emotions into an opaque mass at the base of his throat. If he'd had any doubts at all about Luanne's feelings for Jeff, those had vanished like a puff of smoke on a windy day…only to replaced by something that felt suspiciously, and cruelly, like envy.

And an even stronger urge to bolt.

But his bolting days were over. All his adult life, Alek had shunned responsibility—personal, emotional, social—for reasons he'd never been able to define, any more than one can define one's instinct for survival. But he'd also grown tired of feeling rudderless, of having no focus to his existence beyond the pursuit of a series of momentary gratifications. So, even before the accident, he'd begun the delayed—and not nearly as arduous as he would have thought—task of growing up. He'd all but given up the racing. And the women. In fact, he'd been celibate for longer than most men would readily admit, not a little surprised to find a certain…serenity in abstinence he wouldn't have believed possible even a year ago. The throne would be his, sooner or later—not even his indomitable grandmother would live forever—and duty beckoned. Or, in his case, bellowed. Carpathia might be small, but his country's stability in an area of the world subject to constant turmoil could not be underestimated, and the prince at last fully understood—and accepted—the importance of his role in years to come.

And that role included protecting those whose responsibility came under his care, whether he—or they—sought it or not.

"Here." Alek turned to see Luanne holding out a glass of orange juice. Her hand was shaking. "Freshly reconstituted."

He took the juice, starting slightly when Luanne suddenly flapped at his shirt. "Give that to me so I can wash out that stain before it sets."

"You don't have to—"

"Hand me the dang shirt, Alek." When he still hesitated, she said, "I have to keep busy, keep moving or I'll go out of my mind."

So he set the juice down on the counter and stripped off the shirt, which she snatched from him, dunking it a moment later into a small basin of suds in the sink, her movements agitated, jerky.

Her son's, however, were another story, Alek noticed as he returned his attention outside. Seated cross-legged in the browning grass underneath a quiescent sycamore, Chase's anguish abraded a wound inside Alek still raw after all these years. His sister had been about Chase's age when their parents died in that plane crash; he remembered watching her muddle through her grief, his own sense of loss rendering him virtually useless. And their grandmother had been heartbroken at the loss of her only child. So the three of them had spun in their own sad, separate orbits, unable to offer—or even accept, really— much in the way of solace. Alek was determined not to let history repeat itself, even if he hadn't a clue how to go about it.

"Chase misses Jeff terribly, doesn't he?"

Luanne's silence behind him was excruciatingly eloquent. He turned, something inside him splintering into myriad white-hot shards at her ravaged expression. Then she averted her eyes, scrubbing the shirt so hard, he feared for the skin on her hands.

Alek closed the distance between them, aching to touch her again, knowing he would be rebuffed if he did. Pride churned through this woman's veins where mere mortals had blood, coloring her actions—and perceptions—far more than her heartache. This time, however, he suspected she'd just about used up even her considerable resources for bouncing back. Despite her valiant attempts to sound on top of things, she couldn't mask the sense of defeat that had obviously taken up bone-chilling residence in her soul.

"Luanne," he said, choosing his words with care, "I have no intention of trying to replace Jeff. I won't…come between the boy and the man he knew as his father." Her back still to him, she nodded stiffly. Alek turned again to the doorway, willing his lungs to work. "I never meant to be the bad guy in all this."

The refrigerator clicked on; outside, the dog yapped for Chase to toss him his ball. He heard Luanne wring out the shirt, plop it into something, then come up beside him. "Jeff got the mutt for Chase's birthday," she said quietly, swiping back her hair with her damp hand. "Since Blue finally died of honorable old age last winter. There are days I swear if it hadn't been for that dog, one or both of us might not have made it." Her gaze flicked to his, then away. "There aren't any 'bad guys' in this, Alek. I made a series of decisions based on what I thought was best at the time. Lettin' myself get all caught up in regrets now is not only pointless but a waste of energy."

He didn't believe her for a minute, but he nodded anyway, then took a sip of the juice, shoving all the things he could never say to the back of his brain. "What happened to the house in Dallas?"

"Sold it." She shifted the plastic basin so it rested on one of her hips.

"Why?"

"Because it was too big. Too fancy. I hated Dallas. I'm a small-town gal. Big cities are okay to visit, but living in 'em gives me the willies. Besides, I want my children to have a normal life, y'know? I want 'em to go to public school and be able to hang out with their friends and go ride their bikes without having to be afraid they might get kidnapped or something."

"You were afraid for Chase?"

"From time to time. Not that Jeff knew. But I always felt, in that big house, we were sitting ducks, especially with him being gone so much. I had no idea—" Her lower lip caught between her teeth for a moment. "I know this sounds real disloyal, but I honestly never dreamed Jeff's career would take off the way it did. I figured, y'know, maybe he'd have a few races, grow out of it, come back home and settle down...."

She rubbed her cheek with her shoulder, swallowed. "I've spent the past ten years of my life bein' scared, holding my breath every time Jeff left for another race, every time Chase went out to play. Don't get me wrong—I miss that man more than I ever thought I could miss another human being. But in a way, now that we're back home, I finally feel like maybe I can breathe again."

She looked at him, tears glinting in her eyes. "Then you showed up."

The screen door slammed behind her as she waddled out and down the steps to hang up the shirt on the clothesline outside.

And Alek stared after her, his hand tightly fisted around the glass, once again thrown back into the past....

The screen door slammed shut behind Alek as he followed Luanne and the dog into the stifling trailer. She hurried to open all the windows to let in the cooling breezes, muttering something about popping into the shower to get the godawful cigarette smoke out of her hair, she wouldn't be but a minute.

Damn. If he'd possessed even a grain of sense, he would have driven away and not looked back. That she trusted him not to leave—that she trusted him, period—he found little short of stunning.

When was the last time he'd been this conflicted about sleeping with a woman? Bloody hell—he'd never expected her to come on to *him,* to do this…this about-face just when he'd decided nothing was going to happen. Or that he should suddenly have an attack of conscience about the whole thing.

Alek heard the shower go on; he let out an enormous sigh, swiftly followed by a groan. All right—so he wanted Luanne Evans more than he'd ever wanted another woman, a realization he found at once frightening, exhilarating and incredibly perplexing. But he'd always, always, been the master of his emotions when it came to his relationships. A state of affairs that had been blown entirely out of the water by the mixture of vulnerability and honesty and goodness now standing naked on the other side of a very thin wall.

Oh, dear God.

Alek dropped onto the futon sofa in the minuscule living room, on some subliminal level taking in the bright pillows and framed prints by assorted Impressionists—Luanne's attempt, he supposed, to bring cheer to the dark, paneled walls and worn furniture.

Then he noticed the books. Thousands of them, it seemed, neatly corralled in several cheap bookcases. Intrigued, and momentarily distracted from the problem at hand, he got up to inspect the case nearest to him. A hodgepodge, to be sure— everything from history to science to religion to novels of every conceivable genre, mostly paperbacks, but some hardbacks as well…

"Mama always said people are more inclined to take a person seriously who is widely read."

Alek looked up to see Luanne towel-drying her hair, her figure hidden underneath what looked like a man's shirt worn over white shorts. As he suspected, she was just as beautiful without her makeup. But what knocked him for a loop was the graciousness she exuded, a sense of being completely comfortable with who she was.

Willing his hammering heart to calm down, Alek glanced back at the bookshelf, tugging out a copy of Hugo's *Les Misérables*. In French. "In...more than one language, I take it?"

She shifted the towel to another section of hair, shrugged. "Mama was part Cajun, so I learned French early on. Or her version of it, leastways. Took four years of it in high school, too."

One eyebrow lifted. "Are you fluent?"

"Pretty much. Although I have the world's worst accent, which you can imagine," she said on a laugh, which immediately dimmed to a soft smile. "At one time I thought I might even apply for one of those student exchange programs, y'know? Except then Mama got sick..."

Her eyes lowered; she rubbed harder at her hair. Ignoring the prick to his heart, Alek leaned one elbow against the bookcase. "And was your mother right? About people taking you more seriously?"

That got another laugh. Her garnet-red nails glistened as she skimmed them through her hair. "To be honest—" she frowned, gathered up the ends of her hair in the towel again "—I can't say as I've found folks around here have been all that impressed, no. I think they see me as some kind of misfit, if you wanna know the truth. Heck—" She tossed the towel over her shoulder and tramped over to the refrigerator. "One of the advantages of livin' way out here—" she yanked open the refrigerator "—is that I can play my classical music loud as I want, nobody's gonna say boo. Oh, shoot—I forgot to make tea before I left."

She grabbed a tray of ice from the freezer, then a pair of purple plastic tumblers from a cupboard. Clunking several pieces of ice into the tumblers, she nodded toward an unopened bottle of Coke sitting on the counter. "This okay?"

Alek nodded, feeling slightly as though he were caught in a whirlwind, then asked, "So what do you like to read most?"

"Oh, heavens—if it's got words, I'll read it. Started when I was four, haven't been able to get my fill yet." She plucked the large bottle off the counter, bracing it against her midsection. "I've been to all sorts of places, just from reading, that most folk don't even know about. Like Carpathia—"

She gave the bottle top a sharp twist...then let out a yelp as the warm soda geysered four feet into the air, instantly drenching everything.

While Luanne shrieked with laughter, they both fumbled for several seconds to get the top back on the still-spewing bottle. At last, the eruption contained, they stood in shock, staring at the streaks of soda meandering down walls and refrigerator, dripping off counters, collecting in puddles on the floor, which the dog was valiantly cleaning up. Then they looked at each other. Luanne collapsed against the counter, howling, as Alek snatched a paper towel off the holder over the counter, swiping a stream of cola off his cheek.

"Is this how you treat all the guys?"

"Only the ones I really, really like," she got out, and something warm and giddy and as bubbly as the soda erupted inside him, and somehow or other, she was in his arms and her mouth was under his....

For a second or two, at least.

With a wistful little sigh, she backed away. "I cannot tell you how this pains me—" she squatted to get a small plastic bucket and a sponge from underneath the sink "—but if we leave this, the ants'll have a field day."

And the fizzies inside Alek's brain deflated enough for him to realize what he'd done. But until he figured out how to gracefully extricate himself from his own idiocy, he took the now-filled bucket from Luanne and started cleaning the refrigerator.

"Now, that is amazing," she said behind him.

"What is?"

"I do not believe I have ever seen a man clean anything that didn't have an engine and wheels."

Their eyes met for an instant before she grabbed another sponge from below the sink and started in on the lower cabinets, which the dog was precleaning for her. For several seconds Alek just watched her, listening to her chatter to the dog, whose tail was going as fast as his tongue. Perhaps sensing she was being observed, she twisted to look up at him, her smile fading when she caught his expression. On a heavy sigh, she sat back on her heels, staring at the cabinet in front of her. "Don't say it."

He dropped the sponge into the pail and squatted beside her, brushing an errant curl off her face, wondering if she had any idea how potent her innocence was. "You can't really think our sleeping together is a good idea?"

Her mouth quirked into a shaky grin. "Was it something I sprayed?"

He laughed in spite of the heaviness gnawing at him. "Hardly. But you're just not the type of woman I usually—"

Her head jerked around, hurt flaring in her eyes. Alek swiped his damp hand on his jeans, then cupped her face in his hands, linking their gazes. The scent of her, the feel of her, winnowed past barriers he'd long thought impenetrable, soothing and exhilarating and terrifying him all at once. "That's not what I meant," he said in a fierce whisper. "You're worth a dozen of those other women, do you know that?"

Amusement flickered across her face. "A dozen? My, my…you do get around, don't you?"

"I wasn't bragging."

She jerked out of his grasp, blinking rapidly as she looked away. "But you don't want me, either."

Again his hand sought out her face, his eyes, hers. "If anything, I'm saying no because I *do* want you. But you deserve something better. Something *real*."

Her expression at once guileless and provocative, she stared at him for several moments, then got up to wring out her sponge. Alek rose, as well, feeling more than a little lost.

After tossing the sponge onto the back of the sink, Luanne braced her hands against it. "Did you not hear a thing I said outside, Alek? I am not looking for permanent. In fact, I don't want it, not now, and especially not with anyone from around here. But it's not like I can just…" Color flooded her cheeks.

"Shoot, between my background, living out here all by myself and working at Ed's…well, thank you for your compliment, but to most folks, I'm just plain old trailer trash, the daughter of a wife-beating drunk and a uneducated waitress. So I've sort of made it a mission of mine not to live up to their expectations, you know? But Lord Almighty," she said quietly, "it's been a long time since anyone's held me."

Alek stilled, as an unnamed monster suddenly loomed up out of that void inside him, one he'd desperately tried to stay one step ahead of his entire life. In the distance, thunder rumbled. Luanne looked toward the window. "Another storm's coming…" The words seemed to catch in her throat; he could see unshed tears pooling at the corners of her eyes. And he wondered just what it had cost that staunch little pride of hers to ask of him what she just had?

And with that thought, he was lost.

"Are you really sure you want your first time to be with a stranger?"

Her gaze whipped to his. "Don't tease me," she whispered.

He took a step toward her, close enough to skim a knuckle down her cheek, keeping her gaze hooked in his as the caress continued southward. Her breathing quickened as his fingers danced over her throat, her collarbone, the sweet swell of one breast. "I'm not," he whispered back, willing the beast back into its hiding place. Willing himself not to look at it.

"Well, then." Pupils already dilated, her eyes bored into his. "You have shown more concern for my feelings in the past few hours than all the men I have ever known put together. So I'm willing to take a chance that your considerateness and attention to detail extends past the bedroom door."

On a sigh that was equal parts longing and frustration, he gathered her into his arms, burying his face in her still-damp hair as a thousand thoughts darted this way and that inside his head like a school of fish, pros and cons and maybes and a good many are-you-out-of-your-minds all but pulverizing what little remained of his resolve. He lifted a hand to her face, stroking one finger down her sticky, child-soft cheek, wondering even then if she was a blessing or a curse. Or whether he really cared which.

Rain began thrumming against the trailer's roof as he lowered his mouth to hers, his conscience all but drowning in a wave of need....

Chase's yelling something at the pup shook him out of his reverie. And not a moment too soon, Alek decided on a strained sigh, creaking open the door. Luanne turned, her expression unreadable as she watched him walk out onto the back porch. The sun bit into his bare shoulders; his gaze drifted first to his shirt, quivering on a clothesline in the airless breeze, only to dart to Luanne's swollen middle—a brittle reminder that the child she now carried was Jeff's, not his. Which alone should have been sufficient to halt the memories.

But like lovemaking carried to the point of no return, images of that one night slipped past the brink of his tenuous control and now pulsated through him—images of soft sighs and uninhibited laughter, of a pair of blue eyes wide with startled delight, of soul-searing cries of fulfillment.

Of the mixture of awe and terror that had ripped through him afterward.

He'd been careful, or so he'd thought. Careful to protect her, both from getting pregnant and from getting hurt. Careful to protect himself from feelings he knew he couldn't deal with.

Or so he'd thought.

The last thing he'd expected to discover, when he finally got around to putting together his racing team more than a year and a half later, was that Jeff Henderson had married Luanne, that they'd had a baby boy. No, that wasn't quite true: the *last* thing he'd expected, even though he knew he was acting like a child who bristles at the sight of another child playing with a rejected gift, was the senseless, pointless jealousy that had pricked and tormented him like a hairshirt. And until today, he hadn't believed the chafing could possibly get any worse.

Once again, his gaze swept over Luanne's rounded belly, then up to those eyes teeming with sorrow, confusion, bitterness. And a fathomless weariness that called to something inside him that was nearly atrophied from disuse. Several feet behind her, Chase looked up, noticed Alek. The child chucked the ball as though it harbored some infectious disease, then took off around the side of the house. A second later the television blared on.

Dear God—what now?

Alek came down the steps, crossing the surprisingly large expanse of yard to where Luanne stood, motionless, the sunlight harshly delineating her fragility.

"Can Chase hear us out here?" he asked.

She shook her head, apprehension hovering in her eyes.

"You look ready to drop."

Her mouth thinned. "I'll manage."

"Can you afford to get in some help?"

"I *said,* I'll manage."

They stared each other down for another second or two before Alek said, "If you'd been able to reach me, back then, would you have told me you were pregnant?"

"No." She snatched the plastic bowl from the wooden picnic table nearby before taking off across the yard, obviously hoping he'd leave things there.

"Why on earth not?"

She halted, facing away, worrying the rim of the bowl with her fingertips for several moments before she finally turned. Her gaze glanced off his bare chest, then back up to his eyes. "For pity's sake, Alek," she said on a mirthless laugh, "you tore out of my house after that night like the very demons from hell were on your heels. So why would I have put myself in the position of makin' you feel obligated to marry me, or take on a responsibility you never wanted to begin with, simply because fate played a nasty trick on us?"

"Aren't you being just a trifle presumptuous?"

A strand of hair caught in her lashes; she yanked it free. "Practical, is more like it. My father got my mother pregnant when they weren't but kids themselves. They 'had' to get married. Daddy stuck around for a few years, sure, except he was as miserable as an animal caught in a trap and he made good and sure we all knew it. He took it out on Mama, mostly, but

I felt his frustration, too, and don't think I didn't. And finally he took off, leaving us in a worse state than if we'd had to fend for ourselves from the get-go. Except Mama didn't have to worry anymore about how to explain the bruises.''

Every muscle in Alek's face tensed with the effort not to explode. "I might have been a jerk for leaving the way I did, Luanne, but I've never hit a woman in my life, I don't get drunk, and I would have taken responsibility for my child! For God's sake—you trusted me enough to let me be the first man to make love to you, but you didn't trust me enough to know I'd never have abandoned you?"

"But that's exactly what you did! I didn't expect forever, Alek, and I know I was the pushy one that night, when it came right down to it—"

"Oh, for the love of God—"

Her hand shot up. "—but I thought I was at least worth a little common courtesy. This is a pointless conversation, Alek. If you were so all-fired intent on taking responsibility, you might've left me some way of getting in touch with you. Or bothered to tell me who you really were. But you didn't, did you?"

The undulating drone of a cicada pierced the silence. Alek twisted away, breathing hard, until Luanne's sigh behind him made him face her again. "Oh, Alek—you were a stranger passin' through. I knew it, you knew it. Neither of us was looking for anything permanent. And happily-ever-afters don't come from one-night stands. Besides, even if I didn't know you were a prince, I sure as heck knew you were way out of my league, that we had no more in common than a sparrow and a peacock." Her head tilted to one side. "But none of that's here nor there because I didn't know who or where you were, and by the time I found all that out, I'd been married for nearly eighteen months and..."

Alek frowned. "What?"

Luanne fidgeted with the bowl a moment, then walked over to the picnic table, banging the bowl back onto its top before settling carefully onto the bench.

Alek joined her. And waited.

Several more seconds passed before she said, "When you're twenty-one and pregnant and an inch away from panic, a White Knight can look pretty dang good, let me tell you. My world, such as it was, had crumbled right out from under me. I hadn't finished my education, I wasn't gonna be able to work for much longer, and had no one to fall back on. Not a single, solitary soul."

Her brow knotted, she swatted at an insect in front of her face. "I was out behind Ed's one night, trying to get ahold of myself—I had no sickness to speak of, but my hormones were just all over the place and I cried, like, every ten minutes— when Jeff suddenly showed up out of nowhere, and before I knew what I was doing...I told him. He offered to marry me on the spot."

I'd do anything for that gal....

Alek's stomach clenched; he waited out the slight surge of nausea. "And he never asked who the father was?"

"Sure he did. First question out of his mouth. I told him it didn't make any difference, sort of indicating it happened around the time of the Simmons wedding, that it was a one-time thing...." Her mouth stretched taut. "He never questioned me after that. All he wanted was my assurance that, if he took me and the baby on, there was no chance of the father's comin' back and making things complicated. I told him we were probably safe on that score...but he made me swear to never tell. Since I didn't figure there'd ever be a problem, I agreed."

Alek swore softly. Luanne crossed her arms.

"Even so, I didn't think it was fair to Jeff, and I told him so, but he finally convinced me it was a blessed sight better than goin' on public assistance when I couldn't work anymore, that this way, I'd be able to get my degree like I'd planned. And we'd always been friends, *good* friends, so it wasn't like we didn't get along. And I trusted him, Alek. More than I'd ever trusted another man." He caught the blush stealing across her cheeks, said nothing. She cleared her throat, looked straight ahead. "Marrying him was strictly a practical decision on my part. The last thing I expected was to..."

She glanced away, tucked an escaped curl behind her ear. "I'd never had a man be so good to me. Not for the long haul. Or to stand up for me the way he did. His parents were dead set against the marriage, but he refused to buckle to their objections. And after Jeff's daddy died, right before Chase was born, his mama came around, treated me like gold until her own passing a couple years back. I remember waking up one morning, I guess when Chase was about six months old or so, and realizing, for the first time in my life, everything was going right for a change. I was gonna go back to school, I had a beautiful, healthy baby and a husband who adored me."

She got awkwardly to her feet, waddled over to the clothesline, felt the shirt. "Then this contract arrives in the mail." She unclipped the shirt from the line, handed it to Alek. "Here—stuff dries real fast in this heat."

Silently, he got up, as well, took the still-damp shirt and slipped it on, all the while watching the gutsy, exhausted woman in front of him fight to keep her emotions in check.

"So what would you have done," she said after a moment, "if you'd've been in my shoes?" Anguished eyes turned to his. "Would you have risked destroying the family you never thought you'd have by tellin' the truth? Would you have found it in yourself to break a promise to the only person with the guts to stand by you when nobody else would, who loved your baby more than your own father ever loved you?"

"Oh, Luanne—"

But she cut him off, even though her nerves were clearly at the breaking point. "So I prayed, and prayed, and prayed until my knees were sore, asking the good Lord what I should do, what was the best in a field of bad choices. And it came to me the only practical thing was to keep my promise. Might've pulled it off, too, if it hadn't been for those blamed tenth-birthday photos." Her gaze slid to his nose. "Didn't take much for Jeff to figure things out after that—"

"There you are!" called a raspy voice from the back steps. Alek looked up to see sunlight flash off a pair of gold-rimmed glasses perched on a shiny brown face underneath a cap of white curls. A shapeless dress in an innocuous print hugged an equally shapeless body held up by a pair of scrawny legs. "That boy of yours said you were out here. I don't suppose you meant to leave the hose runnin', so I shut it off, hope that was okay—" The woman lifted her hand to shield her eyes from the sun. "Oh, I'm sorry! Didn't know you had company! I just this minute took some biscuits outta the oven, thought maybe you and Chase might like some, you know, and then he told me to go on back…" The woman's words drifted into an ether of curiosity and embarrassment.

Beside him, Luanne took several deep breaths to regain her control, then struggled to stand; instinctively, Alek rose at the same time, bracing his palm around one of her elbows to help her up. She darted a surprised, wary glance at him, but said nothing.

When they got closer to the house, Luanne introduced them. "Odella Stillwater, Alek Vlastos. An old friend of Jeff's," she added, a forced calm to her voice that put Alek on immediate alert. "Odella's my neighbor to the east."

Alek took Odella's softly wrinkled hand in his. "Pleased to meet you."

Clasping her other hand on top of his, the old woman squinted for a moment, as if trying to place him. Then, on a soft gasp, she gently squeezed his hand between both of hers. "Oh, land—you're that prince fella, ain'tcha? That used to race with Jeff a while back?" A wealth of understanding—and compassion, Alek thought—seemed to flood her words.

He nodded.

Odella scrutinized him for another few seconds before at last releasing his hand, then ushered them all back inside as if the house were hers, not Luanne's, insisting they get to those biscuits before they went stone cold.

One glance at Luanne's strained features told Alek she was obviously no more in the mood for a chitchat over a plate of biscuits than he was. But neither would she have hurt Odella's feeling for the world. When she went to call Chase into the kitchen from the living room, however, and the boy flat-out refused to come, Alek saw her cheeks blaze.

Perhaps Alek had had little experience with kids, and perhaps—no, probably—he was about to screw up yet again, but he refused to let the kid get away with treating his mother with less respect than he did the dog. Calmly, and before Luanne had a chance to react, Alek walked out to the living room where the boy was sprawled on the floor on his stomach, chin propped in hands, watching something on TV. Knowing full well how the child—not to mention the mother—were likely to react, Alek grabbed the remote from the table beside the sofa and clicked the off button.

"Hey!" Chase whipped around just as Luanne breathed "Alek!" sharply behind him.

Alek carefully replaced the remote on the table. "I believe your mother called you?"

"Geez! I *said*, in a minute!" The child lunged for the remote; Alek snatched it out of his reach. "Give that back! I was right in the middle of a program!"

"Alek, I can handle this," Luanne said, obviously fighting for control. Over herself, the situation or her child, he wasn't sure which. Maybe all of the above.

He turned to her. "For once," he said softly, "you don't have to."

She ignored him. "Chase, there is no cause for your being rude like that. None. Not to me, not to Alek and certainly not to Odella who made those biscuits especially for you."

"Like I give a damn."

Shock drained what little color was left from Luanne's face. She opened her mouth, but only to say, "Oh, Chase," in the saddest voice Alek had ever heard, then quickly walked out of the room.

Alek was over to the child in a heartbeat, grabbing him by the back of his T-shirt and hauling him to his feet.

"Hey—!"

He began marching him toward the kitchen. Or rather, dragging, since the child was not in the least bit interested in co-operating. "You will apologize to your mother and Odella both—"

"No!" the kid yelled, wriggling in Alek's grasp like a just-caught fish. "Not fair! Everybody's always tellin' me what to do! When's somebody gonna ask me what *I* want? Let *go* of me—''

With that, he kicked out, grazing Alek's shin with the toe of one of those oversize cowboy boots. Alek dodged the second kick, grasping the child by the shoulders and squatting just enough to lock their gazes. "Kick me again, buster," he said, "and those boots are history!"

Furious tears welled in the bright-blue eyes. "You can't do that! They're my daddy's boots!"

Alek's heart cramped in empathy, but he refused to let it derail him. "Then I suggest you give serious consideration to not using them as deadly weapons."

The child stilled, but he looked away, his brows nearly meeting in a tight frown. "Chase," Alek went on, more gently, "nobody is ever asked if they want to lose someone they love. But that doesn't give you the right to act as if you're the only person in the world who's ever been hurt." His heart twinged again at the single tear that streaked down the boy's cheek. "Your mother didn't take your father away, but you bloody well are acting as if she did. And how do you think that makes her feel?"

After a good five seconds, Chase said, very quietly and with more venom than Alek could have believed possible from a ten-year-old child, "Go to hell."

Alek's first reaction was anger. Hot, vicious anger that literally made him see red. Until the haze cleared long enough for him to see reflected in his son's eyes a sixteen-year-old boy too old for tears, yet too young to handle overwhelming feelings he neither understood nor wanted.

"I have a better idea," he said, straightening. "How about you go to your room instead?"

The blue gaze narrowed. "You're not my—"

"I agree, Chase," came from behind them. Alek turned to see Luanne standing in the doorway, clinging to the tatters of her composure like a beggar his threadbare cloak. "Go on to your room until you've done some good, hard thinking about your behavior."

"I'm sorry—" he began, but Luanne shook her head.

"Go on."

After a moment's glare, equally lobbed at the two of them, the child stomped out of the room and up the stairs. Luanne sagged against the wide door frame to the living room, staring down the hall.

Alek wasn't sure which was more clear: that she was in way over her head, or that she would cut off a limb before she'd admit it. Then, slamming right up against those first two thoughts with a breathless *oomph* came an idea of just how he might be able to rescue the woman without her realizing that's what he was doing.

"Can you imagine him running around a palace?" Luanne suddenly said, startling him. He turned to catch her wry, sad smile. "He'd just charm the pants right off everybody, wouldn't he?"

Swallowing his irritation at the self-censure in her voice, he said, "About as much as I did at that age, I imagine."

"You sayin' you were a handful?"

"According to my grandmother, I was a holy terror."

A little of that humor that had at once time stolen his breath sparked in her eyes. "And I'm supposed to find that reassuring?" she said, then let out a weighted sigh, as worry once again creased her brow. "He wasn't always like this." He saw her swallow and look away, rubbing her belly. "Everything just seems to have gotten away from me."

The urge to hold her—and the terror of what the feel of her softness in his arms would do to him—was so strong Alek shook with it. Barely five feet separated them, a space he could cover in two strides…a space that spelled the difference between sanity and folly. But dear God—the only other time he'd ever heard her admit to needing something beyond herself was the night they'd made the child currently having a sulk-fest in his room. The night Alek had run from the very things now staring him in the face and demanding his attention.

Whether or not he was now any better equipped to deal with any of it, he had no idea. And there was the very real chance that his clumsy attempts to atone for his youthful cowardice could well make things worse. But what choice did he have?

All his life Alek had gone to extraordinary lengths to avoid letting another human being lean on him. Now, in one breath-stealing, epiphanous flash, he realized what a precious thing it was to earn someone's trust enough to be considered *worthy* of being leaned on.

Especially the trust of a woman who would choke on her own pride before she admitted she needed help.

Be that as it may, the fact was that too many people had turned their backs on Luanne Evans Henderson. The least Alek could do was reverse the trend.

"I have an idea," he said.

Chapter 4

Luanne simply stared at Alek for several seconds, wondering if stress caused hallucinations, because the man could not possibly have suggested—

"Come back with you to Carpathia?" she finally got out. "Are you out of your ever-lovin' *mind?*"

"Undoubtedly. But school doesn't start for a few weeks yet, correct?"

"For heaven's sake—I can't just pick up and leave!"

"Why not?"

The kitchen. Things would make more sense in the kitchen, where poor Odella was probably sitting and wondering if anyone was ever gonna come eat her biscuits. So Luanne clumsily turned around and tromped back toward Odella and her biscuits and, hopefully, sanity.

"You didn't answer my question," Alek said behind her, just as she got to the kitchen door, dashing *that* hope all to heck. Odella, who was sitting at the table and talking to the dog, didn't seem much perturbed at all, although she did give them both a bright, hopeful smile.

"I don't intend to." Luanne plucked a biscuit from the basket, slamming it onto a plate and sticking it into the microwave, wishing she could zap all these masculine, take-charge vibrations that she was in no mood or condition to be dealing with just at the moment in the same manner.

Odella looked from one to the other, clearly hoping someone would take pity on an old woman and fill her in on what was going on sometime before the Second Coming. To Luanne's shock, Alek obliged.

"You're an objective bystander," he said to her neighbor, crossing his arms, which was when she realized that putting a shirt back on him—it hadn't even been completely dry—had been a good idea. Because, even as distraught as she was, she had been finding his naked chest far too distracting. And besides, there was no sense in him risking a sunburn—didn't do diddly to keep her from gawking at him. He wasn't even all that built, really. But solid. Real solid.

"If you were in Luanne's situation," Alek was saying, "and somebody just offered you and your child a two-week vacation, would you accept?"

The old woman pursed her lips for a minute, then reached over and took one of her own biscuits, started to slowly pull it apart with knobby, loose-skinned fingers. "Don't rightly know. Suppose it'd depend."

"On?"

"Oh, I don't know…" Frowning, she carefully slathered the bottom half of the biscuit with a thick layer of margarine. "She'd be stayin' in your palace?"

"She would."

She twisted around slightly, glanced at Luanne, then turned her bird-like gaze back on Alek. "Y'all got servants?"

"A few."

"So she—" a nod toward Luanne "—wouldn't have to lift a finger the whole time she was there?"

"Not unless she wanted to."

Odella looked back at Luanne. "Then all I have to say is—girl, if you don't take this man up on his offer, you are ten kinds of fool."

The microwave dinged. Alek laughed. Luanne sighed. Harshly.

"I cannot disrupt Chase again so soon after moving here." She brought her biscuit to the table, slapped the plate down. At the place farthest from Alek. "Which I only did because he wasn't any too happy back in Dallas," she said, trying not to let herself get all caught up in wondering whether she'd ever stop making mistakes where Chase was concerned. "We need to get settled, establish some sense of normalcy before school starts. How're we gonna do that if I yank him away again?" She saw Alek look to his new ally, but she was busy feeding the dog the end of her biscuit. "Besides, what on earth is he gonna do in Carpathia?"

"It's not the moon, for goodness' sake. We even have a video rental shop in the village. Not to mention a Taco Bell. Besides, it's just for two weeks. And—" He leaned forward, pressing his hands against the table. Long-fingered, strong hands, with a simple, gold signet ring on the fourth finger of his right hand. "—this would give me an opportunity to get to know—"

He caught himself. Just about the time Odella caught on.

She got up from the table, brushing crumbs from her lap. "Seems to me y'all got some things to work out, which clearly ain't gonna happen with no old woman hangin' around." As she shuffled from the kitchen, she reminded Luanne to give her a call if there was anything she needed and not to bother seein' her to the door, she could find her own way out.

Luanne waited until she heard the front screen door slam shut, then said, "You want to get to know Chase, you can stay right here." Not that she wanted Alek around, heaven knew, but at least this way, she could call the shots.

"I wish I could. But I've got obligations at home I've already put off." Surprise must have shown itself in her expression, because Alek then said, "I told you, I've changed."

Except, she knew all about boy-men now. Men who'd never wanted the responsibility of family didn't magically change their minds just because they were forced to get married; men who got their biggest thrills from racing expensive machinery around a track didn't suddenly decide there was more fulfillment at home; men who took off after a single night of lovemaking, who dated a million women over the next eleven years, didn't suddenly become models of stability.

It wasn't that she doubted Alek's good intentions. Clearly, he cared what happened to Chase, and would probably even grow to care about him. But how long would that last? Until the next big car race? Until the next movie star or princess or socialite moved into his line of sight?

"It's a preposterous idea, Alek."

"As befits a preposterous situation."

She leaned back in her chair, crossing her arms over the child squirming inside her. "And I don't supposed it even once occurred to you that this would be a good way to begin weaning Chase away from me?"

He looked genuinely shocked. And hurt. He held her gaze for some time, then abruptly walked over to the sink. After another several seconds of staring out the window, he said quietly, "How can I convince you I'm not the same bastard who turned tail and ran the night we made love?"

His words seared straight through to a spot she'd convinced herself had grown numb. When he pivoted back, wearing about as earnest an expression as she imagined a man could, she willed him not to see how her cheeks burned. "Of course I want to get to know my son. That's not an unreasonable desire. And that's going to be difficult if we're thousands of miles apart. But what's also true is that you and Chase desperately need a change. You're both so busy grappling with the same demons, you're not really of much use to each other, are you?"

Luanne turned away, from the gentleness, from the memories, realizing at that moment that what had her most shook up about this whole thing was that seeing him again…it was as if no time at all had passed. That the peculiar, unexplained sense of connection that had ignited all those sexual sparks so long ago still existed, still pulled.

Still deceived.

"No," she admitted. "But yanking him away from what he knows, again—"

"Couldn't possibly make things worse, could it?"

Her sigh could probably be heard clear to Amarillo. She pinched the bridge of her nose, thinking about all the boxes yet to be unpacked, and Chase's belligerence, and the awful heat, and how Carpathia was supposed to be so green and cool, even in the summer, a peaceful little fairy-tale kingdom tucked away in the mountains of central Europe. Then the baby kicked, reminding her. "I don't even know if I can travel this late in the pregnancy. It's only eight weeks until my due date. And I can't leave the dog."

His mouth did this little half-smile thing that reminded her so much of Chase, she nearly lost her breath. Not to mention her resolve. "Surely Odella would keep him?"

"Over Chase's dead body."

"Then we'll take him. As long as his shots are up to date—"

"Well, of course they are," she said, only then realizing that she was being snowballed. The baby kicked again. She skimmed a palm over her belly, remembering she did have an appointment with Doc Patterson that afternoon....

"I can see him kicking from here."

She jerked her gaze to Alek's. His voice held the wonder of a child's, setting loose those dang hormones of hers. As well as her mouth. "You want to feel?"

His brows popped up. "Are you sure?"

Eyes stinging—again—she nodded. Alek squatted by her chair, hesitated, then laid his hand on her belly.

"No. Here." She slipped her hand over his, sliding it to where she'd felt the last kick. Barely a second later Alek laughed. "Strong little beggar, isn't he?"

"Or she," Luanne said, keeping very still, as if immobility would somehow keep her from reacting to the sensation of his hand on her stomach. Like, if she didn't move, she wouldn't remember that same look of amazement on Jeff's face, the first time he felt Chase kick.

Alek grinned up at her, then gently rubbed her belly, sending unexpected shockwaves hurtling through her. "How much did Chase weigh at birth?"

"Eight pounds, two ounces," she said evenly.

"That's pretty big, isn't it?"

"He was a real healthy baby, Alek. You'd've—"

Silence screamed between them until she thought she'd scream, too. "We'd go by private jet," Alek finally said, rising. "No crowds, no hassles. If your doctor says it's okay to travel…"

Luanne looked up at him, into those silver eyes that had so effortlessly seduced her all those years ago. And saw in them something of the same yearning she'd seen then, although she supposed now it had more to do with wanting to make things up to her than anything else, combined with a new strength and sense of purpose that only made them all the more seductive.

And all the more dangerous.

She lowered her gaze to what was left of her lap. "I don't want to lose Chase," she whispered, only to jump when she felt his fingers on her chin, gently tilting her face back up. Her heart rate shifted into a harsh staccato as she desperately, desperately tried not to react.

"Then perhaps," Alek said with the barest twitch of a smile, "this is a way to make sure you don't."

Before she could even begin to sort out his meaning, he let go to pull his wallet from his back pocket, extracting some kind of business card which he tossed onto the table in front of her. "This is where I'm staying. When you decide what you want to do, let me know."

Then he was gone, leaving her in quite a state of consternation.

Odella trundled over to her morning-glory-smothered fence the moment Alek set foot on her section of the sidewalk. "She say she'd go?"

Although he would have liked a few minutes alone to sort out his agitated thoughts, he smiled into the concerned dark eyes a foot or so below his. "Not exactly, no."

The old woman clucked, then cocked her head at him. "I couldn't come right out and ask you with Luanne sittin' right there, but how are *you* gettin' on? I mean, from your injuries? I heard you was hurt some in the accident, too.''

"Not seriously. A broken wrist, a few cracked ribs…" He tried to shrug it off, not wishing to offend the obviously well-intentioned woman. But the fact was, the last thing he wanted to do was talk about the accident, or relive those horrifying seconds when he realized Jeff's car had somehow gone careening out of control and was spinning toward the wall. The shock had made Alek lose his own concentration, just long enough to misjudge the next curve and glance off the wall himself. But all Alek's race cars were equipped with a HANS device, a head-and-neck restraint which might have prevented the severe head trauma that caused Jeff's death. Jeff, however, had insisted he'd made it through more than 800 races without one, he wasn't about to start wearing the damned thing now….

Jeff had left behind a pregnant wife, a child who adored him. And all because he had to have things his own way.

"Sometimes there's a lot more to an injury," Odella said softly, "than a few broken bones."

Refusing to go down that road, Alek said, "Have you known Luanne long?"

"Land, yes. Her and my granddaughter went to school together, used to hang out quite a bit before my daughter Sharice and her husband moved on up to Tulsa, fifteen years ago now. You're not from around these parts, so you may not be aware that a white child takin' up with a black one wasn't something everybody accepted back then. Still ain't. So folks talked. Luanne, though, she didn't care. Said she'd be friends with whoever she wanted, and anyone who didn't like it could just go jump in a lake. Although I think she may have used a stronger expression than that," she ended with a light laugh.

He barely felt her featherlike touch on his arm. "She fights for what she feels is right. And for the people she cares about. But she's real practical, too, if you know what I mean. The two of those things, though—fightin' for what's right and being practical—they sometimes get all balled up inside of her, causing her no small amount of confusion. I 'spect she's pretty confused right now," she said, shooting a glance toward

Luanne's house, then letting her shrewd gaze drift back to him. "She's also not given to burdening others with her problems."

Alek glanced away, expelling a troubled sigh.

"And something tells me she's not the only one who's confused." He looked at her; she let out a soft laugh. "I remember seein' you when you came to town, more'n ten years ago. We don't get many strangers here, and one as good-lookin' as you is bound to stand out. 'Course, your hair was longer, and you looked kinda scruffy, if memory serves, but you ain't changed that much. Then, out of the blue, I see this weddin' notice in the paper, that Luanne and Jeff Henderson are gettin' married, and I remember thinkin' to myself at the time that there was somethin' off about that. That they'd be gettin' married without courtin' or nothin'. And I thought to myself, oh, Lord—that poor girl's done gone and got herself pregnant, is what. And not by Jeff Henderson, either, I didn't imagine."

When Alek couldn't think of a thing to say, a gentle smile spread across the old woman's cheeks. "She kept the child a secret from you, didn't she?"

Tension knifed his shoulders. "She had her reasons."

"I suppose she did. And now you want to fix things, is that it?"

Alek rammed his hands in his pockets, squinted in the early-morning glare. "I don't know that I can."

Odella laughed, a wheezy little thing that sounded as though she was going to start coughing any second. "A body can usually accomplish anything it puts its mind to, y'know. Oh—! There's my phone, so I better be goin'." She turned and began a sort of odd hopping gait back up her uneven walk, yelling, "Nice to meet you," over her shoulder as she disappeared into the heavy shade of Luanne's mulberry tree.

Alek stood for a moment, staring back at Luanne's house, almost wishing he'd asked Odella what, if anything, she knew of Luanne and Jeff's marriage, only to decide it was just as well he hadn't. Besides, he imagined he already knew more than she did, anyway. Certainly more than he probably wanted to.

And definitely more than he would ever reveal.

* * *

Oh, Lord. Now what d'you suppose those two were goin' on about?

As if she didn't know.

Luanne had been on her way up to Chase's room with a buttered and jellied biscuit when she noticed Alek and Odella out in front of her neighbor's house. Stopped her plumb dead in her tracks. Now the biscuit was all cold, but since it was highly unlikely that Chase would eat it, anyway, there was little sense in trekking back to the kitchen to warm it up again. So Luanne kept on up the stairs, all the while wondering what in heaven's name had possessed her to rent a house with stairs when she had a baby on the way?

Halfway up, she had to stop to catch her breath. Leaning against the wall—getting after the landlord to remove the peeling wallpaper was right at the top of the list, soon as this baby was born—she closed her eyes for a second, thinking about Alek's offer. She had to admit, the thought of two weeks of being pampered was sorely tempting. Not that she had the slightest idea what living in a palace would be like, but she supposed she could handle it. If she could make the trip at all, that is.

But…she wasn't about to do anything that might upset Chase more than he already was. And considering that he and Alek didn't exactly hit it off, how was two weeks of forced proximity gonna work out?

Then again—mercy, this was getting tiresome—it wasn't like any of this was going to go away simply because she was exhausted and pregnant and was in no fit condition to be making major decisions. One way or the other, Alek was going to get time with his son.

Which, she thought as a painfully loud, steady thumping began to assault her eardrums from overhead, wasn't nearly as awful an idea as she might have thought two hours ago. For all she didn't trust Alek as far as she could throw him, the idea of letting someone else deal with Chase's perpetual foul mood from time to time was nearly as appealing as the idea of not having to bend over to pick up a single, solitary thing for two whole weeks.

She opened her eyes and glanced up the stairs, ignoring the pup who was begging for the biscuit, then hauled her inflated, achy body up the rest of the way. When she opened Chase's door, he glared up at her from the floor. He was lying on his stomach, building something out of Legos and slowly banging the toe of one cowboy boot against the strip of bare wooden floor edging the multicolored braided rug taking up most of the room, while Tim McGraw warbled from the CD player he'd gotten for his birthday. His daddy's—Jeff's—favorite, she realized. And someone Chase'd never listened to of his own volition before, having declared some time ago that country-western music was "dorky".

"I brought you a biscuit. With strawberry jam."

He shrugged.

She took in a breath, counted to ten. Well, seven, maybe, because that's all it took for her mind to make itself up. "And I have a surprise for you."

With obvious effort Chase finally deigned to look at her, his expression that a cross between disgusted and bored.

"Alek's invited us to come stay with him in Carpathia for a couple weeks."

Pale brows dipped into a frown. "Where's *that?*"

Luanne set the biscuit on his desk, then pointed to the atlas on the shelf crammed with a couple hundred books. "Look it up," she said, then left the room, her glow of triumph almost immediately extinguished by her wondering if she had a single, solitary thing to wear that wouldn't embarrass her to pieces.

"For heaven's sake, guys," Alek heard his sister say away from the phone. "Shove off, would you? I can't hear a bloody thing!"

The din lessened. Somewhat. "Sorry. The twins had a sleep-over last night and they're all just now up—oh, blast. Hold on a minute, would you?" And the receiver clunked in his ear.

Alek smiled. Despite Sophie's words, contentment radiated in her voice. On impulse a few months ago, his ultrarespon-sible, plain-to-the-point-of-dowdy sister had run away from her royal life to a tiny Michigan township, where she'd somehow managed to hire out as a housekeeper, of all things, to a man with five wards, of all things, and—of all things—they'd fallen in love and gotten married. Well, it hadn't been quite that cut-and-dried—there had been the odd identity and royalty/commoner issues to work through—but all good sense to the contrary, Sophie seemed blissfully happy and determined to make a go of it.

And he couldn't be happier for her—

"I'm back," she announced on a whoosh of air. "Goodness—where are you calling from?"

He glanced out the second-floor window of his obsessively Victorianized room, which faced...well, not much, actually. A parched garden, another house or two, then nothing save sky and prairie as far as he could see, the monotony broken only by a cloud of dust left in the wake of somebody's pickup. "Sandy Springs, Texas."

She went very quiet. "You've seen him, then?"

"Yes."

"And?"

"He's bright. Tall. Thin. Looks like me. Hates my guts."

Sophie had the nerve to laugh. "Finally found someone impervious to the Vlastos charm, have we?"

"Very funny."

"Sorry, Alek. I know this is hard. But he probably hates everyone right now. I mean, since he's just lost his—" She drew in a breath. "Sorry. Again." Then, "He doesn't know, does he?"

"Good God! Did you think I was going to just march in there and—"

"No, no, of course not. But someone else might have let it slip, you know."

Alek swiped a hand over his face. "His mother wouldn't have for the world. And obviously, Jeff wouldn't." He waited out the tremor of pain before asking, "You haven't told anyone else, have you?"

"If you mean Baba, no. That's your province, old thing. Steven knows, of course. But he won't tell."

Steven Koleski, Sophie's new husband, had taken on the five

orphaned children after their parents' deaths in a house fire, less than a year before he and Sophie met. A more honorable man Alek had never known. And one who, he gathered from brief conversations at their wedding, had known little more about caring for children—let alone recently bereaved children—than Alek did. His sister, on the other hand, had spent much of her adult life working for and with children whose lives had been mangled by tragedy, and was, by all accounts, working miracles with Steve's brood.

"Was I truly horrible?" Alek suddenly asked. "After Mum and Dad died?"

After a pause Sophie said gently, "You didn't know what to do with your grief—"

"I was a brat, in other words."

He could hear his sister's smile on the other end of the line. "Pretty much, yes. Alek, if you're asking in your typical roundabout way about Chase, you have to understand that there's nothing magical about this. You just have to be patient. And loving. I don't know the child, certainly, but finding out the truth is bound to be a huge blow. I don't envy you, frankly."

The truth. Alek nearly winced. When had such a noble concept begun to leave such a bitter taste in his mouth? "I've…asked Luanne to bring Chase back home for a couple of weeks."

"Oh, my heavens! So soon? Are you sure?"

"I'm not sure of anything, Soph. Nothing at all."

More silence. Then, "And…Chase's mother?"

"What about her?"

He heard a child's laughter in the background, a man's low voice gently scolding. Then Sophie said, "Just wondering what your feelings were on that score, that's all."

He opened his mouth, but nothing came out.

"That's what I thought," Sophie said quietly, then sighed. "Crisis in the other room, got to run. Call me later, darling! I love you!"

He'd no sooner hung up the phone when it rang.

"Hel—"

"The doctor says it's okay to go as long as I get back here no later than September first, but I'm not going anywhere until I get my hair and nails done, you hear me?"

Chapter 5

"*Now* how long's it gonna be?" Chase groused for about the millionth time as they settled into the limo for the last leg of what even Luanne had to admit had been a very long trip. Seated across from them, Alek lifted one corner of his mouth, looking as together and unruffled in his blue oxford cloth shirt and khakis as he had when they started this journey. Luanne, on the other hand—despite her wrinkle-resistant, prissy-as-all-get-out maternity dress—felt like something from the bottom of the give-it-to-Goodwill bag. And Lord knew what her hair looked like, what with it being smashed up against an airplane seat back for the last eighteen hours.

"About an hour," Alek replied. "I don't imagine there will be much traffic this early in the morning."

Chase focused outside the window and muttered something Luanne was just as glad she didn't hear, since she was too wiped out to bother.

Although, considering she wasn't what you'd call a seasoned traveler—and that just getting to the bathroom winded her these days—she'd fared pretty well. Odella had helped her pack, insisting Luanne wasn't to worry about a thing while they were gone, she'd look after the house and collect her mail, keep an eye on the garden. But still and all, by the time Luanne had waded through Lord-knew-how-many tussles with Chase—who had made it more than clear that he thought this was the stupidest idea anyone, anywhere, had ever come up with—and fretted over what to take and asked herself about a million times if she was doing the right thing, she had been too tired to even care if the plane fell into the Atlantic Ocean. Just at the moment, the idea of crawling into bed and sleeping for the entire two weeks was extremely appealing.

Once out of Budapest, where they'd landed, they let Bo out of his carrier, and the pup had planted his happy little butt on Alek's lap in order to look out the window, as fascinated by the countryside as his human companions. Everything was so green, Luanne's eyes hurt, but still she felt something like the beginnings of peace stir through her. Then they crossed the border into Carpathia, and she could see, past what looked like one great big forest, the slate-blue mountains in the distance and, closer, lush fields and wildflower-choked meadows dotted with stone cottages and clumps of grazing livestock....

Luanne felt as if she'd been plopped smack-dab in the middle of a fairy tale.

Even old Grumpybones next to her seemed to perk up. Of course, he'd lived in the country most of his life, but to a Texan, "country" meant flat, pale and vast. Stripped down to the basics, Luanne had always thought, when she'd be driving out on the highway and there'd be nothing to occupy her but sky and God and her own thoughts. Heaven knew, there were plenty of people who couldn't handle the stark, unapologetic emptiness, where the only noise you might hear for hours on end was the constant rush of the prairie wind. But then, solitude had never scared her like it did some folks. Shoot, look at all the people she'd grown up with who'd left Sandy Springs and never come back. Now, seeing Chase's frown ease off as he watched the picture-puzzle scenery flash by, she got to wondering if her own son might be one of those people.

She craned her neck to look out Chase's window at a tiny village they were just then passing, complete with a white-spired church. "You know what this reminds me of, honey? That old fashioned village that Granna Henderson used to set up at Christmas every year. You know, the one with the lights in the windows?"

Chase shrugged. "Yeah. I s'pose."

Lord, how she wanted her baby back, the child who'd always had a smile for everyone from the time he was itty-bitty. While the boy's quiet nature and lack of interest in sports had set him apart from most of the other kids, he'd never seemed to let that worry him overmuch. Like her, Chase loved to read. And he liked building things, too. Hadn't ever had much interest in cars, though, which she knew disappointed Jeff some, even though he didn't let on....

She shut her eyes, deciding she was far too tired to be doing this much thinking. Starting right this minute, she wasn't going to worry about a blessed thing these next two weeks except showing Chase how much she loved him.

Then she opened her eyes to find Alek looking very intently at his son with a combination of awe and apprehension, and she allowed as how maybe there were one or two other things she'd have to worry about. Like the fact that for all Alek's insistence that this was a vacation, she didn't dare forget for a minute that this was really all about a father getting to know his son—a prince, his heir. Which led naturally to her thinking that despite having made a baby with this man, she didn't really know him, even though in a bizarre kind of way she felt like she'd known him forever. That her skin fairly hummed with awareness of him, that it was all she could do to ignore the achy, hollow feeling inside her that she couldn't explain...which was pretty much what had led to the situation they now found themselves in. At twenty-one, however, she had been better able to put aside the illogicalness of such a feeling than she was at thirty-two, and being a new widow besides. Whatever they ended up working out about Chase, Luanne had no more delusions now about her long-term place in the scheme of things than she'd had the night their son had been conceived.

Alek was staring at her, she realized. And the look in those soft-silver eyes set her skin to prickling so bad, she almost couldn't sit still.

"Tired?" he asked. She nodded.

"Won't be much longer now," he said gently, and the kindness in his voice nearly sent her right over the edge, which only went to show what exhaustion, grief and hormonal overload could do to a body.

He had been kind then, too, hadn't he? Whatever his intentions had been to begin with, the upshot was that he'd done her a favor. Yet she'd never regretted it. Oh, she might regret some of the choices she'd made later on—although having Chase would never be one of them—but she had indeed captured a little bit of magic that night. And whether that magic came about because of kindness or lust or boredom or loneliness or because the moon was full, she didn't rightly care.

Beside her Chase suddenly let out a gasp. "Is that it? The palace? Mama! It's huge!" Chase tugged at her hand while Luanne's stomach took a slow, tortuous turn. Now that they'd gotten this far, she suddenly wasn't at all sure she was ready. "It must have, like, a thousand rooms or somethin'!"

Alek laughed. "Only seventy."

"Only?" Luanne said on a squeak.

"The palace had to be renovated after a fire nearly destroyed the original structure in 1843. I suppose my great-great-grandfather got a little carried away."

Fascinated in spite of herself, Luanne listened as Alek went on about the gardens and the grounds, the stables and the swimming pool—Chase stirred a little at that—as well as some of the history of the palace, including the royal family's tacit aid to certain local resistance factions during World War II.

Luanne turned wide eyes on him. "But I thought Carpathia was neutral!"

"And that's exactly what we intended the world to think," Alek said with a shrug, even as obvious pride colored his words. "But the 'new' palace is built on top of the original building's foundations, which include a veritable maze of underground passages...." He let the sentence fade as his expression grew more serious again. "As a young girl, my grandmother had made friends with several Jewish students she'd met while traveling through Austria right before the war. And once Hitler's plans became clear, she couldn't stand the thought of Carpathia's doing nothing to counteract the madness. Yet we had no army or real resources to add to the war effort, and my great-grandfather was equally insistent we not put ourselves in any position that would threaten the peace we'd enjoyed for five centuries. However, he adored his daughter, certainly had no great love for egocentric maniacs and sympathized with the plight of the Jews, so he agreed to turn a blind eye to whatever she wanted to do, as long as she was discreet.''

''You're sayin' your grandmother worked for the Resistance?''

The smile broadened. And for the first time since their reunion, Luanne saw the young man who'd made her believe in magic, all those summers ago.

This was not a good thing for the prickles.

''When you meet her,'' Alek said, ''you'll understand. Ah— we're here.''

Luanne's stomach took another tumble as the car pulled in through a pair of imposing wrought-iron gates, then past gardens and fountains and statues and more gardens until, finally, the palace itself came into view.

She barely managed not to let her mouth sag open.

It was almost too much to take in—the sweeping stone staircases and stately columns; the carved stonework over every multipaned window, sparkling like diamonds in the early-morning sunlight; the silvery-gray stone walls topped with a series of darker gray roofs and any number of chimneys—and she thought, oh, dear Lord...if this is what Cinderella faced when she showed up to that ball, she must've just about wet her pants.

The car didn't stop in front, however, instead pulling on around to the back. ''There's a garden entrance in the back that might be easier for you to negotiate in your condition,'' Alek said, and those dadburned tears tried to make another appearance.

Minutes later she was standing on a bricked terrace nearly

hidden by assorted vine-choked trellises and arbors, breathing in a sweet, cool breeze that almost didn't feel real. Trying not to gawk, she let her gaze sweep down yet another wide, stone-banistered staircase at the far end of the terrace to where, like a liquid sapphire set into a border of mosaic tiles, a large rectangular swimming pool glittered in the breeze.

"It's beautiful," she whispered, only to nearly jump out of her skin when Alek's breath teased the hair at her temple.

"Welcome to my home, Luanne Evans Henderson."

His use of her married name bothered her on some level she couldn't even begin to figure out. But that was nothing to the almost electric shock she got when it hit her that, one day, this house would belong to the sullen, skinny kid with the sticky-uppy hair traipsing over to the pool in too-big cowboy boots, the pup bouncing in excitement at his heels.

"Aleksander! You're early!"

Luanne awkwardly turned to find herself face-to-face with a tiny, white-haired woman in a simple cotton blouse tucked into a pair of beige pleated slacks. She was flanked by a pair of white German Shepherds who immediately broke ranks to check out Bo, who in turn went all to pieces at the prospect of having new friends to play with.

"Now, girls," the old woman said in delicately accented English, "he is just a baby. You be good." Then she looked up at Luanne, kindness and generosity radiating from bright, nearly black eyes. Although her short waves had been elegantly styled, her makeup was nearly nonexistent, her jewelry confined to a pair of pearl studs in her ears. "And you must be Luanne." Before Luanne could reply, she found her hand encased in the woman's surprisingly strong grip. "Welcome, my dear. I am Ivana Vlastos, this scroundel's grandmother." Except she promptly let go of Luanne's hand to grab the scoundrel and yank him down for a hug, which he enthusiastically returned.

That done, the old woman returned her attention to Luanne, her smile now one of deepest sympathy. "There are no words to express how sorry I am for your loss. You are holding up as well as may be expected, yes?"

No sooner were the words out of the princess's mouth than Luanne felt Alek's touch at her back. A gesture of support was all it was, and she knew it. Still, all she could do was nod in response to the older woman's question, afraid to speak for the torrent of emotions buffeting her.

"It is good that you have come here," the princess went on. "I promise, we will take excellent care of you. And your children," she added, her focus now on Chase, who had been drawn to the pool like a dolphin. Luanne followed the princess's gaze, aching for her son's sadness, even as she nearly shivered from her awareness of Alek, who was standing closer than he needed to. Lord, but it was hard not to wish she could make her apologies, call a taxi and just go on back home where maybe she'd still have a mountain of troubles to deal with but at least she still felt comfortable inside her own skin.

"It has been difficult for the child, I imagine?"

"Yes, ma'am," she said automatically, only to immediately wonder if it was okay to call princesses "ma'am."

Chase chose that moment to lean precariously over the edge of the pool; Luanne had to smile when Alek took off down the stairs, although he at least had enough sense to know to keep his distance…and his mouth shut.

"Does he swim?" the princess asked.

A breeze ruffled Luanne's hair, making her swipe it out of her eyes, which is when she noticed her hand was shaking. "Well enough to keep from drownin', although there always seems to be twice as many elbows and knees flailing about as there should be."

Ivana chuckled softly. "Well then, he will have to spend as much time as possible in the pool while he's here, if the warm weather holds. Autumn tends to come quite early in this part of the world." The princess hesitated, then said quietly, "My grandson went through quite a rough patch when his parents died. Perhaps he can be of help to the boy while he's here."

Luanne's heart bolted into her throat. *Oh, my word…Alek hasn't told her—*

"Now, if you would be so kind as to introduce me…?"

Luanne called Chase over and did just that. And even though

he sure wouldn't have won any congeniality awards, at least he wasn't acting like he'd hatched from a tumbleweed. However, Luanne caught the brief look of puzzlement, rapidly followed by a flash of recognition in Ivana's eyes.

Which were littered with a thousand questions when the princess looked up. She apparently chose to keep her suspicions to herself, however, at least for the time being. "But now—you must be exhausted, my dear, after such a long trip. And no doubt in need of the rest room," she added with a mischievous smile all too reminiscent of her grandson's—and Chase's, too, Luanne thought with a start. She slipped her arm through Luanne's, gently guiding her back toward a set of French doors. "When is the baby due?"

"Around the middle of October."

"So soon! And you let my grandson drag you halfway around the world?"

But before Luanne could come up with some sort of reasonable response to the princess's comment, Alek's grandmother turned toward a stout, middle-aged blonde in a gray uniform and white apron who'd just appeared. "Ah, there you are, Elena. Would you please show Mrs. Henderson the powder room, then take her on up to her suite—" the elderly woman turned back to Luanne "—if that's all right? Or would you rather have a little something to eat first? I remember being hungry constantly when I carried Alek's mother."

It was a shame, really, because Princess Ivana was the kind of person a body takes to right away. But there was no getting around the fact that this was a woman people called Your Highness, that this was a palace and that the tension level had zoomed off the charts the instant the princess had gotten a good look at Chase. So Luanne allowed as how she wasn't really hungry, thank you, and she wouldn't mind at all being able to lie down for a while.

"Then that's settled." Ivana then turned to Chase, who was nearly as tall as she was. And whether it was imagination or just plain hope that made Luanne think she saw something soften in the old woman's features, she couldn't say. "But what about you, young man? Are you hungry?"

"Uh-huh."

"Chase!" Luanne said, which got a muttered, "Yes, ma'am, I am."

"Then after the boy's mother is settled in, Elena, why don't you escort our young guest down to the kitchen to see what Gizela might have to offer?"

"*Da*, Your Highness," Elena said with a smile, then gestured toward the open French doors. "Come this way, please?"

Just before she stepped inside, however, Luanne turned and caught a glimpse of Alek, standing at the edge of the terrace with his hands crammed into his pockets. He stared off into the distance, his mouth pulled into a grimace, looking for all the world like the you-know-what was about to hit the fan.

She was almost tempted to feel sorry for him.

"You could have at least *warned* me, Alek!"

Annoyed at being separated from Luanne before he'd had even a few minutes in which to put her more at ease, Alek stood stiffly a few feet inside his grandmother's second-floor, chintz-drenched study, waiting for the storm to pass. "He looks so much like you did at that age, it's uncanny," she continued. "I nearly had a stroke when I saw him!"

For the moment, guilt shouldered aside the annoyance, even as both dogs slunk past him to collapse in a broad swath of sunlight on the rose-patterned carpet. For all the elderly princess's seeming invincibility, she was no longer a young woman. "I know it's a shock, Grandmother. And I apologize. But I had to see him for myself first, before I said anything. And then I didn't think it was the kind of thing you'd want to hear over the phone."

After a moment Ivana let out a heavy sigh. "No. No, I suppose not." She rapped her knuckles against an ornately carved and gilded eighteenth-century desk that held, among other things, a state-of-the-art personal computer, printer and fax machine, and looked levelly at him. "How long have you known?"

The question was inevitable. Complete candor about the details surrounding Alek's discovery, however, was not. "Not long. And not from Luanne, to answer your next question. She'd never had any intention of telling me, since the... circumstances of Chase's conception weren't exactly—"

One delicate hand shot up. "Never mind. I get the picture, as the Americans say." Her brow creased, the princess walked around the desk, sinking into the chair behind it. "You know how much latitude I gave you when you were younger, how little I interfered in your comings and goings. I did so because, at heart, I trusted you not to do anything that would bring dishonor to either this monarchy or yourself. I trusted you not to be careless."

He crossed his arms, frowning. "We were using protection. Nor have I left a string of bastards circling the globe, if that's what you're implying."

One incredulous eyebrow lifted. Alek let out a dry, airless laugh.

"Knowing the other women with whom I've...been intimate, I would say the chances are slim to none that I would still be ignorant of any children that might have resulted from those liaisons."

"Then why not in this instance?"

He blew a stiff stream of air through his lips, then admitted, "Because Luanne was the only woman who didn't know how to reach me afterward. She was also the only one who didn't know who I was, not at the time."

The resulting silence was so profound he could hear his brain working. "And why was that, Alek?" the princess asked at last.

He supposed *Because I was a bloody idiot* would do quite nicely, but he imagined the princess had long since figured that out for herself. "I don't know," he said with a shrug that almost hurt. "I don't suppose I ever will."

His grandmother's quiet grunt told him she didn't buy his explanation—or lack of one—for a minute. But instead of pushing, she got up, crossing to the open Palladian window overlooking the back gardens. From a mantel over the marble fireplace, the crystal clock that had been there for as long as Alek could remember softly chimed. As a child, he used to stand on tiptoe to watch the intricate workings visible through the casing. Each part, no matter how small, was perfectly aligned with every other part, all working flawlessly as a single unit, each passing second marching in orderly fashion to the next. That had been his childhood, he now thought—orderly, predictable, its function more or less prescribed by forces he paid little attention to and never questioned. An idyllic existence, certainly. And safe. But one ill suited to teaching a child about the responsibility that comes with having to make hard choices.

His thoughts veered to Luanne, and how very different her life had been from his. Now there was someone who knew all about hard choices and responsibility—

"So if Luanne didn't tell you," he heard his grandmother ask from across the room, "how did you find out?"

"From Jeff," he said simply, and left it at that. Except his grandmother turned sharply around, her brow knotted.

"Why would he have done that?"

"How the hell should I know?"

Obviously unaffected by his outburst, the princess moved toward him, her determined expression making her seem far younger than she was. The same determination, he imagined, that had convinced Alek's great-grandfather, Prince Hans-Fredrik, to let a nineteen-year-old princess help Jews escape certain death during the war.

"And then Jeff died in that horrible accident."

He waited out the flash of pain. "Yes."

"And you sought out this son of yours."

"Of course. What else would I have done? Once I knew, I was hardly going to ignore his existence."

Ivana drifted into a thoughtful silence for several moments, then said, "Chase's mother seems very sweet. And she's quite pretty, even after such a long journey and in her present condition. I can certainly see why you were...attracted to her. But I question her suitability as your princess."

Alek nearly choked. "My *princess?* For God's sake—who said anything about that? In any case, you couldn't very well object on those grounds, considering who Sophie just married.''

''Sophie isn't in direct line for the throne. You are. Whoever you marry will be much more in the public eye than Steven Koleski ever will be. And it's obvious he has…how shall I put this? Overcome his background more than Luanne has—''

''And you've arrived at this conclusion on the basis of a single five-minute conversation?''

She merely shrugged. ''But what difference does it make, if you do not intend to marry her?''

Alek felt suddenly off balance, despite his immediate, ''I don't.''

''Then what, may I ask, was your purpose in bringing mother and child here? I assume the boy doesn't know?''

''This is hardly the time to spring the truth on him, Grandmother.'' Alek rammed his hands into his pockets, sucked in a sharp breath. ''Look—eleven years ago I screwed up. No question about that. Even if I didn't know I had a child, I should have had the decency to at least check up on Luanne at some point. However, I didn't, and there was no way she could have told me, and here we are. But I do intend to sort it out, Grandmother, one way or the other. And I thought I could start by offering our home as a refuge to this woman and her son—*my* son—even if only for a couple of weeks.''

Ivana's eyes narrowed. ''Then you truly have no feelings for her?''

''Of course I have *feelings* for her. Just not the sort that lead to the altar.'' Alek glanced down at the floor, willing his stomach to unknot, then back at his grandmother. ''We weren't right for each other then, and we aren't now. Though not for the reasons you suggest,'' he added with a stern look. ''Even from our brief association, I can tell you Luanne Evans Henderson has far more to recommend her than any woman I've ever known. She's intelligent, good-hearted, and…'' He hesitated. ''And it's quite obvious how much she loved Jeff, a man who was to her what I should have been, but which I doubt I ever *could* have been. Or could *be*. I respect her, and what she's been through, far too much to suggest a sham marriage.''

"I see," his grandmother said, her lips pursed. "Then…how do you intend to handle the matter of the child?"

Alek walked over to the mantel, frowned at the clock. "Legal adoption. When the time's right."

"Surely you do not intend to take him away from his mother?"

He whipped back around, frowning. "Give me *some* credit, for God's sake. Apart from visits, there's no reason he can't stay with Luanne until he's of age. Both of them have been through enough without having to worry about an international custody battle. I wouldn't hurt her or my son for the world. It's not perfect, but it's the best I can I do."

His grandmother was silent for a moment, then crossed to him, lightly touching his arm. "Is it?"

"What do you mean?"

"I wasn't talking about ensuring Chase's inheritance. I was talking about your eventually taking your place as his father—"

"I told you. I fully intend to carry out my responsibilities—"

"And responsibility without emotional commitment is worthless, child. And that's going to be extremely difficult if the two of you aren't together enough to get to know each other, for you to *fall in love* with the child you created. I realize the difficulty of the logistics involved, and I can only admire your not wishing to take the boy away from his mother, but…"

"But…?"

The princess's brow furrowed as she said on a sigh, "The boy looks like you. If I saw it, so will others."

Alek nearly laughed at her implied suggestion. "I can't very well simply introduce Chase to the world as my just-discovered illegitimate son."

"Perhaps not. But the longer you delay telling the boy, the more you run the risk that someone else *will*."

Alek linked his arms across his chest. "And I told you, I cannot—I will not—tell him so soon after Jeff's death." The image of Luanne's ravaged expression a few days before tore through him, making him nearly stumble over his next words. "It would be cruel. And I won't do that, to either of them."

"You mean, you won't do that to *yourself*."

"And what's that supposed to mean?"

The princess narrowed her eyes at him. "All your life, Aleksander, you have avoided anything that might cause you pain. Well, my precious boy, telling the truth *hurts*. Putting that spoiled, pampered royal backside of yours on the line *hurts*. And unfortunately in this case, there is no getting around either of those things. There is no easy way out of this situation, and you damn well know it. And as long as you keep looking for one, things are only going to get worse."

Alek matched the princess's glare with one of his own. "If I'd been looking for an *easy* solution, Grandmother," he said after several tense seconds, "trust me—bringing Luanne and Chase here would not even have made the short list."

After Alek's angry departure, Ivana called the dogs to her, then sank back into her desk chair with a long sigh. Then she chuckled to herself.

Oh, she'd seen the way Alek had kept such careful watch over the dark-haired beauty, the look of combined adoration and terror coloring his features...the way his face lit up whenever she smiled or laughed. She *was* a sweet girl, and even from that brief first meeting, Ivana could tell Luanne's ingenuousness might very well bring a breath of fresh air to the palace. Especially in a country where a great many of the population were still enthralled by reruns of *Dallas,* Ivana thought with another smile.

And hadn't Alek taken the bait beautifully? Her comments about Luanne's unsuitability had provoked exactly the response she'd intuited they would, bringing her grandson eloquently to her defense. Had he been so wrapped up in himself all these years that he'd forgotten he'd never brought another woman to the palace for more than a weekend? That no other woman had inspired him to such fervor...and such obvious admiration?

Oh, yes—she'd bet her fortune that, for the first time in his life, Prince Aleksander Mikael Vlastos had lost his heart.

She just wondered how long it would take him to realize *where*.

Chapter 6

Feeling like somebody'd stuffed her head with wadded-up socks, Luanne fumbled for her Timex on the nightstand by the canopied bed on which she'd lain down to take a short nap—she blinked, then let out a yelp—nearly five hours before!

And, oh, *mercy,* did she have to use the little girls' room.

She hauled herself and her little passenger off the bed and headed for the bathroom, pausing just long enough to hit the intercom buzzer by the telephone that Elena had told her to use if she needed anything. By the time she staggered back into the high-ceilinged, blue-and-ivory bedroom, the servant had appeared like a genie out of the bottle, smiling enormously while transferring Luanne's meager wardrobe from suitcase to dresser drawers, as if waiting on Luanne was the consummation of her dearest wish.

"Ah! There you are!" Bright smile. "Madam is ready for luncheon, yes?"

"What? Oh, shoot, I don't know. Oh, *Lordy!*" Luanne got a load of herself in the vanity mirror and nearly had heart failure. She planted her fanny on the striped satin seat and began whacking at her hair with a brush, not that it would do much good. "Do you know where my son is?"

"Master Chase is quite happily occupied," the woman replied as if Luanne didn't need to bother her pretty little head with such trivial matters. "Madam would like to change clothes before joining Their Highnesses for lunch, yes?"

Luanne briefly shut her eyes, partly to avoid looking at her hair, partly in hopes that when she opened them again, she'd be back in Texas where she could just throw on a pair of shorts and a ratty old T-shirt, then go on down to the kitchen to fix herself a tuna sandwich. Lord only knew what lunch was going to be here, although at least she hadn't been plagued with heart-burn with this baby the way she had with Chase, so even if she didn't recognize what was being served, she could at least eat it without worrying too hard. However, when she opened her eyes, the room—which reminded her of a fancy hotel lobby, except with a bed in the middle of it—as well as the ever-grinning Elena were both still there.

Luanne's breath left her lungs in a rush as she surveyed her sorry-looking self in the mirror. "I suppose I'd better," she said, plucking at the neckline of the wrinkled, wadded dress. She started to push herself up off the seat to pick out something to wear, only to run smack into Elena's oh-no-you-don't glare.

"You tell me what you wish to wear, madam, and I will get for you, yes?"

Two more minutes of this and she'd scream. Two more *weeks* of this...

"Elena? Listen, it's not that I don't appreciate your wanting to help, but I'm real used to doin' things on my own, and well..." She sighed again in the face of the woman's slightly puzzled smile. "I really don't need help gettin' dressed, or pickin' out my clothes."

Elena cocked her head, like Bo did when he didn't understand what you were saying. "But His Highness said madam is not to lift single finger while here, that you are here to rest. The prince, he is very concerned about you."

It was dumb, the way Luanne's heart fluttered a little at that. "I don't think he included my dressin' myself in that directive,

Elena,'' she said gently. "And considering the nap I just had, I'm obviously resting up just fine. And I'd still like to know where my son is." She waddled over to the dresser, only to grimace at the available choices. True, the princess hadn't been wearing a long gown and tiara or anything, but somehow, Luanne didn't think she picked up that blouse and slacks at Wal-Mart. Oh, when they'd lived in Dallas, Jeff had prodded Luanne into going to Neiman's and Saks—it wasn't like they couldn't afford it—but honestly, those places just weren't for her—

She jumped at Elena's sudden presence at her side. "Princess Ivana said to tell you they take luncheon on east terrace, there is no need to dress, so…I think, perhaps…" The maid lifted out a blue, teal and purple floral-patterned short-sleeved top and matching shorts. "This would be good choice, yes?"

Luanne quirked up the side of her mouth. "You think?"

"Oh, *da,* madam."

She sighed, took the dang clothes, then lumbered into the bathroom to change, leaving the door open.

"As for your son—"

Yes, she wondered when they'd finally get around to that.

"—the cook has grandson who stays here while his parents are on business trip and who complains loudly about being bored, that there is no one his age to keep him company. The last I heard, Zoltan and your Chase were playing the video games in media room on first floor."

Her clothes changed, the wrinkled dress clutched in one hand, Luanne stepped back into the bedroom. "The media room? Video games?"

"Oh, *da.*" Elena snatched the dress from Luanne's hand, tucking it between beefy arm and ample, ever-quivering bosom as she went about undoing the damage Luanne had inflicted on the white down comforter. "The princess recently has big-screen television put in. Of course, she has smaller one in own rooms, but is not good for watching films, she says. There!" the maid said with obvious pride. "Is good, now." Then she turned to Luanne, appraising her with shrewd brown eyes.

"You fix hair, you fix makeup, you be ready when prince comes—" she glanced at her watch "—in five minutes?"

Satisfied, Elena tromped out of the room.

Horrified, Luanne plunked herself back down in front of the vanity mirror, not sure whether to laugh or bawl her eyes out.

When Alek carefully, and with every ounce of charm he could muster, asked Gizela Pandova, the undisputed doyenne of the palace kitchen since well before Alek's birth, to hold luncheon until Luanne awakened, the long-faced cook had slammed the pin down onto the dough she was rolling out, muttering something in her native Slovak that would have been cause for beheading in an earlier generation. So Alek had leaned across the butcher-block island in the cavernous kitchen and, as he'd done hundreds of times before, grinned up into her scowling face.

"Now, *milenka*," he cajoled in the same language, "surely you could prepare something that will keep until she's ready? Salad and sandwiches, perhaps? Some cold roast beef or salmon? Nothing too spicy, though, as I gather women who are expecting sometimes have delicate stomachs."

Gizela had given him a very odd look, then grumbled that she would do her best, only to blush scarlet when Alek bussed her on the cheek. A move that did not, however, deter her from swiping at him with her wooden spoon when he tried to filch a raspberry tart she'd planned on serving with afternoon tea.

And that had been the highlight of a morning that had otherwise crept along with excruciating slowness, as time had a nasty habit of doing when one's life is a jumble of unresolved issues. That conversation with his grandmother had shot Alek's concentration to hell: he barely remembered a word of what his foreign secretary had said about the current situation in Stolvia, a neighboring country not much larger than Carpathia, whose leaders Alek was to meet early the following week in an attempt to stave off yet another territorial skirmish. His volunteering to mediate had clearly both surprised and delighted the princess, who he gathered was growing weary of such tasks. But nothing on earth could have kept him from at least attempting to help, even though he believed that his efforts would, in all probability, prove futile.

My God—he really *was* growing up, he mused as he sat with Luanne on the terrace off the library after their lunch of cold roast beef, fresh rolls and vinaigrette-dressed salad. No mean feat when so many people here only remembered him as a child, or, at best, a hellion of a teenager.

"You know, where I come from, people usually expect a little conversation with their lunch," Luanne said.

Leaning back in one of the wrought-iron chairs, his cheek propped in his hand, Alek allowed an apologetic smile. The princess had excused herself some time ago to run some errands in the village, while Chase and Zoltan—whom the boy had insisted join them—were romping around in the vast lawn below, trying to teach Bo to catch Zoltan's Frisbee. Which left Alek and Luanne on the shady terrace, unsure of what to say to or do with each other.

"Sorry. I suppose I drifted off."

"I suppose you did." Her chiding was gentle, however, perhaps a by-product of a need to quell her own nervousness, if her ceaseless torture of her napkin was any indication. She did look somewhat more refreshed after her long nap, however, not to mention much more pulled together. Still, when she tilted her head at him, a breeze teasing the loose, dark waves held barely in check by a slim silver headband, there was no masking the worry lines etched at the corners of her mouth. She sighed, then focused on the two boys.

"This is so strange."

He didn't need her to explain. "Perhaps it will get less so, the more we're around each other."

One side of her mouth lifted. "I somehow doubt it. I mean, I feel like I'm in a dream. Like it's too perfect to be real."

Chuckling, Alek lifted a crystal pitcher filled with fruit juice, refilled Luanne's empty glass. "One can become acclimated, you know."

"Not me," she insisted, nodding her thanks for her drink which she then lifted to her lips.

"Can't? Or don't wish to?"

She shrugged. "A little of both, maybe. I can't help who I am, Alek. Or you, who you are. It's just the way things are. And frankly, it gives me the willies, whenever I try to imagine Chase in this environment. I mean, how on earth is he supposed to have a normal life if all this—'' she waved her glass to include the palace behind her "—is part of that life?''

More amused than he'd let on, Alek angled his head at her. "Are you implying I didn't have a normal childhood?''

"I hate to break this to you, but living in a seventy-room house with a million servants and having people call you 'Your Highness' is not normal.''

"I suppose that depends on your definition of *normal*.'' She rolled her eyes. Alek laughed. "But if it makes you feel any better, while I may have been a brat, I wasn't spoiled.'' When she gave him a dubious look, he grinned. "One day, I'll take you to meet my nanny. If you think my grandmother is formidable…''

She laughed softly, but only for a moment. Alek leaned forward.

"Luanne, I assure you…I promise not to spoil Chase. Although I suppose that means I'll have to cancel the plans to turn the west garden into an amusement park.''

Their color intensified by the colors in her outfit, her eyes widened, then she burst into laughter, a sound that winnowed straight through to the empty space in his chest, settling in like a large, purring cat.

"Things could be worse, you know,'' he said as her laugh died down.

"And how do you figure that?''

"At least we don't hate each other.'' Then he frowned. "You don't, do you?''

Her mouth quirked, she looked away, shaking her head. "No.'' Then again, on a rush of air, "No, I don't *hate* you.''

He didn't miss the emphasis. "Well, I suppose that's something, then—''

"Oh, Lord, Alek—what are we going to do?''

Without thinking, he leaned across the table and captured

one of her slender, warm hands in his. "Take things one day at a time, *mila.*"

"*Mila?*"

"An endearment, like sweetheart in English."

She withdrew her hand, a flush sweeping over her cheeks.

"Luanne, I didn't mean anything—"

"No, no. It's okay. It's just—" She shook her head, then said, "I take it you told your grandmother about Chase?"

"What makes you say that?"

"Maybe it had something to do with my hardly being able to breathe during lunch, what with all the tension hanging in the air between the two of you."

A tight smile pulled at Alek's mouth. He tore off the end of a roll, tossed it to Sasha, one of the dogs, who was whining at his elbow. "I didn't have to tell her, as it happens. She guessed...Luanne? Are you all right?"

One hand pressed to her abdomen, she held up the other at his question, breathing slowly and deeply for several seconds before finally giving him something resembling a smile. "I'm fine," she said on a whoosh of air. "Just a preliminary contraction. The doctor said they're real normal, especially in a second pregnancy. They just sometimes catch me by surprise, is all."

"Do they hurt?"

"Uh-uh. Just feels like someone's wringing me out inside." Then she leaned over, tried to tug one of the other chairs over to her.

"What are you doing?"

"Swollen ankles," she said on a grunt. "Gotta get my feet up."

Alek stood immediately, the chair scraping over the flagstone as he shifted it into the right position. "It wouldn't kill you to ask for help, you know."

"The few times in my life I let someone help," she said as she slowly lifted her bare feet up onto the seat of the chair, "I only ended up sufferin' for it. So I just kinda got out of the habit, y'know?"

Driven by something totally outside his volition, he clamped both hands on the arms of her chair and loomed over her, his stance eerily reminiscent of one he'd taken eleven years before, on a twin bed in a tiny mobile home in Sandy Springs, Texas. At that moment he didn't give a damn that their closeness breached acceptable parameters between a man and a woman who had just buried her husband a few weeks before. All he knew was that her adamancy infuriated him, even as the proximity of her swollen ripeness, her sweet scent, seared through him in a jolt of raw sexual awareness that nearly ripped the breath from his lungs. Their gazes locked, his heart thundering in his chest, he felt like a man gripping a live wire, unable to break a connection he knows will destroy him.

"I swear by Almighty *God* that you can trust me not to hurt you, Luanne. Not anymore."

He could see her pulse beating frantically, like a bird's, at the base of her throat. "You can't guarantee that," she whispered.

On a growl of frustration, he pushed away.

Trembling worse than Bo in a thunderstorm, Luanne sat with Sasha's head on what there was of her lap, waiting for that unbelievable electrical charge to clear from the air. Well, now she knew for sure—whatever it was that had drawn her to Alek all those years ago was still alive and kicking, boy.

Only bigger and badder than ever.

She didn't doubt his sincerity for a second. He meant every word he'd said, about not wanting to hurt her or spoil Chase. But right now, he'd say just about anything, wouldn't he, to make sure she didn't stand in the way of his getting to know his son? Not that she blamed him—in his position, she'd probably do the same thing—but she knew, from recent experience, there was a big, big difference between understanding a person's motives and trusting him.

"Comfortable?"

Startled out of the state she was doing a real good job of working herself into, Luanne glanced up to see Alek leaning against the stone balustrade a few feet in front of her, his arms crossed in such a way that every fiber of his shirt had cozied right on up to those shoulders of his. And it was dang unfair, the way he sat there, radiating coolness, when she knew for a fact it was going to take her a good two or three hours to corral her stampeding hormones.

"Wh-what?"

"I asked if you were comfortable." But now she thought maybe his voice was *too* level, his jaw set in that way that men do when they don't want you to know what they're really thinking.

She grimaced. For several reasons. "I'm seven months pregnant. What do you think?"

Another second or two passed before he asked, "Do you mind if I ask you something personal?"

Something about his tone put her on guard, although she couldn't have said why. "You've seen me naked. I think we're kinda beyond your having to ask me if it's okay to get personal."

His brows shot up, like she'd surprised him some, but then he said, "Even if it involves Jeff?"

She stared real hard at some tree off in the distance. "If I don't want to answer, I won't. How's that?"

"Fair enough." He paused, then asked, "Is there any reason why you and Jeff didn't have more children before this one?"

"It wasn't for lack of trying, if that's what you're aimin' to find out." She waited for his reaction, only to then wonder why she should feel chagrin when there wasn't much of one. "Jeff was away a lot. Obviously. The timin' just didn't seem to be in our favor was all. When it finally happened, we were both flabbergasted."

His eyes didn't leave her face. "So Jeff was happy about this baby?"

Now what do you suppose was behind that question? Right on the heels of her wondering about that, however, came an almost crushing sense of regret.

"He actually went out onto the driveway in the middle of the night after I told him and yelled, 'My wife's gonna have a baby!' " She looked at Alek. "This child meant the world to him. Oh, he loved Chase, and he'd told me a million times not to fret if we didn't have more kids, but you can't tell me that old male ego didn't get off on knowing he was going to have one of his own.''

The words had come out with more of an edge to them than she'd expected, but when she quickly searched Alek's face for signs that he might have heard, all she saw was a kind of sadness that might have echoed her own, if she didn't know better. As if—

From the lawn below came shouts of approval from the two boys as Bo managed to catch his first Frisbee. Grateful for the distraction, she said, ''Sometimes it's nice to be able to forget how unhappy you are. Even if it's just for a little while.''

''Do you? Even for a little while?''

She looked down at her hands, at the diamond wedding band flashing in a bit of sunlight. *Forgetting* was for children, wasn't it? For folks who still believed in magic and promises and happily-ever-afters. ''Not really, no.''

Suddenly he was squatting in front of her, her left hand captured in his, his thumb tracing the stones on her ring. Then he looked up at her, the fire in his eyes nearly shorting out her brain. ''If there was any way I could erase the sadness I see in your eyes right now, I would.''

It was everything she could do not to gasp, let alone to heave herself out of her chair and haul her pregnant carcass back to her room where she could hide until it was time to leave. Since she didn't figure such an exit, especially in her current condition, would be either feasible or dignified, she mumbled something about his being very sweet, then changed the subject. Or rather, got it back on track. ''What exactly did your grandmother say? About Chase?''

Alek got to his feet, walked back to the balustrade. ''Other than berating me for being an idiot?''

''Oh, for heaven's sake, Alek…I was the one who pushed for us to—''

''And I stayed, didn't I?''

A flush swept over her skin. ''It wasn't just you makin' that baby, is all I'm sayin'. So it doesn't seem right for you to take all the blame.''

"Trust me. It's less complicated this way."

She bristled. "You're not tellin' me everything, are you?"

He pivoted, frowning. "Why do you say that?"

"Because that's what men do, keep things from women."

Alek's mouth flattened into a grim line, then relaxed enough for him to say, "My grandmother thinks I should tell Chase the truth. Before others notice the resemblance."

"No! Alek—it would destroy him!"

"Which is what I told her."

She fought back a wave of panic. "Oh, for heaven's sake, the similarity's not *that* noticeable—"

"And we wouldn't be sitting here right now if it wasn't, would we?"

A brittle, fragile silence hummed between them for several seconds. Finally Luanne said, "We can't tell him. Not yet."

"And what if someone does make the connection?"

"I'll take that chance."

His jaw tight, Alek dropped back into the chair across from her. "Does Chase know Jeff's not his biological father?"

She let out a harsh sigh.

"And that means?"

Her heart felt like a lump of ice inside her chest. "After Jeff saw those photos of Chase, things got real tense for a while, right up until he left for France. We…argued. More than once, in fact." She looked at Alek, unwilling to even attempt to read what was in his eyes. "Chase may have overheard part of one of those arguments."

"*What?*" With a particularly ripe oath, Alek shot up from his chair and strode a few feet away, only to immediately spin back around, his eyes glittering. "Why the bloody *hell* didn't you tell me this before?"

"Because I've been a little preoccupied and I simply forgot, okay? And I don't know that he really heard anything. He'd come home a little early from school, we were in the kitchen." She pressed the heel of one hand against her forehead, then let it drop to her lap. "No matter how hard I try, I can't for the life of me remember the conversation well enough to even guess at what he might've heard."

Alek let out a harsh sigh, shoved his hand into his pocket. "You think Jeff might have said something to him?"

"I don't know. On the one hand I keep thinking Chase would've come right out and said something, if he he'd actually heard your name used. Although…" She struggled to her feet, stretching out her back as she closed the space between them. "Chase also has this tendency to think about things a real long time before he's ready to talk about them. For all I know he's been turning this over in his mind for some months. And now that Jeff's gone…"

After a long moment Alek turned and leaned his elbows on the top of the stone, linking his long-fingered, graceful hands in front of him. He gazed into the distance, his features pinched with worry. "And what if he hasn't said anything yet because he's afraid of the truth? What if he *does* think I'm his father, and that thought makes him positively ill?"

Oh, my word, if he didn't look like a little boy himself just then, afraid of being judged and found wanting by the other kids on the playground. Heaven knew, she'd seen that very look on her son's face any number of times over the past few years. And Luanne, whose need to comfort folks in distress had not diminished over time, had to force her hand to stay where it was and not go getting her in any more trouble by brushing back that wave of hair that had fallen over his forehead. But what she couldn't control was her heart, which swelled up something fierce at the realization that Alek wasn't worried about whether he would like his son, but whether his son would like *him*.

"Things'll work out, Alek," she surprised herself by saying.

Alek looked at her, his mouth pulled into a rueful half smile. "You really believe that, don't you?"

"Well, shoot," she said, even though the words didn't come as easily as they might have, once upon a time, "if I didn't, I'd've been tempted to do myself in long before this."

Something dark and cold settled into Alek's eyes before he glanced back at the boys. Chase picked that moment to look up, his own grin immediately collapsing when he caught sight of Alek watching him. Then, deliberately, he snatched the fallen Frisbee out of the grass and tramped away.

Mortification made Luanne's cheeks burn. "He had no cause to act like that. And you better believe he's gonna hear about it—"

Except her words just dried right up the instant she felt Alek's arm go around her shoulders. "Sh, sh, sh," he said, as he might to a child. "I have a much better idea." Her mouth still open, Luanne looked at him. He nodded back at the palace. "How about a tour?"

"Well...sure. But—"

He gave her shoulders a squeeze, then steered her back inside. "As you say, things will work out."

And if his words hadn't rung quite so hollow, maybe she would've felt better about the whole thing.

Chapter 7

"**W**ill that be all, Your Highness?"

Seated at the desk in his study, Alek glanced up at his aide, his vision slightly blurred from the vast amount of background material he'd been plowing through for the meeting with the Stolvian leaders the following day. Behind him rain slashed against the leaded glass window, as it had been for most of the past week. "What time is it?"

"After five, sir." Behind his wire-rimmed glasses, Tomas's green eyes sparkled; spidery fingers tugged at the hem of his navy cardigan.

The corners of Alek's mouth lifted. "Sonya again, is it?"

Twin dots of color bloomed in the aide's pale cheeks, softening the almost macabre effect of the spiky black bangs which lay like a row of insect legs across the young man's forehead. A subtly patterned bow tie bobbed at his throat. "Yes, Your Highness."

Outside, thunder growled in the distance. "You're a damn lucky man, Tomas," Alek said, and meant it. The bookshop clerk was cute and dimpled and as sweet as they came. "Off with you, then. Mustn't keep her waiting."

"Yes, sir. Thank you, sir. Good night, sir."

Alek's chuckle turned into a dispirited sigh, though, as another grumble of thunder nagged. Thus far, "things" weren't working out at all. And the blasted weather wasn't helping. At best, the downpour had occasionally tapered off to a cold, nasty drizzle, prompting even Alek, who usually loved the rain, to admit the relentless, chilly gloom was getting to him. Especially as he could see how much it was also getting to his son, who clearly blamed Alek for every horrible thing that had ever happened to him, including, but not limited to, the rotten weather. *It almost never rains back home,* he'd hurled at Alek a couple of days before. *If I was there, I could've been swimming or out on my bike or anything except bein' stuck in this dumb old palace with nothin' to do!*

Alek pushed himself up from his desk and walked over to stare at the fire, his arms folded over his fisherman's sweater.

At least Luanne was apparently getting the rest she needed. When she wasn't busy winning over the palace staff, that is. But that meant he rarely saw her, except at dinnertime. And then she seemed ill at ease, her attention focused almost exclusively on her son. Not that she babied him or excused his behavior, but Alek got the feeling she was watching for some sign, perhaps, that would give her more of a clue as to how much Chase knew.

Dammit to hell—relations between mother and son were more strained than ever. Chase wouldn't let Alek get anywhere near him, emotionally or physically, and Luanne was obviously miserable....

"Ah. Hard at work, I see."

He turned, managing to dredge up a smile for his grandmother, who looked as soft and harmless as a kitten in her gray cashmere turtleneck sweater and slacks. "You've found me out."

She smiled in return, then came into the room, lowering herself into one of the leather wing chairs in front of the fire. "You might be interested to know I got a call from the president of the United States this morning, sending you his best wishes for your success."

Alek snorted. "Nothing like piling on the pressure."

"The U.S. would be very grateful if this could be resolved quickly and without their aid. No one wants more bloodshed, Alek. Or more orphans. And you know as well as I do how easily even a minor skirmish can flare into full-fledged war." She paused, approval shining from her dark eyes. "It is a wonderful thing, what you are attempting to do."

"Nothing less than you would have done."

Her lips tilted. "No, I suppose not. But I cannot tell you what a relief it is, to at last have some of the burden removed from my shoulders. And how proud I am of you, Aleksander. Not to mention how grateful I am that I can say that and mean it. I had my doubts, you know."

Alek returned his attention to the fire. "Yes, I imagine you did."

"But not anymore. Now I know you have both the determination and the humility to be a good leader."

He looked back. "Humility?"

"Oh, yes. There is no more direct route to failure than believing one has all the answers. But a person who is willing to listen, to be open to solutions he or she perhaps has not thought of before…that is the person worthy of wearing a crown." She smiled. "Determination, you always had. Humility, however…" Her fingers spread, she wiggled one hand back and forth.

One side of his mouth lifted, then he sighed. "Well, I'll certainly be the first to admit I don't have all the answers. Or, at the moment, any of them."

"I assume you mean concerning the boy? And…his mother?"

He grunted an affirmative reply.

She stood, her hands clasped together. "It has only been a week, child. Give it time."

"I know, I know. But it's killing me to see her—them—so unhappy."

He could almost feel the princess go into speculative mode. "Then the logical thing to do would be to find out why they are so unhappy and fix it."

"Oh, and that's all? Now, why didn't I think of that?"

One dark brow arched, almost coquettishly. "I have no idea, my dear."

Alek angled his head at her. "Is it my imagination, or have you changed your mind about Luanne?"

"Have *you?*" she said, her expression inscrutable, then left.

Alek dropped into another chair, glowering at the seventeenth-century Dutch still-life on the opposite wall. He could ignore his grandmother's last comment—and fully intended to—but as for her earlier one... Oh, for God's sake—he'd twist himself into bloody knots to ease the impending crisis in Stolvia, yet here in his own home, he was standing back and watching a situation deteriorate that was every bit as critical, as if he were completely helpless.

At that thought he dragged his hands down his face, then let out a strangled laugh. Helplessness had nothing to do with it, even though the idea of actually having to make an effort to repair something—as opposed to simply changing course and avoiding the problem altogether—was rather an alien concept. But that wasn't what unnerved him. Nor did the actual struggle necessary to achieve his goal. It was what happened after that, wasn't it?

Congratulations, Alek... you may proceed to the head of the queue.

If he succeeded in alleviating Luanne's distress, getting her to smile and laugh again, resurrecting the woman who'd stolen his breath, not to mention his good sense, so long ago, what the bloody hell was to prevent her stealing his breath and good sense all over again?

Only this time, walking away wouldn't be an option. This time, they had a child, a child Alek couldn't ignore simply because he was afraid of...

Of what? Falling in love?

No, it couldn't be that. How could one fear the impossible? But revealing secrets he'd sworn to himself he never would...ah, now *that* was worth the odd spate of anxiety.

Alek expelled a ragged sigh: sidestepping the truth was definitely easier from a distance. But there was no getting around the fact that he would never win his son's trust without winning that of the child's mother.

And that meant going about things far differently than he had been.

The room suddenly lightened. For a moment Alek was tempted to attribute it to all the revelations pummeling his brain, until he twisted around, squinting out the window at the glorious, golden sunlight flooding the landscape.

Even he knew a sign when he saw one.

"Sun's out! Anyone up for a drive?"

From where she reclined in one corner of the beige leather sectional in the informally furnished media room, trying to read a novel from the palace library, Luanne's gaze popped to Alek's. He wore a sweater and jeans underneath a black leather jacket—*the* leather jacket, she realized with a hitch to her midsection—as well as an endearing, little-boy grin that just plumb stole her breath. They hadn't seen each other all that much since that lunch on the terrace, and now she remembered why she'd been just as glad they hadn't. However, a palace is no better than a trailer if you're stuck inside, and the prospect of getting out—even if that meant getting out with Alek—made her downright giddy.

Luanne let out a whoop of joy, even though her grouchy son, splayed on his stomach on the floor, using up his one-hour-per-day video game allotment, pretended he hadn't heard.

She slammed shut the book. "Where?"

Alek laughed, a real laugh, which was something she couldn't recall seeing him do all that often and which made her insides go all tickley and warm. "It's a small country," he said, long dimples carving into his stubble-shadowed cheeks. "We can take in the whole thing in an hour."

"You're on." She struggled up off the sofa, tugging down the hem of a bright-red sweatshirt over a pair of black maternity leggings, then said to Chase, "Okay, buddy. Unplug yourself and come on."

"I ain't going."

Luanne bristled. "Yes, you are. You've been doin' nothing

but moan your head off about the lousy weather all week and how there was nothing to do. Well, now there is. And the next time you say 'ain't,' you can say goodbye to the video games for a month.''

Chase flipped around to glower at her. "You can't do that!"

"You want to test me, you go right ahead and try. But right now I need you to get up off your posterior and go get ready." Grumbling, the kid got to his feet and shuffled toward the door, the boots scraping against the wooden floor. "And pick up your feet, Chase Eugene! Wood floors scratch something terrible!"

Behind her, Alek laughed again. "You're rather formidable yourself."

She turned around, her heart flip-flopping at the spark in those silver eyes. "Not that it always works, which you well know... oh, shoot." She grabbed for Alek's arm, just because it was the nearest thing to grab onto, you understand, as a contraction strangled her midsection. In turn Alek roped his other arm around her back, supporting her until the stupid thing passed. She let go, embarrassed.

"That's it," he said. "You're seeing the doctor. Tomorrow morning."

There was an edge to his concern she found amusing. At least, that's the word she chose to use for what she felt, since it was safer than any number of others she might come up with. "Oh, for heaven's sake, I just saw my own doctor before I left, and he said everything's just fine—"

"Were you having so many contractions before you left?"

"Yes."

He hooked her chin with one knuckle, forcing her to meet his gaze. "Look me in the eye and say that."

She tried, she really did, but he looked so serious, and what with all the tension of the past several days, her second *yes* came out as a giggle.

Alek let go of her chin, but only to practically jab his index finger in her face. "Tomorrow. Doctor. And that's final."

She opened her mouth to protest, then decided, oh, what the hey? If it put his mind at ease, it wasn't like it could hurt or anything. So she excused herself to visit the rest room, relieved to see Chase ready to go by the time she got back, even if the corners of his mouth just about rested on his chest.

Alek led them through the palace and out yet another door, this one facing a large, simple building mostly covered in vines a hundred feet or so away.

"Would you rather wait here, or walk out to the garage with me?"

"Walk—"

"Wait."

She ignored Chase. "Walk. I'm beginning to forget why I have legs."

Alek smiled, then looked at Chase, who was standing with his hands tucked into the armpits of his baggy Texas Rangers sweatshirt, staring off into space. The frayed edges of the awful ratty jeans he'd insisted on taking skirted the damp ground, even with the raised heels of the cowboy boots. "Maybe you'd like to choose which car to take, Chase."

Luanne felt her heart drop to her swollen ankles, but it was too late to avert—

"Cars are stupid."

She gripped her son's shoulders and did that thing she did with her nails she knew he hated. "That was uncalled for," she said quietly. "Apologize."

"No."

But before she could say anything else, Alek twisted Chase around to face him. And, boy, she'd've had heart failure if any adult had ever looked at her the way Alek was at her son right now. Her first instinct was to run interference, but then it hit her that she couldn't do that. This was between Chase and his father, whether that made her uneasy or not. So she crammed her hands into her sweatshirt pockets and bit her tongue and ignored the way her heart was hammering against her ribs, especially when the idea trickled past her apprehension that, well, maybe she could trust Alek. A little, anyway.

"If you have a bone to pick, young man," Alek said in a low voice, "pick it with me. Not your mother. I thought you'd enjoy getting out for a bit, that's all. If you don't wish to go, fine. But let's not ruin it for your mum, all right?"

"Alek—"

But he lifted one hand to cut her off.

And, after what seemed like an eternity, Chase swiveled more or less in Luanne's direction, still scowling, and mumbled something that sounded like "Sorry, Mama." It came across about as sincere as a politician's promise, and heaven only knew what was going through his head, but it was a start.

"Thank you, honey," she said over the knot in her throat, then nodded back toward the door. "Okay, go on."

Startled blue eyes shot to hers. "Go on?"

"Well, yes. Alek's right." She risked a glance at Alek's face, only to chicken out before she could read his expression. "If you don't want to go, there's no point in forcing you. So you might as well stay here with…" Now she did look at Alek. "You think maybe Gizela could find something for him to do?"

"Oh, I'm sure she could." Alek hooked his hands on his hips, his expression thoughtful. "She used to make me scrub out her mixing bowls. And with guests coming tomorrow, she's bound to have used, oh, I don't know, dozens by now…."

Somehow Luanne managed to keep a straight face as horror streaked across her son's. Chase's first comment after meeting Gizela that first day was that the cook "creeped him out."

"Uh…" Oh, she could see pride battling it out with self-preservation in those big blue eyes. The child licked his lips, shuffled one foot, swiped an arm across his nose—Luanne let out an "Honestly, Chase!"—until he finally, quietly, red-facedly allowed as how maybe he wouldn't mind going for a ride after all. If that was okay?

And the question was directed at Alek.

Alek seemed to ponder this for several seconds. "I don't know…" He bent over, his hands on his knees. "Are you sure you can stand that much time in my company?"

"Better you than Gizela," Chase muttered.

She watched Alek try, without much success, to suppress a grin. "Well," he said, straightening up, "if it's all right with your mother—"

"Please, Mama?" The words spewed from her son's mouth

as he whipped around. And, oh, Lord, he looked so much like he did when he was still little, when even the smallest things had the power to render him awestruck.

"I suppose—" But her words were cut off by a huge hug and a muffled thank-you, followed by a laugh when the baby kicked him.

"Well, then," Alek said, his voice oddly tight. Luanne lifted her eyes to see that same sort of wonderment in his. "We're all set. But we'd better get on with it, or we'll all have to answer to Gizela if we're late for dinner. And we don't want *that*, do we?"

"Uh-*uh*," Chase said with an emphatic shake of his head.

Chuckling, Alek hesitated, then held his hand out to the child. Luanne held her breath, counting her heartbeats until, almost in slow motion, her son slipped his hand into his father's.

Their feet crunching fallen twigs and wet leaves plastered to the brick walk, they wordlessly made their way to the garage, as if speaking might somehow break the spell. Alek's own lungs tight with the same tension that radiated from Luanne, he caught her sneaking glances several times at Chase and him.

He was holding his son's hand.

The realization rocketed through him, cramping his heart. He wanted to sweep the child into his arms, make promises the like of which he'd never made—or wanted to—to a living soul before. Inevitably, he was sure, would come the regret and anger over what he'd missed, but this moment was too precious—and too brief, he thought, as Chase wriggled his hand free and walked on a few feet ahead of them—to allow anything to sully it.

Not knowing how much, if anything, the boy knew was agony. But now more than ever, Alek didn't dare broach the subject. Timing was everything. If Chase didn't know, his discovery of the truth before he was ready to deal with it—whenever the hell that might be—could very likely annihilate this first tenuous, fragile thread shimmering between them.

Luanne touched Alek's arm, just briefly. "Good job," she

said with a half smile, and Alek wondered at how, of all the things he'd ever been given, of all the races he'd won and the women he'd dated, nothing had ever given him one-tenth of the satisfaction, or poleaxed him quite the same way, as had those two words from this woman.

Alek tapped on the window to the lounge beside the garage where Gregori, the chauffeur, spent much of his down time in front of the television. The pewter-haired man glanced up from the recliner, immediately slamming the chair into an upright position and tugging his suspenders back into place on his shoulders, only to wave and nod in understanding as Alek indicated his intention to do the driving. Alek punched in the code to lift the door to the first bay, almost laughing aloud at Chase's gasp when he caught sight of the ten vintage models in the garage. So much for "hating cars."

Luanne seemed equally impressed. "Oh, my word..." She reverently skimmed her hand over the hood of a cherry-red Ferrari F-40. "Jeff would've given his right arm for one of these."

"You know what it is?"

"You kidding?" She moved on to the next car, a deep-green Jag Alek had bought off an Oxford colleague. "You're forgetting who I lived with for more than ten years."

The softly spoken sentence pierced the space between them like a row of rusty spikes. Forget? How could he? Never mind that for reasons he knew better than to examine any too closely, Alek would have liked nothing better than to forget that. He pushed back his jacket, shoved his hands into his pockets. "I'm sorry—"

"It's okay," she said quietly, offering him a hint of a smile. He saw her dart a glance at her son, who'd found his way to the other side of the garage and Alek's grandfather's gleaming white, fin-tailed '59 Lincoln. Her eyes drifted back to his. "Not talking about it doesn't make it hurt any less."

Alek nodded and looked away, patting the Jag's hood. "So...Jeff didn't collect cars, then?"

"No." She hugged her middle, her breath clouding in the damp, chilly air. "Oh, I think he might've gotten around to it, one day, but…oh, would you look at this!'' She inhaled sharply at the sight of the 1934 black Rolls that had belonged to his great-grandfather. "These all family cars?''

"Except for the Ferrari, which was an admitted indulgence.'' Alek wondered why he felt the need to justify himself. He stopped in front of a golden-beige '68 Mercedes convertible, its chromework glistening even in the dimly lit garage. "This one belonged to my mother.''

Luanne moved beside him. "And you've never driven it, have you?''

He felt a sad smile pull at his lips, but he didn't look at her. "Does reading minds come as naturally to you as bossing your children?''

His circumnavigation of the garage apparently complete, Chase joined them in front of the Mercedes, sagging against his mother. Surprise flashed across her features before she draped one arm around the child's thin shoulders and hugged him to her. "I guess maybe it does,'' she finally answered.

"I like this one best,'' Chase announced, then looked up at Alek. "Did you mean it, when you said I could pick the car to go for a ride in?''

Alek swallowed past the knot at the base of his throat and nodded. "I did. But why this one?''

"I dunno.'' Underneath his sweatshirt, one shoulder hitched. "I just like the way it looks. Not all flashy or nothin'.''

"Or *anything*,'' Luanne muttered, then said to Alek, "But if you don't want to—''

"No, no…that's fine. I'll just have to get the keys from Gregori—''

Chase pointed. "Isn't that them in the car?''

Which they were, since the chauffeur's duties included driving all the cars every so often to keep them in prime condition. Apparently, the Mercedes had had her turn that morning. So they all climbed in, Alek refusing to kowtow to any suggestion of unease about being behind the wheel of the only car he ever remembered seeing his mother drive. No, he could *not* smell her perfume after twenty years, for God's sake. Gregori had thoroughly cleaned out the car years ago, glove compartment and all. There was nothing left of his mother in this car.

Except memories.

But once out on the open road, he could feel all three of them relax. Thick, apricot-hued sunlight had set the rain-kissed fields and trees ablaze; dozens of birds, obviously relieved to discover the world had not come to an end, trilled and chirped and cawed their little hearts out. Luanne laughed; Alek looked over, saw her enormous smile, and his heart took a slow, almost painful tumble in his suddenly far-too-tight chest. Her smile immediately dimmed.

"You okay?" she asked, and he nearly jumped.

"Why do you ask?"

She shrugged, one hand clamped on her hair whipping about her face. "Just wondered. Because this is your mother's car and all." She glanced at him, then away. "And because you have a very peculiar look on your face."

Her compassion was unfeigned. Uncomplicated. And unfettered by the million-and-one "shoulds" concomitant to the disparity of their positions, he realized. Although Luanne expected—demanded—nothing more of him now than she had eleven years ago, when she didn't know who he was, neither was she about to allow either personal tragedy or social "convention" to hinder her ability—or, apparently, her desire—to give.

Alek felt oddly humbled. And even more oddly…blessed.

They crested the hill that would take them down into the village. "The peculiar look would be due to Gizela's sausage-and-sauerkraut casserole," he said, hoping to hear her laugh again. Which she did.

"Hey, I liked it. But then, you're talkin' to a gal who teethed on Tex-Mex cooking. A little spice isn't going to bother me—Oh! Is this the village?"

"Don't blink or you might miss it entirely."

Another laugh. "Like Sandy Springs."

Although her attention was riveted to the succession of charming buildings and shops, some of which had been standing literally for centuries, Alek couldn't miss the wistfulness in her voice.

"You're homesick, aren't you?"

Now it was her turn to look startled. She smoothed one hand over her abdomen. "I miss the sky."

"We have sky."

She gave him an indulgent smile. But that was all.

They inched down the narrow, cobblestoned streets to the village square, in the middle of which stood a worn, pigeon-stained stone fountain dating back to the sixteenth century, and Alek heard himself prattling about how the farmers still set up their booths every Friday and Saturday, just as they'd been doing since medieval times. At one point he stopped by a cluster of villagers who clearly would have been offended had he not, introducing Luanne and Chase to them. Most Carpathians younger than fifty spoke English fairly fluently—it had been a required subject in all schools since the mid fifties—but many of the old-timers still spoke Carpathian, a dialect of Slovak. When Luanne smiled at the two old men in the group, however, all language barriers simply dissolved in the face of her genuine, all-encompassing affection. One of them indicated her swollen middle with a grandfatherly smile, then cradled his arms.

"*Ditete,*" he said. *Baby.* Luanne nodded and laughed, then repeated the word in her Texas twang, much to everyone's delight.

Luanne Evans Henderson was one of the most gracious human beings he'd ever known, Alek thought with a start as they pulled away, after he'd sworn to bring Luanne and Chase back to visit this one's bakery or that one's bookshop. And she was dead wrong about not fitting in. In fact—

His heart jerked to a halt, even as he forced his thoughts to do the same.

Five minutes later they'd passed the Baroque cathedral on the village's outskirts and were back out in the country, zipping past neat little farms, a candy factory, the pottery works. Alek yammered like a hyper tour guide; Luanne listened; Chase issued periodic, noncommittal yawns.

Eventually they circled back to the palace grounds, by way of the stables. Chase, who had remained ominously quiet the entire time, now clamored to get out, to Luanne's obvious surprise. The instant Alek stopped, the boy bounded from the car and straight toward an open stall, from which protruded the intelligent, blazed face of a bay mare, her ears twitching in curiosity.

Luanne clumsily followed. "Oh, Lord! Chase—!"

"It's all right," Alek said, laughing, as he halted her lunge across the muddy stableyard. The pungent smells of hay and horse, damp earth and fireplace smoke assaulted both Alek's nose and his memory as he guided her around assorted puddles and bogs. "Starlight's twenty if she's a day, and she adores children. Watch," he whispered, leaning close enough to let another scent override all the others.

But Luanne was far too intent on making sure the beast didn't bite off her child's head to notice Alek's sudden respiratory problems. Her breath hitched softly as the horse lowered her head, whuffling in Chase's face before bumping him with her nose, as gently as a kitten. Chase laughed, stroking the mare's blaze, then turned to them, his face alight.

"She likes me, Mama!"

"I can see that."

"What's her name, Alek?"

"Starlight."

"Starlight, star bright," Chase chanted, then gave her one last pat before starting back toward them. Reluctantly.

Luanne sighed. "You'd think a kid raised in Texas would learn how to ride practically before he learned how to walk. But when I took him out to the Carlisles' place to ride, couple of times when he was about six or so, he didn't seem to care for it much, so I didn't bother after that." She shook her head. "Now look at him, acting like it's just about killin' him to leave her. You just never know, do you?"

Why that simple, rhetorical question seemed particularly significant at that moment, Alek couldn't have said. All he knew was that a feeling he hadn't acknowledged for years sat up inside him, whining for attention...that feeling of wanting *more.* More of whatever it was that was causing this sweet, achy feeling inside him, this bizarre combination of fear and peace and longing for things he'd never wanted before, wasn't sure what to do with now.

And yet, even though every logical brain cell he had tried to convince him he'd accomplished his short-term mission, that she seemed more at ease now, that he should take her back to the palace, he heard himself say, "If you're not too tired, there's one more spot I'd like to show you before we go back."

An almost childlike expectancy radiated from her eyes as she said that would be just fine, so he shepherded them back into the car, acutely aware of Chase's last, yearning glance back at the horse. While grief and shock had perhaps provoked the child into moroseness these last few weeks, like his mother, Chase wasn't one to beg. When meant, Alek realized, it was up to him to make the offer the kid obviously wanted so badly he could taste it.

He started up the car, pulling out of the stableyard. Then, praying Luanne wouldn't think he was trying to buy his son's affection, Alek said, very casually, "I don't suppose you'd be interested in learning how to ride while you're here?"

"You mean that?"

"Of course I mean it," Alek said over this extremely odd bubbly feeling inside him. "I'm sure Fritz or one of his sons would be thrilled to have someone to teach again."

"Could I ride Starlight?"

"If Fritz thinks she's up to it, I don't see why not. She was my sister's when she was younger. And I believe some of Sophie's step-children-to-be rode her when they were here for her wedding last month."

That got a "cool" from the back seat and a curious look from the front. So Alek explained all about Sophie and her Yank and his wards and how she now lived, most of the time, at least, in a farmhouse in Michigan.

After a few very telling moments, Luanne said, "Your sister became a farmer's wife?"

Alek laughed, steering the car up a hillside leading to a certain ridge. "Not exactly. He's an electrician-turned-photographer and she's up to her eyeballs as the new President of the World Relief Fund.'' He glanced over at Luanne, who was still sitting there wearing a stunned expression. ''There's a housekeeper to keep things from falling apart. But that's it. Okay...close your eyes.''

''Why?''

''Just do it, all right?''

She gave him a wary look, but on a little huff, did as he asked.

''You, too, Chase,'' he directed toward the back seat, then steered the car into a clearing some fifty metres or so off the road. He got out, helped Chase from the car with a whispered order to not say a *word*, then went around to get Luanne, who looked as though she was about to succumb to a fit of the giggles. Since he'd instructed her to keep her eyes closed until further notice, he had to clamp one hand around her waist, the other to her hand, and carefully nudge her over the rocky surface of the clearing. When he had her exactly where he wanted her, he whispered, ''Now tell me if this isn't almost as good as Texas.''

She opened her eyes, letting out a gasp that made his heart cramp.

Chapter 8

"**O**h, my word, Alek—oh, Chase!" Luanne twisted around, presumably looking for her son, who had already climbed up onto a large boulder facing the view, where he sat huddled over, grasping his knees as he stared. "Have you even seen anything like this in your whole life, baby?"

Chase only shook his head.

Luanne then returned her attention to the panorama that stretched endlessly before them. The bluff just above the palace overlooked not only all of Carpathia—which admittedly wasn't saying much—but well beyond. To the north, the Carpathian mountains, majestic and snowcapped, jutted up into a blue mist. In every other direction, there were fields, forests and—

"Sky," Luanne whispered, her hands bracketing her face as she slowly turned all the way around, at last meeting his gaze. Tears shimmered in her eyes. "Oh, thank you, Alek. *Thank* you." She threw her arms around his neck and pressed her cheek to his, so briefly he barely had time to register the sensation. When she let go, however, she flung out her arms, as if to embrace...everything. The childlike gesture touched him, warmed him, started that *more, more, more* chant all over again.

"Come on." Alek grabbed her hand. "There's a place where you can sit and be more comfortable." She tried to extract her hand, but he wouldn't let her as he turned to Chase, still enthralled on his rock. The feel of Luanne's hand in his, the look of wonder on his son's face, revved the chant to fever pitch, teasing him with promises of things he'd never let himself want before, still wasn't sure should be his. Or that he could handle. "Want to come with us, or are you all right there?"

The boy distractedly waved them off.

When they reached the grassy slope nearby, Alek removed his jacket, spreading it on the still-damp ground, then settled the pregnant, protesting woman on it. Then he plopped down beside her. But not too close.

And not nearly close enough.

Luanne leaned back on her hands, grimacing at her swollen ankles for a moment before looking again up into the vast stretch of deepening blue, as if willing it to absorb her. "Well, it's not west Texas," she said with good humor, shifting to flap at the scenery. "Too many of those mountains and things impeding the view. But it'll do. It'll do just fine."

Alek reclined on one elbow, his head in his hand, fascinated by her rapturous expression. "I used to come up here quite a bit when I was younger. Much younger," he added, frowning at the frisson of sadness that shuddered through him. Oh, yes, he'd come up here a lot, especially around the time his parents' marriage had begun to go sour. As a child he remembered the way his parents couldn't even be in the same room without touching, the blazingly intimate shared glances they probably thought no one else—let alone their son—noticed. That their love should somehow simply die made no sense. That *they* should, made even less.

The emptiness ached, yes. But at least that was a dull and bearable thing, far preferable to the searing agony of loss and disappointment. Only, in this woman's presence, that philosophy no longer seemed to make quite as much sense as it once did.

Luanne tilted back her head, the breeze making a strand of hair dance enticingly over her throat. "Did you ever just lie back and stare up at the sky, tryin' to wrap your mind around the concept of infinity?"

"No. Infinity scares me."

"Really?" she said, but without judgment. Then she let out a deep, contented sigh. "Not me. I look up and see all that sky, and get to thinking about how it never, ever ends, and I think...that's God, isn't it?"

"You mean, like looking up into heaven?"

She shook her head, then lowered herself onto her elbows, skimming one hand over her undulating belly. "No," she said after a moment. "Not that God was up there in heaven, but that the up there *was* God. I guess..." She stopped, another slight flush washing over her pale cheeks. She'd worn little makeup since they'd arrived, he realized.

"You guess...?" he encouraged.

Her smile was hesitant. Almost shy. "I don't talk about this with many people. I mean, since faith is such a personal thing, you know?" She tucked the errant strand of hair back behind her ear. "Most folks aren't really interested."

"I am," he said, stunned to realize how long it had been since another human being had confided in him. Since he'd wanted one to.

Her glance was brief, assessing. Then she nodded, as if to herself, and said, almost in a rush, "Thinking about God and infinity and all that just reassures me, somehow, that He really does have all the answers. That no matter what happens, things will work out."

Alek squinted off into the distance. Damn, but he envied her the simplicity of her faith, her almost childlike trust in something unseen. When he said as much, her eyes widened. Then she grinned, a sassy little thing that made her nose wrinkle and Alek's heart thump in his chest.

"Childlike?"

This time, when that strand of hair broke ranks, drifting across her cheek, his hand lifted to brush it away. Except something stopped him from completing the action. His hand slapped against his hip. "That's not a bad thing, Luanne."

Her eyes had followed his hand's aborted flight, he saw, her brow slightly puckered. Then, on a quick sigh, she said, "It's just that I've never been able to swallow the idea that God causes the bad stuff. Not that I've figured out what does, mind, but, well…I just look up there and I think, there's gotta be an answer. A way out of whatever mess we find ourselves in." Before he could figure out what to say to that, she said, "You know the story of the Prodigal Son?"

He thought of his own recent return to the fold and smirked. "Vaguely."

She struggled to sit up, her earnestness infectious, intoxicating and—there was little point in denying it—arousing. "Okay—here's this kid who figures life's better 'out there', so he asks his father to give him what he's got coming to him and leaves. Except, not being exactly the sharpest tool in the shed, he spends it all like that." She snapped her fingers. "Which leaves him so broke he's ready to eat pig food. Then it dawns on him—hey! Here I am, like to starve to death, when the servants back home are living the high life in comparison. And all this time, his father was just waiting patiently for the fool to come to his senses and see the light."

Alek frowned. "And your point is?"

"That his father didn't throw him out—he left of his own accord. His father didn't punish him—the kid got himself in hot water because of his own dumb choices. I mean, what with the way kids are, there probably wasn't a single blessed thing the father could've said that the kid would've listened to. He just had to go on out there and find out for himself. But here's the important thing—soon as he went home, he realized his father's love, and everything he needed, had always been right there all along, just waiting for him to accept it." She looked down, twining a long piece of grass around her finger, then shrugged. And said with a wistfulness that pierced Alek's heart, "The father didn't even say 'I told you so.'"

The intricate, burbling song of a wren pierced the ensuing silence, momentarily followed by an answering call from its mate, as a dozen emotions wrestled for dominance in Alek's brain.

"So you really believe in a God of forgiveness?" he asked.

She looked at him, frowning slightly. "I have to. Or I'd go plumb nuts."

He nodded and glanced away.

Alek's turning away like that ripped right through the thin veil of serenity Luanne had managed to wrap around herself the past hour or so, despite the tension of being so close to a man who had the ability to provoke such unseemly reactions inside her. More than once she'd been sure he was going to touch her, and her disappointment that he hadn't made her feel about three inches tall. She now put all those confused feelings aside, however, to try to clarify a few things.

"I'm not talking about forgiving *you*, if that's what's eatin' at you."

Now he looked chagrined. "No, not exactly. But since you brought it up…"

"I told you—I had no expectations goin' in, so there's nothing to forgive on that score." She glanced over at him, but he didn't look much relieved, which puzzled her even more. "I'd like to think I'd be able to forgive anything. But I'm as beset with human weakness as the next person. I suppose it would depend on the circumstances."

Her words made his jaw tighten, she could see that much, as if she'd said something hurtful. "Alek? What is it?"

"Mama?"

Her head snapped up; Chase stood a few feet away, his hands fisted inside his pockets. The breeze had ruffled his hair and pinked his cheeks, and she thought how unfair it was, that his innocence should have been yanked from him so early. But then, life hadn't exactly been kind to her, either, and she had survived. Although, come to think of it, maybe she'd like to move past "surviving" to "living" sometime soon.

"C'n we go now, Mama? I'm gettin' hungry."

Frankly, his timing was perfect. If he hadn't come along, she probably would have pursued the conversation, if for no other reason than to find out what was causing Alek so much obvious distress. Only she wasn't all that sure she wanted to know, when it came right down to it. Not this time. Not now. Besides which, she needed to use the rest room.

"Sure, honey," she said, more than a little annoyed at having to accept Alek's offer of help to get up, since she'd apparently left her center of gravity somewhere over the Atlantic Ocean. He hauled her swiftly to her feet, his grip so strong and gentle it set her insides to hopping about like a flock of fleas. But when she glanced at him to thank him, she saw that haunted look back in his eyes, worse than she'd ever seen it. And although she couldn't discern what exactly was causing it, she had a bad feeling it had something to do with her.

"What's the best way to keep a skunk from smellin'?"

Luanne watched Alek, seated to her left at the head of the dinner table, frown in mock concentration at her son's riddle as they waited for dessert to be served. Although they were eating in the smaller, less ostentatious family dining room rather than the formal one with the soaring, beamed ceiling and the crystal chandeliers and the table that seated about a million people, Luanne still couldn't exactly see chowing down barbecued ribs and corn on the cob in here. The sauce would stain the pretty linen napkins something terrible, for one thing.

"I give up," Alek said at last.

Chase nearly exploded with laughter. "Hold his nose!"

Luanne smiled. The excursion had done wonders for Chase. For the first time since they'd arrived, the child's bad mood wasn't fouling the atmosphere like the smell of rotten vegetables. In fact, even before the riddle marathon, he'd been chattering away all through dinner about getting to ride. And he'd seemed real pleased when Alek said he thought he had a pair of riding boots left over from when he was a boy that might fit Chase, at least well enough to start.

To start.

Her smile dimmed. Of course. Far as Alek was concerned, this wasn't just a one-time thing, but the first step to building a real relationship with his son.

Which would eventually separate Luanne from hers.

Not that Chase was gonna turn over his affection for Jeff to another man, just like that. But whether she liked it or not, the fact was the man who had just reduced their son to even more helpless laughter by telling some of the worst knock-knock jokes she'd ever heard in her life was not the same man who'd breezed through Sandy Springs eleven years ago. This was a man who she thought maybe, just maybe, she could eventually trust with her son's heart.

Hers was something else again.

Chase suddenly twisted around in his chair, demanding more milk from the waiting servant, a man who looked like he'd been around as long as the palace. *Before* it had been rebuilt. But before Luanne could even blush, Alek leaned over to whisper something in Chase's ear. A moment later the child not only apologized to the servant, but asked if he might have some more milk, *please.*

Well, shoot. Alek really was trying to meet the child where he was, wasn't he, unlike a lot of adults who think bullying a child's the only way to get him to behave? Jeff had been a good father, for the most part, certainly better than anything Luanne had had in her experience, but he was gone. And Chase was going to need someone to be for him what Jeff would have been had he lived.

That that person should turn out to be his biological father was an irony that was going to take some getting used to on her part.

A soft touch jerked her out of her musings. Luanne glanced over at the princess's smile.

"You were lost in thought, my dear," the princess said kindly, the candlelight making her white hair shimmer like the angel hair her mother always put on the Christmas tree every year. "Are you feeling well?"

Luanne nodded, anxious to deflect the old woman's concern. "Yes, ma'am, I'm just fine."

"Still, it will not hurt to have Dr. Palachek stop by in the morning, no?"

Just what she needed, some old grizzled doctor who probably hadn't delivered a baby in a hundred years poking and prodding her. "I really don't want to inconvenience anybody—"

"Nonsense. The doctor is an old family friend. It will be no problem at all."

Luanne stifled a sigh, then returned her attention to Alek and Chase. Her son was giggling so hard Luanne worried he'd make himself sick. Then Alek looked over, beaming with pride, and her heart slowly cracked in two.

"In the midst of tragedy," the princess said, "it is sometimes hard to see the blessings, yes?"

Her eyes suddenly stinging, Luanne stared hard at the slice of chocolate-raspberry torte on her gold-bordered plate, the ornate silver fork clutched tightly in her fingers. "Yes, ma'am," she whispered.

Nothing if not diplomatic, the princess redirected her conversation to Alek and Chase, who soon left the table to finish watching a movie he'd started before dinner, all three dogs tagging along after him.

"So, Alek," the princess then asked, "are you ready for tomorrow?"

"As much as I'll ever be, Grandmother," Alek said with a smile before polishing off the single glass of wine he'd taken with dinner.

Luanne couldn't have missed all the buzz about the upcoming visit from the pair of leaders from neighboring Stolvia, or that Alek had volunteered to act as mediator between the two sides. Even Elena—whose hovering presence Luanne had finally come to terms with, especially as the woman had more stories up her sleeve than a library—had gone on and on about how proud everyone was of the prince. *Relieved* was probably more like it, which even Elena's stilted English could not disguise.

"What time are they coming, again?"

"Marek said he'd be here by 9:00 a.m. Peclov, a little later."

The princess gave one sharp nod of her head, then excused herself, declaring she needed to tend to some correspondence.

"I think maybe I'll just go on, too, if you don't mind,"

Luanne said, trying to gracefully negotiate her huge middle around the edge of the table as she stood.

"Running away?"

Alek's quiet question startled her. The look of yearning— for what, she wondered?—in his eyes just about rendered her senseless. Luanne laughed, even though that was the last thing she felt like doing. "Run? Heck, I can barely get up to a good waddle at this point."

A slight smile blurring the angles of his beard-shadowed face, Alek got up and came around to ease her chair back, guide her away from the table. "Please stay," he said, guiding her into, then down, the hallway. "For a little while, at least. I could use some company this evening."

She glanced up into his face, but trying to read his expression was futile. "You nervous about tomorrow?"

The smile tightened as he led her into his study, a handsomely decorated room with leather furniture in tans and browns. "More than I'd admit to my grandmother, certainly. Not wanting to look like a fool does that."

"Oh, please..." Luanne lowered herself with a slight grunt into the corner of a tufted leather sofa as Alek crouched in front of the slumbering fire, stabbing at it with a poker. "Anyone who can handle a ten-year-old boy the way you did Chase today can certainly set straight a couple of old fogies with their heads in their rears."

Alek glanced over his shoulder, then burst out laughing. Rising, he replaced the poker on its wrought iron rack. "How much do you know about Stolvia?"

"Enough to know if they don't quit their infernal squabbling, their country's going to go down the tubes. While Carpathia's got one of the highest standards of living in Europe, they have one of the lowest, simply because of their refusal to figure out how to work out their differences."

His mouth twitched. "Perhaps *you* should mediate the conference tomorrow instead of me."

"And set back relations between Stolvia and Carpathia a hundred years? In case you missed it, I'm not exactly the most diplomatic person on the planet."

He didn't say anything to that, but his staring at her the way he was wasn't doing a thing to settle her nerves. Then he closed the few feet between them and dropped into the opposite corner of the sofa, angling his long frame to face her, his head propped in one hand. As usual, a wave of mahogany hair was flirting with his right eyebrow. As usual, her fingers itched to push it back.

She looked away.

"Do you really think I'm doing all right with Chase?"

The simple earnestness of his question only served to painfully jostle her already mangled heart. "It's...a little early to tell. I mean, Chase isn't the easiest child in the world to get along with." She glanced over, was nearly bowled over by both the resolve and hope shining in his eyes. "I think you're doin' fine, Alek. Long as you don't spoil him."

"I won't. I promise." He smiled. "My father certainly didn't spoil me. But he never for an instant let me forget how much he loved me, either. If I can live up to that example, I'll be a very happy man."

If only... if only... A pointless mantra, the sort only starry-eyed, foolish little girls let hang around in their heads for very long—

"I have a proposal to make. About...our son."

Her gaze darted to his. "Oh?"

"When the time is right," he said softly, "I'd like to legally adopt him. He would still live with you, most of the year," he quickly added in reaction to her obviously horror-stricken expression. "But then there would be no question of either his inheritance or his eventual accession to the throne." He leaned forward, taking her suddenly cold hand in his, his thumb gliding back and forth across her knuckles as if he had no idea the effect even that innocent skin-to-skin contact would provoke. "Luanne," he said, those soft-silver eyes linked with hers, "think about it—this way, if he *doesn't* know, we'd never have to tell him. And it seems a better solution than our getting married."

"*Mar*—" Her throat closed, strangling the second syllable. Heaven knew, that was the very last word she expected to hear come out of his mouth, but what was even less expected was her reaction to hearing it in such a negative context. Of course marriage to Alek was out of the question, even if her husband hadn't been barely cold in his grave. Any fool could see that.

"You deserve more than a marriage of convenience, Luanne," Alek was saying. "And frankly, that's all I could offer. On that score I haven't changed. I'm here for our son— and for you, you know that—but it would hardly be fair to either of us to make that kind of commitment—"

"No. No, you're absolutely right," she said stiffly, trying both to keep her emotions in check and wondering at the same time why it should be such a struggle to do so. Eleven years ago it had been illogical to entertain the idea of anything real and permanent with the man she thought Alek to be; it was even more illogical to entertain such notions now that she knew who he was. Jeff had been the logical choice, Jeff was the man who'd deserved her heart....

Luanne withdrew her hand from Alek's, laying it on her belly. "I won't stand in the way of the adoption. On two conditions."

"Which are?"

On a deep breath, she lifted her chin, staring at some obviously royal portrait over the mantel. "That the adoption in no way infringes on my legal claim to Chase, and that you not start proceedings for at least a year, until enough time has passed—"

Her eyes burning, she planted both hands on the arm of the sofa and willed herself to stand in one relatively smooth motion, needing to flee, to get away from those eyes that she knew were boring into her at this very moment.

"I'm about ready to keel over," she said, heading toward the door. Except Alek caught up with her, gently turning her back. She would have looked down at her feet if she could have seen them.

"Luanne..." Oh, Lord, it just wasn't fair, him having a voice like that, the way it provoked the memories the way it did. They practically shrieked inside her, tearing at her heart like a pack of hungry dogs. He slipped one knuckle under her chin, lifting her face so that she had no choice but to meet his gaze, still earnest, still kind, but overlaid with a veil of confusion, like he couldn't for the life of him understand why she was reacting this way. His breath, warm and chocolate-scented, washed over her, stirring a totally inappropriate longing inside her. "I swear, I didn't mean to upset you. I just thought, after today…"

"I'm not upset. I told you, I'm just tired—"

"You're a terrible liar, Luanne."

She opened her mouth to say something, but knew if she tried to talk, she'd start blubbering like an idiot. How dare he look at her like this, treat her like this, as if he really cared, when hadn't he just admitted he didn't? Still, in the take-whatever-you-can-get department, she sure didn't fight him any too hard when he gathered her as close as he could, resting his chin on the top of her head and stroking her back.

"You've got your year, *mila,*" he murmured into her hair, and she thought she'd die, both from the tenderness and the knowledge that it wasn't meant for her. Not really. "I'm not going to take him from you. Ever." His hands cupped her jaw, his eyes once again capturing her gaze in his. "Please believe me…the last thing I want to do is hurt you."

"If only…if only…

Bitterness sliced through her like shards from an exploded glass. What on earth was he doing? Trying to secure his position with his son by sweet-talking her? And what on earth was she doing, lettin' him get away with it?

"No," she said on a soft cry, pulling out of his arms and running—after a fashion—from the room.

Alek stared at the doorway through which Luanne had just trundled, feeling like…like…

Like ten kinds of fool, as Odella would say.

His grandmother's words exploded in his brain—*Responsibility without emotional commitment is worthless.*

But, if that was the best he could do…? Surely that counted for something.

Didn't it?

Then why the hell had he taken her into his arms? True, all he'd meant to do was comfort her, to try to ease her obvious distress—distress which he'd brought on with his truly brilliant timing, he thought with a wince—but all he'd succeeded in doing was upsetting her even more. He knew what the boundaries were, damn it, and yet he'd violated them all the same. And for what? *What?*

For the second time that day, frustration roared through him, made all the worse since he couldn't get a handle on what, exactly was making him feel treacherously close to smashing something. His own head, preferably. More pent-up than he'd ever been before a race, he began to pace the floor, the intricate pattern of the Moroccan carpet blurring underfoot as he dug his fingers into the back of his neck. Dear God—if he hadn't known why he'd never let a woman get to him before this, he sure as hell knew why now. In the space of a few hours he'd managed to bring a smile to Luanne's lips and tears to her eyes. The first had made his heart swell with a kind of joy unlike anything he'd ever known; the second had nearly torn him to pieces.

And as buffeted as he felt by these rampaging, totally off-the-chart emotions, there wasn't a bloody thing he could do to stop them. Alek laughed aloud, the laugh of a man perilously close to losing it.

How the bloody hell did he expect to rule a country when he couldn't even rule *himself?*

"Mama? You okay?"

Luanne surreptitiously swiped at her eyes, then laid down the book she hadn't been getting a whole lot out of, forcing a smile for Chase as he clamored up onto her bed, already in his pajamas. Bo yipped and whined something pitiful on the floor beside them until Chase reached over and dragged him on up, too.

"Pregnant women get weepy, I told you that," she said as he snuggled down next to her under the down comforter. "Just hormones, is all."

"Oh. I thought maybe it was because you were missing Daddy."

A fresh wave of discombobulation threatened her already fragile composure. "Well, and that. I suppose I'll always miss him, you know. Your father—" she had to talk fast to keep from tripping over the words "—was a good man." And she wasn't lying about that, either about missing Jeff or her praise of him. Oh, sure, he'd been real pushy at times, intent on getting his own way, but that was a small price to pay for everything he'd done for her. Her biggest regret was that he died before they'd had a chance to work things out, to patch up the gaping hole in their marriage, their friendship.

Chase got real quiet, like there was something he wanted to say, and she held her breath. Only what he said was, "Alek said I could probably have my first ridin' lesson day after tomorrow." He shifted, his eyes the brightest they'd been in a long, long time. But she saw ambivalence in their blue depths, too.

Luanne managed a smile. "You excited about that?"

His brow all crumpled up, Chase directed his attention to the dog, who had flopped onto his back to get his belly rubbed. "It'll be okay, I guess. The boots were in my room when I got back after finishing the movie. They fit real good, too. Although I still don't see why I can't wear Daddy's boots."

"Alek said they were too big, remember? He was afraid your foot would slip out and leave the boot in the stirrup."

"Oh." Then he said, "I guess Alek's not so bad."

She reached over to rub the dog's belly, too. "Oh?"

"Uh-uh."

She let another few seconds drift by, then said, "Don't knock yourself out gettin' too enthusiastic, now."

Chase grinned a little, then wiggled around to hug her huge middle. "It's just weird, how sometimes I almost feel like nothin's wrong at all, and then I remember that Daddy died, and then I feel all guilty and stuff."

"For…not feeling so sad, or for liking Alek?"

"I didn't say I *liked* him."

"Okay, for not *dis*liking him."

"Both, I guess."

Her heart trembling, Luanne held her oldest baby close for a long time, then planted a kiss on his hair. "Doesn't matter how much we miss someone, or how bad we feel that they're gone. It still won't bring them back."

"I know," Chase said on a sigh. "It just makes me feel confused, is all."

Oh, my, yes, she knew all about being confused. She thought about Alek's offer and how he would be the only father figure in Chase's life, since she didn't figure on ever marrying again—a thought that slapped her like a cold fish—and how that meant she couldn't simply up and leave and never come back.

She thought about how, if Jeff hadn't died, she would be right now working to repair a marriage that maybe couldn't've even been repaired.

That maybe shouldn't've been, she thought with a jolt to her stomach.

And that made her more confused than ever.

She noticed Chase flicking over and over again at an imaginary spot on the comforter, an activity he only indulged in when he was working up to confessing about something. Luanne's heart leaped right up into her throat, but she still said, "You got something to say, spit it out."

"Well…" More skootching and settling. Then, "Alek asked me if I thought I'd like to come back on a regular basis. Like on vacations and stuff."

Compared with what he might have come out with, this was almost a relief. "I see. Well, would you?"

"I don't know. Maybe. Alek was tellin' me at dinner how they do this real big enormous tree in the front hall at Christmas with like a thousand lights on it, an' then another one in the family room where they open the presents. And that the town does this big celebration where they sing carols an' everything, an' everyone goes to Midnight Mass an' how there's almost always snow, and Alek said he's promised to play Father Christmas—that's what they call Santa Claus here—at the Children's Home this year, and how the princess and Alek's sister,

Sophie, spend weeks buying and wrapping presents for all the children, 'cuz they don't have any parents to give them anything. And that Gizela spends a *month* baking Christmas cookies for the big open house the palace always has for anyone who wants to come, the Sunday before Christmas.'' *And I'd give my eyeteeth to be a part of that.* That's what the light shining in his eyes said, clear as day.

Christmases when she'd been growing up had been meager, presentwise, but happy enough, once her father had gone and left her mother and her in peace. They'd always had ham and candied sweet potatoes and a small tree and watched *It's a Wonderful Life* and counted their blessings, and Luanne could honestly say she'd never felt deprived. Then, after she and Jeff got married and Jeff started doing so well with his racing, the holidays had gotten a little flashy for her taste, what with all the lights Jeff loved to put up and the holiday parties Jeff insisted on having. But all the to-do had made her husband happy, and Luanne had figured the least she could do was go along with it, for heaven's sake.

But what Chase had just described…well, it was downright magical, wasn't it? "Sounds like a lot of fun."

"I suppose," he said, but the longing in his voice was unmistakable. Then he said, "D'you feel like readin' tonight?"

Even though Chase was ten, Luanne still read to him most nights, a practice she'd kept up since coming here, thanks to a set of C.S. Lewis's *The Chronicles of Narnia* she'd found in the library. Now she smiled, dragging over the book and opening to where they'd left off the night before. And when Chase snuggled close, she reminded herself that, at least for the moment, he was still hers.

Chapter 9

"Hmm..." Anka Palachek, a slender—and anything but old and wrinkled—blonde in khakis and a white man-tailored shirt unplugged her stethoscope from her ears, then freed Luanne's arm from the blood pressure cuff, all the while giving her as stern a look as her soft brown eyes could muster. "Your reading is higher than I'd like to see it."

She'd arrived at eight that morning, apologizing for needing to fit Luanne in before the village clinic opened in half an hour, then efficiently shooed the ever-helpful Elena and the ever-nosy Chase from Luanne's room before beginning the cursory exam. Now, however, a pair of twin creases had taken root between her sandy brows. "Although I suppose," she continued kindly in her musical accent, "considering the circumstances, that's to be expected. Why don't you lie back—that's it—and let me take it again while you're flat, see if I get a better reading. And I can check out the baby at the same time."

Luanne skootched back on her bed, trying not to frown as the scrub-faced young doctor—her short, almost boyish hairstyle accentuating her sharp features and full mouth—reattached the blood pressure cuff, pumped it up again. Considering the brawl going on inside her head, Luanne was surprised her veins hadn't just exploded sometime during the night.

"One-forty over ninety. Not wonderful, but I'll take it." The doctor then *tsked* at Luanne's ankles. "How long have they been swollen like that?"

Luanne struggled up onto her elbows, except she couldn't see anything south of her navel. "Since I got here. I think it's the humidity. We don't have any in Texas."

Dr. Palachek chuckled, gesturing for her to lie back again. "Are you sleeping well?"

"Some."

"The bags under your eyes tell another story…oh! Contraction?"

Luanne nodded over her wince; the doctor lifted Luanne's maternity blouse to lay her smooth, cool hand over the tightening muscles as she checked her watch, obviously timing things. "And are you having many of these?"

"Now and again."

"More than a couple times a day?"

"Some days, maybe."

"Are they ever painful?"

"Not really, no."

"I see." Then the doctor began carefully palpating Luanne's belly to ascertain the baby's position. "You might have a point about the humidity—ah, there's the little bottom, right where it's supposed to be—but I want you to keep your feet up as much as possible, anyway. His Highness said you were planning to return to the States in a week?"

"Yes." An odd mixture of relief and regret swirled through her. "That's all right, isn't it?"

The doctor stretched a measuring tape over the mountain, frowning a little. "Yes, but I wouldn't stick around a day longer than that. Have you had any ultrasounds during this pregnancy?"

"Both my doctors gave me the option. I declined."

"Mm. Well, goodness knows millions of healthy babies have been delivered without them, yes?" Then the doctor grinned. "Would you like to listen to your baby's heartbeat?"

Luanne nodded; the doctor placed her stethoscope on Luanne's belly, then the earpieces in Luanne's ears. The heartbeat was firm and steady—*whooshwhooshwhooshwhoosh*—and Luanne gasped in delight, only to feel a great wave of sadness come over her right after.

Dr. Palachck barely dented the bed when she sat on it. She tugged Luanne's blouse back down, sympathy swimming in her eyes. "Are you all right?"

No, Luanne was definitely not all right. In fact, she was beginning to wonder if she'd ever be "all right" again. But she said, "As well as can be expected," before letting the doctor hoist her upright. "Is the baby okay?"

"The baby is fine. It's Mama I'm much more concerned about. Grief and pregnancy are a wicked combination on the body." She stood, replacing her things in her black bag. "No wonder His Highness sounded so worried when he spoke to me yesterday evening."

Luanne swung her feet off the bed. "Worried?"

"Oh, heavens, yes. As much, if not more, than many of my expectant fathers. But then, that's not really surprising." She snapped shut her bag. "My father served as royal family physician for many years, and I was a school chum of Princess Sophie—the royal children have always attended the village schools, did you know that? In any case, I always remember Prince Alek as being very kind. At least," she added with a smile as she picked up her bag, "he was kind enough not to torment a gawky young girl with a mad crush on him."

That certainly grabbed Luanne's attention. "Do you still?"

The doctor laughed. "Oh, please—that was just one of those schoolgirl things that disappears about the same time the braces do. Now you be sure to keep those feet up and try to get as much rest as possible. I'll be back in a few days to see if that pressure's down."

"And if it isn't?"

The doctor laid her hand on Luanne's shoulder, and as much as Luanne truly liked the woman, she sure did not like the look in those brown eyes. "Let's just know that it will be, all right?"

"Would you like some coffee, Doctor? I could buzz Tomas, have him bring you a cup."

Standing just inside his study, her frumpy brown oxfords contrasting with the rich reds and blues of the carpet underneath them, Anka grinned. *"Doctor?"* Mischief sparking in her brown eyes, she swung her black bag around to her front, clutching it in both hands. "Does this mean I have to call you Your Highness?"

Alek laughed softly, remembering Anka Palachek as a skinny, flat-chested adolescent with braces and frizzy blond hair who sighed and giggled in equally copious amounts. What a startling contrast to the handsome, very together woman now standing in front of him. "God forbid. In any case..."

"No coffee, no, I only have a few minutes. As do you, I gather?"

Alek fingered his tie, pushing aside the uneasiness that had kept him awake most of the night, an uneasiness that had little to do with his morning's schedule. An uneasiness that went up a good two or three notches at the now-serious expression on Anka's face. "She's all right, isn't she?"

"Yes...and maybe. The baby is fine, yes, but I'm concerned about Mrs. Henderson's blood pressure and the fluid retention in her hands and feet. So far, neither are outside the normal range for a woman so advanced in her pregnancy, but she is borderline. And...well, I'd need to do an ultrasound to be sure, but I think she might be farther along than she's been told. Not much," she added at Alek's lifted brows. "A couple of weeks, perhaps—but at this point, I'm not comfortable with the idea of her making the long trip back to the States."

"You mean, she should stay here until after the baby's born?"

"I'm not sure she's going to have much choice."

"What if she left sooner, perhaps in a day or two—"

But the doctor was shaking her head. "Travel right now is definitely out of the question. But we can wait a week. If her pressure's down, we'll see. I don't think she's high risk otherwise—she told me the first pregnancy went off without a hitch, and the birth was quick and uncomplicated—but we're talking a fairly narrow window of opportunity." Her huge, fawn-like eyes were far too discerning for Alek's comfort. "Is there some problem with her staying?"

"Not from my standpoint, no, of course not." Alek leaned one hip on his desk and crossed his arms, frowning down at the gold cufflink winking at him. "I brought her here to give her a break from everything she's been through recently, but…" He looked up. "I'm not sure it's working."

Anka's head tilted. "Because of you, you mean?" His gaze shot to hers. "Oh, for heaven's sake, Alek—her husband was a friend of yours. How can she be around you and not be reminded of him?"

Tomas burst into the room, his brown suit jacket flapping about, begging the doctor's forgiveness for the interruption. "Marek is early, Your Highness! His car has just now pulled up in front of the palace!"

Although no one could hold a candle to Tomas's dedication and efficiency, poise under fire was not his strong suit. "Take a couple of deep breaths, Tomas—yes, like that—then would you please inform my grandmother? The others know what to do, you needn't concern yourself."

A moment later, Alek was alone in the study, his stomach none too steady as he grabbed his charcoal-gray double-breasted jacket from the back of his chair. As he slipped it on, however, his gaze lit on the kindly faced portrait of his great-grandfather, Prince Hans-Fredrik Vlastos, that he'd brought over from some obscure room in the north wing upon his return a few months ago. His grandmother had said this likeness of her father was her favorite, the one that reminded her most of the man she'd known and loved.

"Just look at the pride shining in those eyes," she'd said after Alek had hung the painting over the fireplace. "He never expected anything more from anyone than he knew they could give. Or anything less."

With a final tug at his cuffs, Alek clicked his heels, then bowed slightly in the portrait's direction. "The prince is in, Great-grandfather," he whispered, then prayed he would not fall short of anyone's expectations.

Anyone's.

* * *

Three hours and several pots of strong coffee later, the Stolvian situation was no nearer to being resolved than it had ever been. And frankly, Alek was ready to wring both men's necks. Never in his life had he seen such bullheadedness, especially over matters that should have been forgotten at least a half dozen generations ago. Yet the proceedings hadn't started out all that badly. Their willingness to meet at all was a positive sign that deep down both wanted to work out their differences. And the two men, dressed like a pair of crows in almost identical, slightly shiny black suits, had actually deigned to shake each other's hands, even managing a few minutes' benign conversation about the weather over their first cups of coffee.

But Stolvians handed down ethnic grudges as if they were heirlooms. When Stanislav Marek, a bombastic little man with pastry crumbs lodged in his bushy salt-and-pepper beard, reiterated for the dozenth time the humiliation his people had endured at the hands of Anatoly Peclov's ancestors two centuries before—to which Peclov, his black eyes aflame underneath heavy white brows, swore everlasting vengeance for a clandestine attack on some villagers in the early thirties—Alek nearly threw up his hands in disgust.

They were meeting in what had been Alek's mother's private parlor. Peclov and Marek sat on matching pale-blue velvet love seats across from each other, Alek on a wing chair at one end between them, while the young, female interpreter—the pair's English was rudimentary, at best, and Stolvian was closer to Hungarian than Slovak—sat across from Alek on the other side of a marble-topped coffee table. Now frustration drove him to stand and circle the grouping as the men continued their argument. The interpreter was clearly becoming more flustered by the second, occasionally hesitating over obvious obscenities.

Alek's pacing eventually led him to one of the open French doors, his eyes drawn to the clear blue sky that seemed to go on forever. He could almost hear Luanne say, "Go on, now. Listen for your answer."

So he shoved aside his skepticism, tuned out the imbroglio

behind him, and listened. After a few minutes he became acutely aware that it had gone stone silent in the room, as if the damask-covered walls had swallowed up all conversation. Alek turned, found all eyes trained on him. He hesitated, then walked back to the group, resting his hands on the back of his chair.

"I certainly wish no disrespect to two men who are not only old enough to be my father, but who have far more experience at being leaders than I," he said softly, pausing to let the interpreter catch up, "but the pair of you have been acting no better than spoiled children. You're wasting your time, you're wasting *my* time, and frankly, you're bloody pissing me off."

Her blue eyes big as dinner plates, the interpreter halted, staring at Alek as if to give him the chance to reword his sentence. He shook his head, gesturing for her to continue. A flush swept up over her neck, but she cleared her throat and did her duty, as Alek mused that he'd just had the shortest diplomatic career in history.

Marek laughed first, a big, booming sound that nearly shook the windows. A second later Peclov joined in, declaring something the interpreter, blushing once more, translated as a compliment to a certain part of Alek's anatomy.

His knees weak, Alek made his way back to his chair, sinking into it and sending up a silent prayer of thanks.

"Can you hear anything?"

Ivana hadn't meant to startle the poor girl, but Luanne whipped around, her hand plastered to her chest. Still, she only put her finger to her lips, then silently shuffled down the Persian runner running the length of the twenty-metre hallway, smoothing one hand over the leopard-print maternity blouse ballooning over a pair of slim black pants. Even in that outfit and in her condition, the young woman exuded a natural grace and confidence that were eminently appealing.

"Not really," she said without the slightest indication of guilt. "Except they were all laughing their heads off a few minutes ago."

The princess's eyebrows shot up. "Are you serious?"

The young woman's crystal-blue eyes glinted with just enough amusement to take the edge off her obvious sadness. "I *know*. I didn't believe it, either. Only now everyone's gotten all quiet again, so I can't tell what's going on."

Princess Ivana's mouth twitched before she linked her arm through Luanne's and led her down the corridor toward her own study. In one way, it had been almost excruciatingly difficult to leave Alek to his own devices this morning—she'd had to sternly remind herself that her grandson was not only well into his thirties, but far removed from the wastrel he'd seemed bent on becoming even a few years earlier—even as in another way it had been deliciously freeing. But for all the tension hovering about due to whatever was going on behind the closed door down the hall, that was nothing compared with whatever was going on between her grandson and her great-grandson's mother.

Ivana had liked Luanne Henderson from the moment of that first meeting, and she'd seen no reason in the days following to alter her initial opinion. If anything, the more she got to know her, the more she saw to admire. What's more, the staff all seemed quite taken with her, as well, which carried a great deal more weight than perhaps some of the princess's royal cousins might recognize.

Now if only her dunderhead grandson would get over himself and see the blessing that had been set before him....

Ivana had sworn to herself she wouldn't interfere. A pledge she was finding extremely difficult to keep as the days ticked by. "And where is your son?"

"Up in his room, reading."

"On such a lovely day?"

"Takes after his mama," Luanne said with a smile. "There were days my mama used to threaten to burn my library card if I didn't get up off my bed and go outside. Think maybe it has somethin' to do with being an only child, the ability to lose yourself in other worlds like that...."

They had reached the door of the princess's study. Ivana casually issued an invitation to Luanne to join her and Alek and the pair of Stolvian leaders for luncheon later on. Not un-expectedly the young woman immediately declined.

"I don't...I couldn't." A short, embarrassed laugh. "You're just invitin' me out of politeness, Your Highness."

Ivana felt something close to annoyance slash through her. "Nonsense, child. And if you think I would jeopardize my grandson's work for mere politeness, you have sorely mis-judged me."

A flush swept over Luanne's cheeks. "I'm sorry. I didn't mean to offend you—"

"That, my dear," the princess said gently, "is almost an impossibility. I do not easily offend, as you will come to find out. I do, however, know you would be an asset to the gath-ering, and that our Stolvian guests would undoubtedly find you charming. Not to mention far more pleasant to look at than an old crone like me, yes?"

A small smile flirted with the young woman's mouth for a second or two before, on a sigh, she shook her head. "Thank you, Your Highness. But, no. It's one thing takin' meals with just you and Alek, but..."

"But you would not be comfortable?"

"No, ma'am. I wouldn't."

After a moment Ivana silently ushered Luanne inside the room, quietly shutting the door behind her. "Please have a seat, my dear. Keep an old woman company for a few minutes."

Luanne's brows lifted, but she settled herself on the sofa, one ruby-nailed hand massaging her middle. Ivana sat on the chair opposite, her hands tucked together in her lap, and men-tally tossed her earlier pledge to herself out the window. Per-haps her grandson had taken the burden of political mediation off her shoulders, but why should all her years of experience go completely to waste?

"I think it is time we both stopped avoiding the one subject that is uppermost in our thoughts, yes?"

Oh, Lord. Luanne wanted to be anywhere but right there, but it was true: they all had to stop pussyfooting around the issue, even if the issue himself had no idea who he was or what this all would mean to him someday. She licked her lips, her lipstick tasting like old flowers.

"I take it you mean Chase?"

"I do."

Luanne looked up. "You know Alek wants to formally adopt him?"

"Yes. But this idea does not appeal to you, does it?"

Luanne heard something in the princess's voice that made her think that maybe, just maybe, she had an ally in the last place she'd expect to find one. "I don't know. Logically, it makes as much sense as anything, I suppose. But in here—" she pressed a hand to her heart "—it just doesn't feel right, you know?"

"You are afraid you will lose your son?"

She felt tears well up in her eyes. "I know Alek wouldn't—"

"No, no...of course not. But I do not think this adoption idea is a good one, either, for many reasons, the main one being that I cannot support perpetuating a lie. This is a monarchy established and maintained on honor and integrity, my dear. While I understand the problems involved in 'coming clean', as you Yanks would say, I cannot help but believe the eventual problems caused by not doing so would only be far worse. But why are you smiling?"

And she was, in spite of yourself. "Because this is the first time in my entire life than anyone has ever called *me* a Yank."

"Ah, yes. I seem to recall that term is not generally used to refer to people from your part of the country?"

"No." But then her smile faded. "But if you don't approve of Alek's idea...?"

"If I had little influence over my grandson's actions and decisions when he was younger, I certainly have even less now. But one or the other of you needs to tell your son the truth, my dear. And the sooner, the better."

"Not yet. Not when he's just now beginning to show signs of comin' to terms with Jeff's death."

"I know the timing is bad. Your Chase is a sensitive child, yes? As was his father, believe me. Eventually, that tenderness will stand him in good stead, enabling him to feel compassion and empathy for those who need both. And under other circumstances, I would agree that to wait would be the kindest thing to do. But how long do you think it will be before others notice the resemblance between Chase and my grandson? Frankly—and please believe me when I say this has nothing to do with my feelings for you, because I find I'm growing quite fond of you—Alek's bringing you here was not perhaps the wisest choice he could have made. But he has, and now Dr. Palachek tells me there is a chance you might not be able to return to the States before this child is born—''

Luanne felt the color leech from her face. "What?"

Embarrassment supplanted the brief flicker of bewilderment in the princess's eyes. "Oh, my dear...I'd assumed she'd discussed this with you...."

The best Luanne could manage was a shake of her head.

"My apologies for overstepping my bounds. But you must understand our dilemma—that the longer you and Chase are here, the more likely it is that people will notice. Granted, the paparazzi do not find the Vlastos family nearly as interesting as the Windsors, but the discovery that the crown prince has an illegitimate son could certainly be seen as a choice enough morsel for at least a secondary headline in any number of tabloids, yes? And trust me, my dear—it is far better to best them at their own game by being the first one to tell the truth.''

If Luanne could have moved, she would have jumped up from the sofa and begun to pace the room. Since she couldn't, she simply stared at the princess, well aware that there wasn't a blessed thing she could say in rebuttal. Alek's grandmother's was right: the longer they put this off, the worse things were likely to be, especially for Chase, who was, of course, the very one whose feelings they were trying to spare.

But... "I'm sorry, Your Highness. I see your point, but it's just too soon. We'll just have to be careful until I can take him back home. And Alek has sworn that Chase can stay with me in Texas—''

"Which is another thing. How practical would that be? Your son is the heir to a surprisingly influential crown. For the people to trust him, to accept him as their monarch eventually, they need to feel he is one of them. No, to answer the question on the tip of your tongue, he doesn't need to live here the entire year, but I doubt young Chase can assimilate our culture—his culture, now—unless he's here at least six months out of the year."

What was the woman trying to do? Get her to have the baby here and now? This time, Luanne did get up, because there was no way she could just go on sitting there with all this turmoil going on inside her. And her blood pressure must be hovering somewhere near Mars about now. "Six months?" She shook her head. "I couldn't stand being away from him that long."

"I didn't think you could. But there is a solution to that, as well."

She twisted around, her heart beating about a thousand times a minute. "And what is that?"

The princess rose, her hands clasped in front of her. "You and my grandson need to marry."

Sheepishness made such infrequent appearances in his grandmother's repertoire of expressions, Alek barely recognized it at first. Especially as she managed to keep it pretty much under wraps until some hours after the Stolvian leaders' departure. While six hours had been hardly enough time to bring Marek and Peclov to an accord on every single issue, progress had definitely been made, with both sides agreeing to continue talks until a formal treaty of some sort could be hashed out. The sooner that happened, the sooner Alek could begin haranguing Carpathia's other, larger neighbors for economic aid to begin rebuilding the decimated country.

All in all, not bad for a day's work, he'd mused wryly as he went in to dinner, only to have his upbeat mood immediately plummet when the princess informed him that Chase and Luanne had taken dinner in their suite.

"Is she all right?"

His grandmother fidgeted with her napkin. His grandmother *never* fidgeted. "I have not heard otherwise," she said quietly.

Too quietly.

Alek remained standing until the servants had left them alone, then demanded to know what was going on. To his grandmother's credit, she told him.

Fury the likes of which he'd never, ever felt before tore through him, obliterating his all-too-brief euphoria over his earlier success.

"What the *hell* were you thinking, Grandmother?"

Her chin came up. "At least *I* was."

"Of what? Your own agenda? *Damn* it!" Alek shut his eyes, trying to get his breathing under control, only to impale his grandmother with his gaze when he reopened them. "I don't suppose it even occurred to you that Luanne and I might have already discussed this issue? Or that we're perfectly capable of navigating this minefield without your 'help.' I told you, I *will* sort this out. In my own time, in my own way, and with the other people involved. Which means Luanne and Chase. Period. So I'd bloody well appreciate your backing off and letting me be about it!"

He stormed from the room, more than a little startled by the desperateness with which he wanted to fix an unfixable situation. He took the stairs two at a time to the east wing, nearly creaming Elena, who was just coming out of Luanne's rooms, a covered tray in her hands.

"Oh!" Small curtsy. "Your Highness—!"

"Is Mrs. Henderson awake?"

The maid's brow crinkled. "She is not here, sir."

Alek stared at the maid as if she'd just spoken in Japanese. "Not here? What do you mean, not here?" A horrified thought sliced through him. "Did she take Chase with her?"

The full-faced woman now looked at him as if he was truly on the verge of madness. Which he supposed he was. "The boy? Oh, no, sir. Master Chase, he is watching TV in his room, but Mrs. Henderson said she was going for a walk."

Alek willed his heart to stop pounding quite so painfully. She couldn't be far, then. "When was this?"

"Perhaps an hour ago?"

"Did she say where she was going?"

"No, sir. Just out for a while."

He opened his mouth to ask—what? The woman had already told him everything she knew. Rephrasing the same questions wasn't going to yield different answers. He briefly entertained the idea of interrogating Chase, then decided that not only was it doubtful the child could provide any more information, but that questioning him might only plant seeds of worry in his mind. So he thanked Elena and left, only to be nearly overcome by the oddest sensation of being off balance, as if someone had let the air out of one tire.

Corridors and passageways blurred in his peripheral vision as he strode through the palace. He would deal with his grandmother and her meddling later. A picture flashed through his brain of Luanne stranded somewhere in the woods in labor, unable to move, unable to get help—

Alek nearly laughed at his own descent into maudlin melodrama, except even a pregnant woman can cover a lot of ground in an hour, and it was getting dark. The palace grounds were too extensive for Alek to search on his own, so his first stop was the staff dining room, where Tomas, who was working late due to the events of the day, and many of the live-in staff were just finishing up their own suppers. Within minutes Alek had enlisted the aid of a dozen men to scout out the gardens and parks closest to the palace itself, all the while fully expecting the lady herself to waddle back and wonder what on earth all the commotion was about. When that initial search, however, came up empty, Alek found himself headed toward the stables. Eschewing the stable hand's offer of help, he saddled up his own horse, a black gelding named Octavian, then yanked on a pair of boots which he'd left to languish in the tack room years before. He had his mobile phone with him; if necessary, he could call Gregori to bring one of the cars, but for now he could more quickly and easily navigate the walking paths on horseback.

The enormous horse pranced in nervous anticipation before Alek kneed him out of the stable yard, only to bring the beast to an immediate halt while he contemplated in which direction to head. The sunset drenched the landscape in remnants of molten copper. After the week of rain, the day had been unseasonably warm, although with the rapid approach of nightfall, a chill teased the air, bringing with it the lush scent of early autumn. The horse whinnied, sniffing the air, clearly anxious to get going—

"Your Highness!"

Alek twisted in the saddle to catch sight of one of the stable hands, a dark-haired teenager in jeans and a plaid shirt, sprinting down the path, a mobile phone clutched in one madly waving hand. "Tomas just called from the palace," he said breathlessly in Carpathian. "One of the men said they ran across a woman from the village who saw a very pregnant woman making her way up to the ridge about an hour ago!"

Even over the pounding of Octavian's hooves against the rocky path, Alek heard Luanne long before he spotted her, her keening spinning out over the valley below like the lamentations of some bereaved spirit.

He reined the horse in by a gorse bush, his dismount clumsy and nearly frantic. Through a scrim of heavily-laden blackberry bushes, he caught sight of her, a slight, ponytailed figure sitting cross-legged in a patch of low-growing wildflowers a few metres down from the bridle path. Wearing her black pants and a sweater he'd lent her when it had been so cold the week before, she hunched over her swollen belly, rocking in tandem with her sobs.

Reins cursorily tethered to the shrub, Alek scrabbled down the incline toward her, his heart ramming inside his chest as he called her name. She jumped, then looked up at him, much of her hair hanging in snarls around her blotched and tear-ravaged face. For a single, infinitely long second, he was sure she was going to tell him to "just go on and leave her be."

Instead she lifted her arms.

He gathered her close, clinging to her nearly as fiercely as she did to him, as if the world would spin off its axis if he let go. Never before had another human being asked for his comfort like this; never before had he so desperately wanted to ease someone else's pain.

And if he'd had even an inkling of what he was supposed

to do, he imagined he wouldn't be feeling half so panicked. But then, was it panic that impelled him to tuck her head underneath his chin, to bury his face and one hand in her tangled hair as he held her, rocked her, his own eyes burning as she cried and cried and cried as if her heart would never be whole again? And was it panic, or something else, that led him to press first one kiss, then another, in her sweet-smelling hair...then her temple, once, twice, three times...then lower, gentle kisses to her red, swollen eyelids, her damp cheeks...

Her mouth.

Her gasp of surprise was quickly swallowed by a guttural moan that reverberated through Alek with a dizzying, frightening intensity, even as it dimly occurred to him he'd never kissed a pregnant woman before and that heaven knew he shouldn't be kissing this one. Not now, at least. Probably not ever. This wasn't...right. Wasn't rational. And not five minutes before he could have listed all the reasons why. But when her fingers tightened in the folds of his sweater, when she opened to him, tasting of tears and explosive need, rational thought vaporized.

Never before had desire felt so much like pain. His breath coming in tortured gasps, Alek bracketed Luanne's flushed face, only briefly noting her spiked, dark lashes before once again crushing his mouth to hers. She moaned, deep in her throat, sending sensations and emotions, both, pounding savagely through his blood as he felt her hands shoot up underneath his sweater, abrading the taut muscles in his back.

"Touch me," she begged against his mouth. "Please...just...touch me."

He laid a shaking hand on her swollen belly, safely sequestered underneath the sweater. *His* sweater, sheltering both Luanne and her unborn child. A wave of tenderness slammed into him, almost literally knocking him off balance, this need to take care of another human being...a need that catapulted light-years beyond responsibility. "Luanne—"

Her blue irises were crystal sharp against the bloodshot whites. "Don't ask. Don't..." She grabbed one of his hands to kiss his palm, then held it against her cheek. "Just help me to forget. Please."

Bad enough she'd asked this man once to make love to her. But a second time? She supposed she could chalk it up to grief or hormones or any number of currently fashionable excuses that people used when they didn't want to accept responsibility for their actions. But, really, it all boiled down to the fact that she simply *wanted* this, just the way she'd wanted it eleven years ago.

Only about a million times more.

Still, that didn't mean Alek felt the same way, especially not after all this time. So while she sat there, staring at her hands and feeling the early-evening breeze wick away the moisture from both her crying jag and the hottest kiss she'd ever experienced in her life, she held her breath, waiting for Alek to point out any number of reasons why he couldn't honor her request. And she wouldn't't've blamed him, not one bit, because even in the midst of this hurricane of emotions swirling inside her, she knew what she was asking made no sense whatsoever.

So when he reached up and smoothed her tangled hair off her face, his fingertips then tracing the path made by about a thousand tears down her cheek, she wasn't quite sure how to read what was in those cloud-soft eyes of his. And when he gently guided her down onto the grass next to him, but spooning her against the front of his hard, lean body, she thought, *So much for that,* especially when he didn't make a move of any kind except to wrap himself around her from behind, linking his fingers with hers.

He didn't know how to let her down easily without hurting her feelings—that's what was going on, wasn't it? And of course, just about the time she reached this conclusion, what did he do but reach around and slip those warm, strong fingers up underneath her sweater, moving them in the kind of deliberately sensuous dance across her taut belly that a man of Alek's experience didn't do without a definite purpose in mind.

Just like that, a new kind of ache spread thickly, languidly along every nerve ending, pooling hot and sharp at her core.

And just like that, Luanne realized the magnitude of her mistake. For eleven years she'd worked to persuade herself that it was only the novelty of a new experience that had her remembering her blood humming and purring and sizzling like this and that it had never hummed or purred or sizzled this way with Jeff—who was a more than adequate lover—because…well, because things just didn't happen that way in real life. That she'd wanted magic that night with Alek, and therefore had convinced herself she'd found it. Yet, as Alek's fingers slowly, tantalizingly, skirted her ribs, flirted with her navel, it hit her that she hadn't imagined a blessed thing about that night. And that brought a whimper, provoked as much by her own foolishness as by the sensations arcing across her skin.

Just what the Sam Hill did she expect he would help her to forget, when this was the very thing guaranteed to unearth the memories she'd kept buried for so long? Once before she'd come right out and asked this man to do her a favor, to stanch the screaming loneliness inside her, even though she knew she'd feel even emptier when it was all over. Why should this time be any different?

If not even worse?

"Are you all right?" Alek whispered.

No.

"Yes," she hissed.

"Soooo…you don't want me to stop?"

Yes.

"No!"

The front hook of her bra popped open, her breast sighing into the cradle of his palm. Oh, *mercy!* She was gonna die from joy and agony both, right there and then. She tried to twist around, but Alek wouldn't let her.

"You want to be touched? Then let me touch," he murmured against her temple as his palm gently rasped across one rigid, tingling nipple, then the other. "Let me do at least this much for you, *mila*. Let me help you to forget…."

Behind her lowered lids tears again bit at her eyes, even though she was now powerless against the whorls of sensation that seemed to radiate from her in pulsing, vibrant waves. She shut her eyes even more tightly, almost afraid to breathe, concentrating on the slow, searing path of his clever, clever fingers, even as a thousand contradictory emotions seared her soul—that this was wrong, that nothing had ever felt more right, that she had a child to think of...that for once maybe it was all right to think about herself....

Her body jerked, both in response to Alek's caresses and in a futile attempt to outdistance the torrent of thoughts threatening to drown her. She bit her lip, forcing herself to hold on to both the anticipation and her last few moments of control. Like being on a roller coaster, she thought, helpless to do anything else but go along for the ride.

His fingers breached the stretchy fabric of her pants, slicking over her distended middle. "This is," he murmured, "incredibly erotic."

Luanne thought she might die from the waiting while he dawdled around her navel for what seemed like forever, while she in turn lay there about to burn up and as close to writhing as she cared to get. Finally, on a whimper of frustration, she covered his hand with hers and encouraged him further south, arching against him again with a shaky, grateful sigh when he caught on. And, oh, how he caught on, his thoroughness more than worth the agonizing wait. Sensations tensed... stretched...swirled and eddied and coiled and *shrieked* as Luanne fought to hang on to the magic for another few precious seconds, fought to hold off a release that would release her from *nothing,* not from the pain of remembering how good Jeff had been to her or the pain of knowing how bad Alek was for her—

A moan, a gasp, then an explosion, as jolt after jolt of something too razor edged to be called pleasure roared through her, ripping a strangled cry from her throat. Then, before the aftershocks could die down, before Luanne even got ten seconds to untangle the guilt from the euphoria or even to say, "Thank you", she cried out a second time as the mother of all contractions knocked her clear into the following week.

Chapter 10

His heart rate still nowhere even close to normal an hour after that little side trip to madness, Alek stood just inside the door to the examining room, his arms crossed, hoping the frown of genuine concern masked his mortification. At least he knew Luanne would be as well taken care of here as anywhere in Europe: Carpathia's sole hospital was small, but extremely up-to-date. And if the set to Anka Palachek's mouth was any indication, the doctor would kill with her bare hands anyone who dared to mess with her patient, brainless princes included.

At least the worst seemed to be over. From a physical standpoint, in any case. Although Luanne's initial contractions had been strong enough to drain the color from her face and shave five years off Alek's life, by the time Gregori brought the limo to the crest a few minutes later, they'd already begun to settle down enough for her to protest Alek's insistence that she go to hospital. Anka had met them there, the frown crimping her brow somewhat dulling the effect of what was meant, Alek was sure, to be a reassuring smile. When a good half hour had passed with no further contractions, the doctor examined Luanne, including giving her an ultrasound, which confirmed her initial assessment that Mama was farther along than she'd been led to believe.

"Almost a month, I'd say," Anka said, her clipboard clamped to her white-coated chest.

"That's not possible!" Luanne sputtered from the exam table, her hands protectively cradling her middle through the blue paper-sack gown the nurse had insisted she put on. For the first time since her admittance, she looked at Alek, as if expecting him to back her up. Her cheeks immediately blazed; she just as immediately looked away. "I had a period in January!"

"A normal one?"

"Well..." She frowned. "Actually, I remember thinkin' it seemed kind of light. But I've always been irregular, so I didn't pay it any mind."

"Which means you actually got pregnant in December, not January. Which means this baby is due in less than a month. Which means your window of opportunity for returning to the States is now officially closed until after this baby comes. Now," she said, bulldozing right over Luanne's "Oh!" of protest, "I want you off your feet for the next three days. Although strong, the baby's a bit small yet, so it wouldn't hurt to buy a little more time. Unfortunately, that time will have to bought on this side of the Atlantic." When Luanne let out a resigned sigh, Anka gently squeezed her shoulder. "I'm sorry. I'm sure you didn't expect your baby to be born a Carpathian citizen—"

"Dr. Palachek?"

The doctor turned to the round-faced, redheaded nurse poking her head around the door. "Yes?"

"Um, Princess Ivana is here, with a child she says is Mrs. Henderson's son? The boy seems quite distraught, wants to know if he can see his mother?"

"Of course he can," Anka said not two seconds before Alek's grandmother and Chase wriggled past the nurse into the room, the boy running right into his mother's outstretched arms. Humility and envy delivered a one-two punch to Alek's gut at the fierceness of Luanne's hug as she raked her hand through Chase's hair, fervently reassuring her child that she was okay, provoking bittersweet memories of his own mother's demonstrations of her unconditional love.

"C'n you come home now, Mama?"

"Oh, honey—the doctor says I have to stay in Carpathia until after the baby comes."

Chase looked perplexed. "I meant back to the palace. Not Texas."

Silence stuttered for a second or two. Alek's grandmother patted his arm—a truce of sorts—but she didn't look at him. Just as well, since Alek couldn't take his eyes off Luanne's face. He saw her swallow, then turn an unnaturally bright smile on Anka. "I suppose, if it's okay with the doctor?"

"Only if you promise to be good," Anka said, then unceremoniously shunted the princess and Chase from the room so the nurse could help Luanne get dressed. Alek followed them out into the hallway, only to feel Anka's hand snag his arm.

"This way, if you don't mind."

Not liking the ominous tone of that one bit, Alek nevertheless let Anka steer him into a small, minimally furnished office down the hall. She sank into the chair behind the gray metal desk and, with a groan, smacked her head into her hands. "Oh, Alek," she said to the desktop, then looked up, accusation sparking in those toffee-colored eyes. "I would have thought, with all your purported experience with women, that you would have known the dangers of fooling around with a woman that far along in pregnancy?"

Alek nearly choked, but managed to rally with, "What makes you think—"

She propelled herself to her feet, leaning over the desk to pluck a twig from his sweater, which she then wiggled in front of his face. "And Mrs. Henderson's clothes were equally embellished. Not to mention that every time she looked at you, she went red as a beet. And no—" she lifted one hand "—I don't care to know the hows or whys. That's none of my business." Then she sighed. "Just keep a lid on the hormones at least for another week, all right?"

He bristled at the censure underlying her words, even though he well understood her attitude. As far as Anka Palachek was concerned, he was still the randy, feckless prince who was used to getting whatever he wanted, *who*ever he wanted, whenever he wanted. That he'd obviously been messing around with a woman that pregnant—the widow of a man who was purportedly a good friend—was hardly going to garner points in the good doctor's book.

"This isn't what you think," he said, not flinching at the directness of her gaze in return. "*I'm* not what you think. Not anymore. Luanne means a great deal to me—"

"Because she's Chase's mother?"

Now he flinched. "You know?"

"I always did score off the charts in deductive reasoning."

Alek shoved his hands in his pockets. "It's a complicated situation."

"Then I suggest you not make it more so."

He managed a tight smile. "Doctor's orders?"

But Anka didn't smile back. "That woman in there is one of the toughest human beings I've ever met, Alek. Or at least she thinks she is. And in my experience those are the ones who fall hardest."

"Tell me something I don't know."

The doctor studied him for a moment, her lips flattened into a thin line, then blew out a sigh. "Then, Your Highness, I suggest you stay the hell out of her way for the next couple of weeks. Because, as they say, if you're not part of the solution, you're part of the problem."

Alek opted to start following the doctor's advice immediately, sending Luanne home with his grandmother and Chase in the limo while he drove the princess's BMW back by himself. As much as Anka's interference nettled, he *didn't* have any business letting things get out of hand, as it were, the way they had. Both he and Luanne were far beyond the stage or age where either one of them could simply blow off a sexual encounter as "nothing."

One hand on the steering wheel, he frowned at the back of the limo some twenty metres ahead of him as they drove onto the palace grounds. Whatever that had been, it hadn't been "nothing." Just as it hadn't been "nothing" the night their child was conceived. Then, as now, Luanne's forthrightness and generosity and trust had burrowed straight through to that still-raw, still-bleeding part of him he'd shut off from light and air—and emotional risk—from the moment his grandmother told him his parents were dead.

Except that no one had warned him about the impossibility of not falling in love with your own child...or that once your heart had been laid bare and trembling to the overwhelmingly sweetness of loving another human being more than your own life, it was all the more vulnerable to attacks from other sources.

He pulled the car into the driveway leading to one of the side entrances, cut the engine, then slammed his palm against the wheel.

"You *idiot,*" he breathed, staring into the darkness.

Ten minutes later Tomas followed Alek into his study, conveying the news that Sophie had called and wished Alek to return her call as soon as possible, that Gizela had kept dinner for him, should he wish it, and that, yes, Mrs. Henderson and Master Chase had gone straight up to their rooms, Mrs. Henderson specifically requesting they not be disturbed until morning.

"Thank you, Tomas," Alek said wearily, then frowned at his aide. "You should have gone home hours ago."

Tomas shrugged off Alek's concern, then said, "I...I trust everything is all right?" Curiosity sparred with discretion in his ivy-colored eyes as he slipped his suit jacket back on in preparation for leaving.

Alek dropped into the leather chair behind his desk, rubbing his eyes. He briefly considered going up to Luanne's rooms anyway to say good-night, but thought better of it. She probably needed a little time to sort out a few things. God knew he did. Morning would come soon enough.

He glanced up at Tomas, then leaned back in his chair, fingering a stray paper clip on the blotter. "Mrs. Henderson had a bout of false labor. She's fine now," he quickly added to assuage the aide's worried gasp. "But she'll be staying with us until the baby's born, since Dr. Palachek feels it would be too risky for Mrs. Henderson to travel now."

To his surprise Tomas's thin, usually serious face brightened considerably. "That will be excellent, Your Highness. And this way, Master Chase and I can continue our chess tournament."

"Your what?"

"I taught him how to play chess the other day during lunch, and already he has beaten me three times out of five."

Alek smiled, the knot in his chest easing just a fraction, then requested dinner be sent to him there. Tomas gave a quick half bow—Alek had given up trying to break the young man of the obsequious habit some months ago—then left, after which Alek dialed up his sister.

"Oh! Thank goodness!" she said the instant she recognized his voice. "I know this is horribly last minute, but *please* tell me you can fill in for me at the Women's and Children's summit meeting in Vienna tomorrow!"

"Tomorrow?" The Women's and Children's Summit was bringing together leading activists for women's and children's rights from more than a hundred nations and a dozen major charitable organizations. As head of the World Relief Fund, Sophie would undoubtedly be a keynote speaker. "Why can't you make it? And what on earth do you expect me to do?"

"I can't make it because three out of the five children are sick, and I haven't been feeling particularly wonderful myself, so I figure the last thing I need to do is spread the flu to representatives from half the world's countries. And I've spent the entire day trying to find a substitute, but everyone else on the board has other commitments. So you're my last hope."

Alek rubbed his eyes. Sophie rarely asked anything of him. Which was a good thing, since he was incapable of saying no to her. "What do I have to—"

"Just read the speech I sent you an hour ago by e-mail. Oh, and sit in on a few meetings. I've sent you a list of those, too. Oh, *thank* you, darling, thank you! So how are things going on the Luanne and Chase front?"

"You know, you're beginning to sound far too American."

"Yeah? Cool," she said, and Alek rolled his eyes, then started to tell Sophie a little—very little—about what had transpired over the last twenty-four hours. Except she suddenly cut him off because she had to go "puke," so any comments or words of wisdom from that source would have to wait, he supposed.

He booted up the computer on his desk and retrieved Sophie's e-mail, realized he'd have to leave before dawn to make the 7:30 a.m. orientation breakfast meeting. And it would be several days before he returned.

Several days in which, God willing, he would have some sort of bloody epiphany about this whole sorry mess.

"Oh, no, madam," Elena said when Luanne protested the breakfast tray descending like a guided missile to her lap the next morning. "Dr. Palachek, she is very insisting that madam not get out of bed, except to use toilet."

"Which I have to do," Luanne pointed out, dodging the tray and swinging her legs over the side of the bed before it could descend again. "Besides, eating off a bed tray when you're this pregnant is kinda an exercise in futility. How's about, if I promise to sit real still, you set the food up over there?" Luanne pointed to a small, lace-covered table set in front of the window. After a second of obvious internal struggle, the maid carried the tray across the room and began to remove the various dishes to the table.

Luanne tugged her plush robe over her cotton nightie, shivering a little as she slowly began the interminable twenty-foot journey to the bathroom. Funny how finding out she was a month further along made her feel five times more pregnant than she had twenty-four hours earlier. "Where's my son?"

"He has gone down to stables already. Andrei, the stable master's son, said he could start his riding lessons today."

Luanne supposed her bladder would remain intact for ten more seconds. "Really? Has the prince gone with him?"

"Oh!" Elena smacked herself on her forehead, then trudged over to Luanne, digging in the pocket of her uniform for an envelope which she handed over. "What a dunce I am, almost forgetting to give this to you. Is from Prince Alek. He had to leave very early this morning for conference in Vienna. He says to tell you he will be back in five days, please to forgive him for leaving without seeing you and Chase. Shall I pour your tea now?''

Luanne nodded, then finally made it to the bathroom, after which she scanned the note, which basically said what Elena just had, except in better English.

Well. She wasn't sure whether to be ticked off or relieved, which was only going to give her a headache if she thought too hard about it. True, she'd been just as glad Alek had taken the other car last night so she wouldn't have to deal with both him and her muddled thoughts in the same confined space, but she'd been pretty much resigned to dealing with...things this morning. Except then he up and leaves.

Of course, maybe by the time he came back, one or both of them would've forgotten the incident up on the hill.

Okay, so maybe that was a little farfetched.

She ran a comb through her snarled hair, then lumbered back to the table, only to wince at the spread in front of her: scrambled eggs and sausage, oatmeal with fresh strawberries, warm rolls, half a grapefruit, orange juice and tea. If Gizela actually expected her to eat all that...

"I will leave you to your breakfast, yes?" Elena said, and Luanne could have kissed her, since she'd yet to master the art of dismissing servants. But halfway to the door the maid turned and said, "I know you are probably unhappy that you cannot go home until baby comes, but everybody here is glad for you to stay."

"You are? Why?"

"You and Master Chase, you are like sunshine in palace. And not since Princess Sophie have we had baby born in palace. So everybody here is very excited." She grinned. "The baby will have many aunts and uncles, I think."

Such overwhelming acceptance...oh, for heaven's sake—at this rate Luanne was gonna be crying over toilet paper commercials. She blinked hard, then nodded. "You betcha. A whole slew of 'em."

Elena cocked her head. "A *slew?* I do not—"

"It means a whole lot. Many, many."

"Ah, yes." Then she hesitated.

"Is there somethin' else, Elena?"

The woman scrutinized her prodigious bosom for a second or two, then peered up from underneath her blond lashes. "Is just that…is not just staff who would be sad to see you leave so soon, we do not think." Her cheeks flamed. "And I think you are too smart woman not to catch my meaning, *da?*"

And then she was gone, leaving Luanne to glare at her grapefruit.

Two days later, Luanne had had about all she could take of lying around and watching her belly dance. She'd been good, but mainly because Elena and Alek's grandmother had threatened to tell Dr. Palachek if she wasn't. But, honestly—she'd read until her eyeballs were like to fall out, there was nothing on television she either understood or cared to watch, and if Elena didn't stop her infernal hovering and fussing, the maid was liable to find herself trussed up and hanging from the nearest chandelier. And when there wasn't anyone around, Luanne was left with her thoughts, which kept straying to Alek and their dilemma and all these tangled-up feelings she didn't know what to do with, and that just made her crankier than ever.

Luanne mused how pregnancy did tend to bring out a body's worst side, in more ways than one.

Her highlight of the past thirty-six hours had been a phone call to Odella, asking her to please go ahead and forward any mail that found its way to Luanne's house and to not bother watering the flowers anymore, seeing as it was getting on to fall. Unfortunately, all it took was ten minutes of hearing Odella's accent—not to mention a few juicy tidbits of local gossip—to make Luanne feel more homesick than ever. And being confined to her bedroom when it looked absolutely glorious outside wasn't helping her mental state any. Especially as it was making her crazy not being able to watch Chase's first riding lessons. Therefore, when Dr. Palachek made a surprise palace call late that afternoon, Luanne decided to plead for parole.

"I haven't had a single contraction for two days, I swear," she said, the instant the doctor walked into her room. "And bein' confined like this just goes so against my nature, I'm sure it can't be any good for my blood pressure."

Without comment the doctor sat on the edge of Luanne's bed, then lifted the sheet to check Luanne's ankles. "Good. Swelling's down."

"Thanks for telling me. I wouldn't know."

That got a chuckle. She checked Luanne's blood pressure, listened to the baby's heartbeat, handed her a plastic stick to go pee on, nodding in approval when Luanne brought it back.

"Well, things certainly seem to be more under control..."

"Then can I—"

"Not so fast. Last time I checked, you were three centimeters dilated and fifty percent effaced. And the baby's head is fully engaged in your pelvis. You could give birth an hour from now, or not for another three weeks. Given those two options, I'd definitely opt for three weeks. Or at least, one more."

Luanne fought against the prickle of tears. Lord, she felt like a little kid. "All I want to do is go watch Chase ride."

At this point Alek's grandmother rapped on the partially open door to Luanne's room, entering without further invitation. "Well?" she said to the doctor, who relayed to the princess what she'd just told Luanne. And what Luanne had just told her. Then Anka turned to Luanne, who was sitting there with her arms linked over her belly, chastising herself for feeling so crabby when these people had shown her and Chase so much kindness over the past little while. "But I don't see any harm, if she's driven to the stables, in her getting out long enough to watch her son's riding lessons."

"That is no problem at all," Princess Ivana said with a shrug. "I would be happy to accompany her."

"As long as she doesn't stay on her feet too long."

"Of course, Doctor," the princess said with a smile for Luanne that the doctor wouldn't have been able to see. "Off her feet. I understand completely."

* * *

Chase had already intimated that the princess drove like a maniac, if his sigh of relief the other night at finding out that Gregori, and not the princess, would be driving them back to the palace was anything to go by. However, they managed the short drive to the stables without mishap; a few minutes later, Luanne had hauled her enormous self up on top of the post-and-rail fence surrounding one of the practice rings, watching her grinning son guide Starlight into a canter for the first time. Andrei, a lanky, sandy-haired young man with the brightest blue eyes Luanne had ever seen, ambled over to where she was sitting, his hands parked on his jeans-clad hips as he kept a careful eye on his student.

"Is true, he has never ridden before?"

"A pony ride when he was six, but I don't suppose that counts."

A grin. "No." Then, "But he is natural. Not at all afraid of horse. Good instinct. Look at way horse and boy move as one, even after only two lessons."

And even Luanne could see what Andrei meant, that Chase and the animal seemed to share a brain. When they got back, she'd have to be sure to find a stable where he could keep up his lessons.

But what she was seeing, she realized, was more than just Chase's newfound affinity for riding. There was a regalness, for lack of a better word, an air of confidence about the way he sat upon that horse, the way he'd begun to conduct himself in his dealings with the princess and the palace staff and even Luanne herself, that both tickled and scared her to death.

She sensed the princess's presence beside her, just about the time Andrei returned to the center of the ring to work with Chase. Shoving aside her ambivalence, Luanne managed a smile for Alek's grandmother, who stood with her hands tucked into the pockets of the brick-red blazer she wore over a white silk blouse and pleated gray skirt. "Care to join me up here?"

Ivana laughed, a breeze teasing her soft white waves. "I am afraid my fence-sitting days are over, my dear." She paused, her expression turning far too meaningful. "As should yours be, I think?"

"Dr. Palachek said to stay off my feet, and that's what I'm doing—"

"I am not speaking literally, child."

Yes, she knew that. "Could we please not go there again, Your Highness?"

"As you wish." The old woman's seemingly benign expression did little to settle Luanne's nerves, however. Especially when she said, "Still, you do not strike me as the kind of woman to deny what is in her heart."

Luanne laughed, shaking her head. "You don't give up, do you?"

"I wish I could, to be honest. But I find I cannot. Not until the problem is solved. One way or the other."

Shivering a little underneath her long-sleeved denim maternity blouse, Luanne watched Chase for a moment, then said, "Okay. Just for the heck of it—what do *you* think is in my heart?"

"That your first child was conceived in more love than the one you now carry."

Her gaze whipped to the princess's, a rush of anger diffused only by the gentleness—and understanding—she saw in the older woman's eyes. Luanne looked away again. "What kind of love can there be in a one-night stand?"

"Perhaps the kind that survives more than a decade of separation?"

She opened her mouth to deny the princess's assessment, only to have the words wither up and die on her tongue. It was pointless, her pretending any more. She did love Alek. Always had, as illogical as that was. But despite her surroundings, this wasn't a fairy tale, this was reality. A cold, harsh reality that didn't allow for such foolishness.

After a moment, Luanne carefully lowered herself to the ground, waving to Chase and saying she'd see him later. Except then she realized a person doesn't exactly walk away from a princess. Especially one who brought you.

Ivana touched her arm. "Come. We will go for a ride—"

"I don't want to go for a ride! I don't want..." She stopped, trying to get her breath, to control her emotions. Then she said, "I'm sorry if I seem disrespectful. Or ungrateful. I don't mean to be either, since y'all have been real good to Chase and me while we've been here. But the thing is..." She looked away, shook her head. "Look—your grandson and I share a son. And I won't deny I'm still attracted to him, maybe even more than I was then. Alek's a good man, and I can see he's going to make a strong leader—"

"Did you love your husband, Luanne?"

Luanne could barely think over her pulse pounding in her ears. "Where on earth did that question come from?"

The princess smiled kindly. "From an old woman's musings about why someone so recently widowed talks so little about her husband."

"That's because it hurts too much," Luanne lobbed back. Which was true. "Jeff was very good to me. I cared—"

"I am not asking about caring. *Did you love him?*"

"Of *course* I loved him!" Which was also true.

"And were you *in love* with him, as well?"

A bench sat nearby, underneath an ancient oak tree. Luanne sagged clumsily onto it before her back gave way, then let out a harsh, defeated sigh as well as another part of the truth she could no long deny. "No." She rammed a hand through her windblown hair, not looking at Alek's grandmother. "Lord knows I wanted to, I tried to—"

"Love cannot be forced, my dear."

Luanne's lips twisted into a wry smile. "I know that. Now."

The princess lowered herself onto the bench beside Luanne. "My grandson is convinced that you were. In love with your husband."

"I know he is."

She heard the slight intake of breath. "But *why*, child?"

Now she met the older woman's puzzled gaze. "Because as long as he thinks that," she said softly, "he doesn't have to feel obligated about trying to feel something for me he doesn't. Or can't. Like you said, love can't be forced."

"You think Alek cannot love?"

"No offense, ma'am, but Alek has attention deficit disorder of the heart. Staying focused on one woman for more than a few months just isn't possible. I mean, if it weren't for Chase, I wouldn't even be here right now, would I?"

"You don't know that."

"Yes, I do." She blew out another sigh, crossing her arms over her middle. "Believe it or not, we did more than make a baby eleven years ago. We actually talked, too. Even though he left out a few little details, like his identity, he still told me all about his parents and how he knew they were about to break up before they were killed. He said then he knew he'd never fall in love, and he as good as reiterated it the other day...."

Unbidden, images of their little encounter up on the mountainside slashed through her brain. Of Alek's tenderness, his protectiveness. The way his hand shook when he touched her face.

That as intimate as his *touches* had been, he hadn't been able to look her in the eye, had he?

"And...and I'm not dumb enough to think I can change a man's mind. I know too many women who let themselves fall into that trap and ended up miserable. Besides, I've been on the other end of that equation, y'know? And lopsided relationships are the pits. Ma'am."

"I agree with you. After all, I was in one."

Luanne gawked at her. The princess shrugged. "I felt great affection for my husband, certainly. Respected him. Genuinely grieved for him when he died. But I always felt that something was...missing. So I was thrilled to see the spark of true love in my daughter's eyes, when she brought her Lloyd home to meet me. And to see the way he could not take his eyes off her."

Then she sighed. "We have no way of knowing whether Alek's parents might have worked out their differences, had they lived." Her mouth twisted. "My daughter still had a lot of growing up to do. I like to think that, given time, she eventually would have. That she would not have thrown away something so precious." Then she looked at Luanne. "But what Alek has not yet learned is that we cannot base our own experiences on another's. Or that there is any safety in cutting ourselves off from feeling.''

"And sometimes feelings aren't enough," Luanne said, more sharply than she meant to. At the princess's raised eyebrows, she let out another sigh. "Even if Alek hadn't locked up his heart good and tight so long ago, what difference would it make? I could no more be a part of all this on a permanent basis than a fish could live on dry land."

Ivana angled her head at her. "The staff adore you, you know."

"That's probably because I'm a lot closer to being one of them than being one of y'all. Well, it's true," she added when the princess snorted her reply. "Your Highness—" Luanne reached over, covered the princess's hand with her own. "I know what you're trying to do. You want Alek and me to get together to make this business with Chase a little less awkward. And you know what? At one time in my life, I might've even gone along with your plan, since in some ways our getting together makes as much sense as anything else I can think of. But I lived a lie for more than ten years, trying to love a man the way he loved me, and spending far too many hours feeling all torn up because of it. I wouldn't put another living soul in that position for all the world, ma'am. Not for you or your country or even for my son."

The princess scrutinized her for a long moment, then got up, nodding toward the car. "Come on. I have something I want to show you."

"I said I don't want—"

"You will find I rarely pull rank, child, but this is one of those times. Now get up off your duff and get in the car."

In spite of herself a laugh sputtered from Luanne's throat. Princess Ivana was the most stubborn, meddlesome old woman she knew—and coming from the South, that was going some— but Luanne had to admit she found herself hoping she had half as much spit-and-vinegar left in her bones when she turned eighty.

A few minutes later the princess carefully steered the car out onto the road that would take them toward the village. A little while after that she said, "There is to be a small dinner party next week, after my grandson returns. Nothing fussy, just some old family friends from France who regularly travel though here this time of year. Their daughter and my Ekaterina, Alek's mother, shared a flat in Paris during Katia's stay there before her marriage. I would like you to join us."

"Oh, no, I couldn't—"

"You can, my dear. And you will charm them no end, I am sure."

Luanne grimaced. "I suppose this is one of those pulling rank times?"

"It is."

She looked at Alek's grandmother, her brow knotted. "Why?"

"Because you are the mother of our future monarch, my dear."

She pushed out a sigh, then said, "I have nothing to wear—"

"That can be arranged."

Further discussion was pointless, Luanne knew. But with any luck she'd go into labor the night of the party and the problem would be solved.

"You are a very…determined young woman, yes?" Ivana said, not unkindly.

"Look who's talking," she said, which got a laugh. "But, yes. I suppose I am."

"Ah, but determination is a good trait in a woman, is it not? We would be hard-pressed to survive otherwise, I would think. And what other trait does a species need to survive?"

Luanne chuckled. What was this? A quiz? But she replied, knowing full well where the princess was taking the conversation. "Adaptability?"

"Exactly. So—as far as your 'fitting in' is concerned…" Ivana glanced over, then back to the road. "You are perhaps forgetting that Alek's father came from working-class roots in Northern England. He never quite lost his Manchester accent, in fact. And my granddaughter just married an American tradesman, although Steven had his work cut out for him to convince my equally *determined* granddaughter that *he* could adapt to our admittedly rarefied way of life.''

Luanne stared out the windshield in silence as the princess went on. ''You have a keen mind, child, as well as a natural poise that cannot be instilled from the outside. The rest of it…oh, for the love of—!''

She leaned on the car's horn, then deftly zipped around a farmer prodding a pair of cows up the road. Luanne bit back a smile, realizing where Alek's affinity for racing must have come from. ''Now, where was I? Oh, yes—the rest is just cosmetic, is it not? A matter of learning our customs and culture, the social graces expected from those in our position…'' The princess hesitated, then said, ''No matter what you and my grandson do or don't work out, there will be functions, some of them quite formal, at which your presence will be expected, *even if,*'' she added as Luanne opened her mouth to protest, ''you both persist in following through on this ridiculous 'adoption' scheme. Although I detest the idea of trying to mold you into someone else, neither would I want you to feel ill at ease.''

Luanne frowned at the scenery flashing outside her window.

''Now. As for your conviction that Aleksander cannot love…'' Ivana turned onto a smaller road that led to a large, mansion-like building sheltered by a forest of maples and elms just beginning to fade. She pulled the car into a circular driveway that took them around to the front of the building, stopped. ''Love sometimes needs to be primed before it flows, yes? Perhaps a person who…believes he cannot love simply needs to be shown what it is to *be* loved?''

Luanne decided not to point out that she'd just said, not five minutes before, that she'd been down that road once and it was a dead end. But she sure couldn't stop turning over in her mind that business about her position in Chase's life. Not that she could ever change who she was on the inside, but the princess was right: like it or not, Luanne was the mother of a prince. And as such, she supposed the least she could do, for Chase's sake, was to not embarrass her son. While she was thinking on all this, she craned her neck to look out the window. "Where are we?"

"The Children's Home Sophie set up some years ago, mainly to house refugee children from other countries until families can be found for them. Since my granddaughter can no longer be here as much as she used to, I have taken up some of the slack, visiting and reading to the children. I...understand you have a degree in education?"

A half dozen children, the oldest no more than six, darted out of the nearest door and across the front lawn, a gray-haired woman in a navy-blue jumpsuit in frantic pursuit. Luanne nodded, her gaze fixed on the giggling children as she wondered what tragedy had brought each of them here, what sort of spirit they each possessed to be able to laugh so freely in spite of that.

And if there were children inside whose spirits had not yet recovered from fate's blows...

"Then perhaps you wouldn't mind putting your skills to use while you are here? An extra pair of hands—not to mention an extra heart—is always welcome."

"Yes, yes," Luanne said distractedly, unhooking her seat belt, only to remain where she was. Fate had just dealt her, if not another blow, exactly, certainly another challenge. She could either meet it or let it flatten her.

"Luanne? What is it, my dear?"

"Show me," she said quietly, then twisted to meet the princess's slightly startled gaze. "Show me what I need to know. How to act. How to dress. What to say to people who are likely to judge Carpathia's future monarch by his mother."

The princess simply stared at her for several seconds, then said, "I would be honored, my dear. But what prompted this...change of heart?"

"I don't want to embarrass my son. Or..." Luanne hauled in a breath, looking out at the children scampering across the lawn. "Or make Alek regret that night eleven years ago any more than he probably already does."

The princess got out of the car; Luanne followed suit. Then Ivana linked her arm through Luanne's and said, with the kind of firmness you'd expect from someone who'd bucked Hitler, "When I am done with you, my dear, the only regret my grandson will have regarding that night is that he walked away to begin with."

Luanne thought better of disabusing the old woman of her notion.

Chapter 11

"Alek!" Seated squarely on Starlight's back in the center of the riding ring, Chase waved madly at Alek's approach, a huge grin splitting the narrow, freckled face underneath his riding helmet. "You're back!"

Alek matched both wave and grin as he approached the ring. Tomas had told him the boy had been riding every day since he'd left, that he was lucky to get even one chess game a day with him now. But his aide's obvious disappointment had been tempered with pride nonetheless. And now, catching sight of the kid who'd been so determined to make everyone's life a living hell a few short weeks ago quietly chattering to the huge animal underneath him, Alek felt a surge of pride, as well.

And something else.

Bo scampered up, a quivering blob of golden fur, and Alek chuckled, leaning over to scratch the beast behind the ears. A second later the pup clumsily scrambled back onto his feet and gallumphed over to Luanne, who was leaning heavily on the top rail of the fence, her swollen form encased in a dusty blue tunic and pants outfit in some soft, plush fabric. She'd turned toward Alek at Chase's greeting, a slight smile playing across her lightly lipsticked mouth.

And his heart ricocheted around his chest.

He'd had his epiphany. Or he'd thought he had: without the flash of light and voice booming from heaven, one couldn't be quite sure. Rather, it had dribbled slowly but steadily into his consciousness like rain through a leaky roof, starting with an awareness of missing Luanne and Chase so much he thought he'd go mad, and ending with the even more profound—and ramification-rich—realization that what had seemed impossible to even contemplate barely a week before now seemed the only logical answer.

He wanted them to stay. Not from any sense of obligation or responsibility, but from a need so strong and deep and awe-inspiring, he couldn't even begin to explain it.

True, he hadn't much cared for the terror that had ripped through him when he'd thought Luanne or the baby might be in danger the other day. But he'd survived it, hadn't he? And that fear, raw and suffocating as it had been, was nothing—*nothing*—compared with the joy that damn near set him on fire at simply seeing her smile or hearing her laugh, of watching the way her expression softened whenever she looked at their son. Whatever this was, he was powerless to fight it. Like it or not, he was committed, at least enough to get it through his thick head that this was his family—*his* family. And that his grandmother was dead-on right, that simply adopting Chase would never work. That the only responsible solution—the only logical solution, despite his avowal to the contrary a week before—was marriage. Surely Luanne—practical, logical Luanne—would see the sense in that?

He caught her hesitant expression as he approached her.

Well, it wasn't as if he didn't know he was facing an uphill battle. Banishing Jeff's ghost was not a given. And attempting to forge a relationship while secrets still lurked in the shadows was risky to the point of foolhardiness. He knew that. But what choice did he have? He wasn't about to jeopardize Luanne's health or fragile peace of mind by revealing something that could easily shatter both, but neither was he about to let the past dictate the solution to their present dilemma. This could—would—work, he was sure of it. Since neither of them was interested in anything romantic, who would get hurt?

As he got closer, he could see her clothes were of a higher quality than she usually wore. Her hair was tamer, too, pulled back into what he thought was called a French braid, a few wisps floating free around her slightly fuller face. She'd gained weight, he noticed with both shock and relief, but there was something else about her that seemed different, something he couldn't put a finger on. All he knew, though, was that by the time he reached her, putting his arm around his shoulders and giving her a hug wasn't even something he'd had to think about. Although her brows lifted, her only response was to politely ask him how the conference had gone.

He hooked his thumbs in the pockets of his jeans, watching the boy. For the first time in many, many years, he felt as though he'd come home. "Very well." Then he grinned. "This being a prince business isn't half-bad, once you get the hang of it."

Luanne laughed, a soft, musical sound he admitted would be very nice to hear for, well, the rest of his life, actually. Except, the moment the laughter died out, silence landed with a dull thud between them. Alek leaned on the fence, his hands linked. "Chase is doing well, isn't he?"

"Andrei can't say enough about his progress. When we go back, I'll have to find a stable that teaches English style."

Alek rubbed his hands together, pretending to ward off the chill. Then he looked at her, frowning. "Aren't you supposed to be off your feet?"

"It's okay. I'll have you know I haven't had a single blessed contraction since you...left."

She went very still. He looked at her, then boldly reached over and swept a tendril of hair off her cheek, deliberately letting his fingertips graze her skin. "If you expect me to apologize for what happened—"

"Oh, for pity's sake, Alek..." Her laugh was unnatural, her cheeks ablaze. "Don't be ridiculous. It's just not something that's gonna happen again, is all. I mean, my letting myself get all shook up like that and puttin' you in the position of havin' to be kind to me."

Alek felt his jaw tighten. "I don't have sexual encounters out of pity, Luanne. And I never have."

He could tell his vehemence caught her by surprise. Almost as much as it caught him, in fact. But only for a moment. "You really expect me to believe that every time you took a woman to bed, it was because you really cared about her?"

"Luanne, look at me." After a moment she did, caution clouding her eyes. "I have no idea how many women I've dated. I stopped keeping track of that years ago. But I can tell you exactly how many women I've slept with—"

"Alek, please—"

"Six, Luanne. *Six.* Not dozens, as the tabloids would have the world believe. And while I will readily admit that love wasn't the motivating factor in any of my affairs, respect and admiration were. Every time. I never, not once, bedded a woman because I felt sorry for her or at the behest of my libido. If you want to know the truth...as a playboy, I would not have gotten full marks."

After a moment, a crooked smile slid across her mouth. But she looked away again, toying with her wedding rings. Alek reached over, deliberately taking her left hand in his. "I know you want to go home," he said softly, watching her watching his thumb skirt across the rings, "but I'm not sorry you have to stay." Not surprisingly, she extricated her hand, her brow pleated.

"If I didn't know better, I'd say you were tryin' to come on to me."

"Perhaps I am."

Her gaze snapped to his, then away. "This conversation is makin' me real nervous, Alek."

"Why?"

"*Why?*" The word flew from her lips on a choked, startled laugh. "Where would you like me to start?"

Alek leaned on the fence, as well, squinting slightly in the sun, his voice low. "Tell me something—when you asked me to...*help you forget* the other day, am I correct in assuming that if any other man had found you up on the ridge in tears, you would not have made the same request of him?''

Silence crackled between them. Bristling, shocked, angry silence.

''Okay, I'll take that as a yes. Then, to save you any further guesswork in the matter, let me just say that if *I* had come upon any other woman crying her eyes out, I daresay my aid would have been limited to a listening ear and a handkerchief.'' He sidled closer, close enough to smell her, to let his breath stir the hair at her temple, to feel his own body stir in response to the subtle shift in her breathing pattern. ''Five days away gave me a lot of time to think. About us. About what we have. Or could have. And I realized that what happened up there on the ridge, Luanne, wasn't about sex or attraction or even grief. It was about caring and affection. And it was genuine.''

Again, her gaze whipped to his. ''What *are* you talkin' about?''

He glanced over to be sure Chase's attention was focused elsewhere, then cupped her jaw in his hand. She flinched, distrust glittering in her eyes, sparking a resolve to annihilate that distrust if it took everything he had in him.

''A man can change, Luanne. A man can suddenly realize he's spent most of his adult life resisting the only thing he really needs, the only thing that makes any sense.... Why are you looking at me like that?''

''You don't have to sweet-talk me to get to Chase, Alek.''

His brows flew up. ''*Sweet-talk?* For the love of God, woman! Why are you being so bloody obtuse? I *care* about you, damn it! You and Chase both!'' He lifted a hand, skimmed one knuckle down her cheek. ''When I touch you, in whatever way you let me touch you, it's because I *care*. I care enough that I don't want to see either of you go. I want us to become a family. And I know this sounds ridiculous, considering our previous conversations...but now I think we *should* get married.''

Luanne glanced away, her heart knocking. And Alek thought *she* was being obtuse? But when she turned back, she had to admit, he certainly looked sincere. Then she narrowed her eyes. "Your grandmother been raggin' on you?"

He actually smiled. "Relentlessly. But that's not why I changed my mind."

But that wasn't gonna cut it. "I know you care, Alek. If you didn't, we wouldn't be here at all. But that doesn't mean…" Oh, this was nuts. She jerked away, her hands in the air, then twisted around and called to Chase. "C'mon, sugar—it's gettin' on to lunchtime—"

"Aw, Mama…"

"The horse isn't goin' anywhere, honey. And, besides, Gizela said she'd show you how to make those pastries you liked so much, remember?"

With a groan and a moan, Chase rode over to the fence and dismounted, he and Andrei then leading Starlight back to his stall. Luanne tried to follow, but Alek handily blocked her path.

"This conversation isn't over," he said, his eyes like steel.

"Oh, yes it is." She stepped forward. "Now get out of my—hey!"

He'd caught her by the shoulders. "I'm not going anywhere until you give me one good reason why this wouldn't work."

"Alek! You can't just go changin' your mind on a dime like that a-and expect me to just fall in line behind you!"

His grip relaxed as he glanced up, a sigh rushing from his lips. "I apologize, *mila*. Of course this must seem…a bit out of the blue. It's just that the more I thought about it, the more this option seems to be the most practical. The one that would disrupt Chase the least—"

"Do you love me, Alek?"

There was no mistaking the panic in his eyes, like a man about to be overtaken by a tidal wave. But his gaze never left hers, she'd give him that. "I *need* you, Luanne. And I care about you more than I've ever cared about another woman—"

"I *cared* about Jeff, Alek." The words just flew out, a knee-jerk reaction. "I *cared* about him so much I wanted to die myself when he did. In every way conceivable, ours was a logical match, y'know? But that didn't change the fact that, no matter how much I wanted to, I still couldn't love him the way he loved me, the way I would have given my right arm to, what with everything he did for me. And that just ate away at me, Alek, that I couldn't give him the only thing he ever really wanted.''

It took a moment or two for her words to register, but when they did, she could feel the shock pulse through his body as his grip tightened.

"Then why the hell did you lead me to believe—"

"I didn't. You assumed."

"But you didn't bother to correct my misapprehension."

"No."

"Why?"

Funny thing about the truth: once it slips out, it's the very devil to rein back in. So Luanne looked into those stunned, disbelieving eyes and said, with a resignation that almost felt like relief, "Think about what you just said, then ask yourself...what would have been the point?"

When she moved to pass him this time, he didn't stop her. But not six feet past him, she turned and said to his back, "And I refuse to do to you what Jeff did to me."

He was staring out the window of his study, his hands stuffed into the back pockets of his jeans, when he heard his grandmother's approach.

"You're home."

He glanced at her, then away, attempting to mask the turbulence that still crippled his lungs, a half hour after that...whatever it had been with Luanne. "In a manner of speaking."

"The conference went well?"

"Yes, fine."

The princess crossed the room, sat on the window seat in front of him. "Chase has made remarkable progress with his riding—"

"I know. I saw him."

"Oh? And...Luanne?"

"Yes."

"She's looking well, don't you thi—"

"Did she tell you of her feelings for me?"

The princess merely lifted her brows, as if expecting his question. "She...might have intimated—"

"When?"

"While you were gone. I haven't been keeping some deep, dark secret from you for weeks, if that's what's bothering you."

No, he didn't imagine she had. Alek frowned, then scrubbed the heel of his hand against one eye. Deep inside him, the hulking, nameless monster he'd harbored for twenty years grumbled in its sleep, annoyed at being disturbed. "I asked her to marry me. More or less."

His grandmother's mouth sagged open. "That is a bit of an about-face, isn't it?" He grunted. "And what was her reaction?"

"She basically told me to shove off."

"Which I suppose accounts for your less-than-jovial mood at present."

Another grunt.

"I don't suppose you happened to mention that you... returned her feelings?"

"She knows how much I care about her."

"Oh, for the love of God, Aleksander...*why* do you think calling something by another name, or not naming it at all, somehow exempts you from its effects? Why can't you simply admit you love the woman?"

The monster jerked awake, roared at having a light shone in its eyes. "I don't—"

"Of course you do. Any fool can see what you feel for Luanne. And while I may be a pain in the backside, Alek, I am not a fool. But somehow you think you can have things both ways. That you can protect your heart while expecting someone else to give you hers—"

"But that's just it. I *didn't* expect her to give me her heart. I thought—I assumed—we'd be able to go into this on an even footing."

"And there is no reason why that is still not a possibility, my dear. Now that you know she loves you, the solution is a simple one, yes?''

He barked out a laugh. "Oh, believe me, Grandmother...there is nothing simple about this." At her perplexed expression, he quickly weighed his options, then crossed to his desk, the carpeted floor groaning under the weight of his strides. He unlocked the bottom drawer, pulled out an envelope, the contents of which he handed to his grandmother.

"Read it."

He watched the old woman go pale as she skimmed the note, her eyes darting to the top of the page to take in the date. "Oh, dear God," she breathed, then lifted her gaze to Alek's. "Then you have known about this since when? Before Sophie's wedding?"

"Yes."

"No wonder you were in such a foul mood all summer! What—"

"—do I intend to do?" One hand streaked through his hair as he shook his head. "I don't know. I honestly don't know."

"*Do* you love her, Alek?"

The monster screamed, begging to be left alone. To be left in peace. "The thought of her finding out about this makes me ill. Is that close enough for you?"

"No. Nor will it be for Luanne, I'll wager."

He looked away, slowly thumping his hand on the back of one of the chairs, as the monster whimpered, cowering into a corner... And Alek reached in, grabbed it by the scruff of the neck, daring at last to stare it in the face. "The prospect...terrifies me."

"Of what? Of being loved? Or of having it ripped from you again?" He turned, meeting his grandmother's exasperatingly discerning gaze, and felt a shudder rip through him as the monster howled in fury at being named. The princess then tilted her head, her expression hopeful. Encouraging. "And if you don't pursue her, you've already lost, haven't you?"

Alek shut his eyes, expelling a sharp breath as the beast, in a rapidly fading voice, begged not to be banished. "And if I do, she'll insist it's only because of Chase."

"Then it's up to you to convince her otherwise," his grand-mother said gently. "You're very used to having things handed to you. This you'll have to fight for." She then scanned the note again before handing it back. "As for this abomina-tion...burn it. Wipe it from your mind as best you can and pretend it never existed. What earthly good would it do for her to know?"

Alek took the letter, folded it, then stared at it for several seconds before saying, "You wouldn't be advising me to be less than completely truthful, would you?"

She toyed with a pleat in her skirt for a moment, then looked up. "At times it is not only best to keep a secret, but morally wrong to do otherwise. This is one of those times. However..." She stood, lifting a hand to his cheek. "Whatever you decide, my dear, I will support you. I trust implicitly in your ability to make the right decision about this."

A wry smile twisted his mouth. "About damn time."

Ivana's expression softened. "Luanne has been through a great deal. She deserves nothing less than your love."

Alek hauled in a breath. "I know."

"Does she have it?"

He met her gaze. Nodded.

And the beast ran howling into nothingness.

The princess smiled. "Then court her. Slowly. Sweetly. Show her, in as many ways as you can think of, how much you love her. Then—and this is the tricky part—you must be willing to give her the space and time she needs to come to her own conclusions."

Alek rubbed the back of his neck, let out a hollow laugh. And realized bringing the Stolvians to some sort of accord was *nothing* compared with winning Luanne Evans Henderson's stubborn, wounded heart.

Over the next week Luanne played a little game she called "dodging Alek." She'd never meant to reveal her feelings to him, but his holding the dang carrot out on a stick like that...well, it had plumb knocked her for a loop, is what. But just as she had tried to twist gratitude into love with Jeff, so was Alek trying to strong-arm his sense of responsibility into some fairy-tale notion of family. She had no doubt he probably even wanted to love her, just as she had wanted to love Jeff, because that would make everything all tidy and neat, wouldn't it? Trouble was, *almost* happily ever after was not gonna cut it, for either of them. Which was a real shame, because that's about as close to it as she was likely to get.

So Alek's having to spend most of three days last week in Stolvia was a blessing. And at least her lessons were going well—and Chase's, too, since she'd managed to get hold of enough fifth-grade material to tutor him so he wouldn't be behind when they went back. So while Chase was navigating his way through a maze of dangling participles and pre-prealgebra and science experiments set up in a corner of the kitchen under Gizela's eagle eye, Luanne was learning how to negotiate a twelve-piece flatware setting, absorbing everything she could find out about Carpathian history and customs and had basically let Marta Nierzdakova, the princess's personal shopper, have her way with her. It was a shame, really, that she'd only get a few weeks' worth of wear out of most of the clothes, but my, oh, my—could the elegantly coiffed Miss Marta work wonders with a pregnant body.

"Zere iz nos-sing more enticing zan a voman who iss vis child, no? Ve celebrate your ripeness, ze fullness of your vomanhood."

Well, Miss Marta certainly had the fullness part right. But tonight, as Elena helped Luanne into the shimmering, low-cut, silver-blue panne velvet evening gown Marta insisted would be perfect for tonight's dinner, Luanne nearly turned *herself* on, she looked so good.

"Wow, Mama." Chase sashayed into her bedroom and flopped on top of her bed. He and Tomas had a hot chess tournament planned while the adults were at dinner, which seemed to suit him fine. In fact, everything about life here seemed to suit him fine, which was a complication she hadn't counted on in a situation that already had more than its fair share of complications. "You look *hot*."

One hand frozen in midair as she was about to pat back a

wave, Luanne glared in stunned surprise at her son in the three-way mirror in the corner of her room. "What did you say?" Then she flapped the hand, went back to primping. "Never mind, I heard. But just for the record, ten-year-old boys do not generally go around calling their own mothers *hot*."

"How about thirty-six-year-old men?" she heard from the sitting room doorway and nearly dropped the baby right then and there. She whirled around, one hand on her heart, only to feel that heart about explode out of her chest at the sight of Alek in a white dinner jacket and black bow tie, looking like something right out of a James Bond movie. He gave her a wink that happened so fast she nearly missed it, then immediately turned the charm on his son, whose attitude toward Alek was still, Luanne couldn't help but notice, a little on the cautious side. As if he was reserving judgment. Or more likely a piece of his heart, she thought. And who could blame him for that? Alek's grandmother was still going on about telling Chase the truth, but Luanne was holding firm to her conviction that the time wasn't right yet.

"I hear you and Tomas have a real showdown planned for tonight," Alek said with a grin, casually walking over to the nightstand and picking up the copy of Madeleine L'Engle's *A Wrinkle Through Time*.

"Uh-huh. Mama's readin' that to me."

Alek turned toward him, the book raised. "You like it?"

"Yeah. It's cool."

A smile played around Alek's mouth as he leaned over far enough to lightly rap Chase's head with the book. Chase giggled, almost against his better judgment, Luanne thought, and her heart took a slow, painful turn in her chest.

Alek replaced the book on the stand. "My father read this to me, when I was about your age. I thought it was pretty cool, too." Then he nodded toward the door. "Off you go, then. Tomas is waiting in the media room with pizza."

With a whoop of delight, the boy vanished, the pup slipping and sliding at his heels. An insouciant grin stretched across his mouth, Alek then turned to Luanne. She swallowed, wishing she had something to grab hold of. Like her sanity. ''How did you get in here, anyway?'' she asked.

''Elena.''

Luanne let out a sigh, then turned back to her mirror, more out of a need to avoid looking directly at the gorgeous, deluded man standing in her bedroom than because she needed to do anything more with herself. Except the gorgeous, deluded man came up behind her and wiggled a long, slender jewelry box over her right shoulder. ''I come bearing gifts.''

She froze, again. ''Alek, I—''

''—*would be honored to wear your mother's necklace tonight,*'' he said, snapping open the box and lifting out a string of perfectly matched pearls spaced with small, brilliant diamonds, which he smoothly draped around her neck before she could get her mouth working properly again. His touch sent a lightning storm dancing over her skin. Which she ignored. Tried to, anyway. Then he traced one finger along the necklace's path, and she just gave it up with a spectacular shiver that set her nipples on full alert.

And it was times like this—times she did her best to avoid— when she thought maybe ''almost'' wouldn't be all that bad. After all, she had no doubt that Alek would be a loyal, attentive, dutiful husband….

Except then she'd remember that she'd been loyal, attentive and more than dutiful to Jeff and look how *that* had turned out.

Luanne shivered again. Alek chuckled. ''Cold, *mila?*''

She shook her head. He removed his hand, smiling at her in the mirror. ''Marta really knows her stuff. But then, look what she had to work with.''

Luanne eyed his reflection. ''Was that supposed to be a compliment?''

''Let's put it this way—I, for one, am going to have a devil of a time forcing myself to look at anyone else in the room tonight.''

She blushed, then watched her image as, of its own bidding, her hand lifted to caress the exquisite necklace, which she had to admit looked pretty dang good with this dress. "It's beautiful."

"My father gave it to my mother for their first anniversary." Alek smiled. "Which meant, since I was born the following day, she was in about the same shape, literally, that you're in right now."

Her sigh lifted her breasts, which set the diamonds in the necklace to twinkling like fireflies. "Thank you for letting me borrow this—"

"It's not a loan, *mila*. It's a gift."

"Oh, Alek! I can't—"

His grip was warm and firm on her upper arms, even through the velvet sleeves. "You're the mother of my child," he whispered against her temple. "If I want to give you an occasional gift, that's my prerogative."

She twisted around, her belly preventing her from getting too close to him, which was a very good thing. Still, she looked directly into those soft-silver eyes, right past the hope she didn't dare trust, shaking her head. "I can't be bought, Alek."

His smile didn't even waver as he leaned over, placed a soft kiss on her forehead. "Which makes the challenge all the sweeter," he whispered, then stood apart, his arm bent. "Now—shall we go down to dinner?"

Well, she got through it without managing to use the wrong fork or spoon or sound stupid, but Lord Almighty, if she wasn't a mess afterward. And it wasn't like the Girards were cold or la-di-da or anything, because they really weren't. In fact, Luanne mused as she ducked into the powder room down the hall before rejoining everyone in one of the drawing rooms for coffee and dessert, they seemed pretty down to earth, considering the women—Marie-Hélène, who'd been Alek's mother's friend; her mother, Brigitte; and Marie-Hélène's daughter, Françoise, who was about Luanne's age—all looked as if they'd just stepped out of the pages of *Vogue*. However, between the family's barrage of questions about Texas, the homesickness that conversation provoked and the way Alek kept looking at her all through the meal, her appetite had gone out the window. But then, she'd been feeling kind of funny all day, anyway.

Luanne slipped out of the powder room, fully intending to go straight to the drawing room where coffee and dessert were being served. But a snatch of conversation from just outside the pair of French doors opening onto a courtyard caught her attention. The past few days had been unseasonably warm; apparently the two younger women had opted to step outside for a few minutes.

And it obviously never occurred to the ladies that Luanne spoke French. She had no idea why she was so shocked. After all, they weren't saying anything more than what she'd said or thought about herself. Perhaps it was the viciousness, though, that she found so hard to fathom. And the horror expressed that, of all the women darling Katia's son could have chosen, he should settle for someone like her.

"And to give her Katia's necklace!" Marie-Hélène whispered, her French rapid-fire but easily understood. "What must have his poor grandmother thought? Did you see her face when Luanne came in?"

Yes, Luanne had noticed the surprise on Ivana's face when she noticed the necklace. She had also seen the princess's gaze slip to Alek's and the small nod of obvious approval.

Nausea swirled though her. For her, the night was definitely over. She made her way to the drawing room to make her excuses to the princess, grateful that Alek wasn't around.

Ivana gave her a piercing look when Luanne allowed as how she wasn't feeling all that well. Seated on a love seat, the princess reached up and grasped Luanne's hand. "Do we need to call Dr. Palachek?"

"No, no—it's nothing like that. I just need to…go lie down, is all."

After a moment, Ivana nodded. "I will make your apologies. They've all had children. They will understand. Alek or I will check on you later."

"That's really not—"

But Ivana tightened her grasp, the corners of her mouth dipped in exasperation. "Surely it has not escaped your notice that there are people here who care about you, child? So let us *care,* for heaven's sake.''

Ah, yes, she thought with a lurch in her stomach. She well knew how much they all *cared.* Luanne gave a smile and a nod, and then skedaddled as fast as her puffy feet would carry her. Her back nagged at her as she rode the elevator to the second floor, even as angry tears burned behind her eyelids. It would be a cold day in Hades before she let herself be subjected to that kind of humiliation again. And Alek thought she could be his *wife?*

She let herself into her empty suite, breathing a sigh of relief that Chase was apparently still with Tomas. Elena was gone, as well, praise the Lord...

What was that?

Her back muscles like to give her five fits, she made her way over to the end table by the sofa, on which sat a large U.S. Global Priority Mail envelope addressed in Odella's neat, flowery script.

Alek was just passing the courtyard on his way back from taking a phone call from his sister when he caught the tail end of a conversation he really wished he hadn't. He'd never much cared for Marie-Hélène, to be honest; but she'd been his mother's best friend, and, as such, Alek had always gone out of his way to be polite whenever their paths crossed. Frankly, he figured she was more interested in keeping her link to the Vlastos name than out of any undying loyalty to the family itself, but since he was rarely around during her visits, he'd been pretty much able to put her snottiness out of his head.

Until now.

Hands in pockets, he stepped out into the courtyard, clearly catching mother and daughter by surprise.

"C'est une nuit plus belle, n'est-ce pas?" he said coldly. "A perfect night," he continued in English, "for cats to be out. Wouldn't you say, Marie-Hélène?"

Even in the dim light spilling outside from the windowed corridor, he could see the color rising in the woman's artificially smooth cheeks. "I beg your pardon?" she said, clutching her flimsy stole to her even flimsier bosom.

Alek stood apart from them, somehow reining in his temper. "Unfortunately, your conversation wasn't nearly as private as you might have preferred. And since you are my grandmother's guests, I will refrain from saying what first comes to mind. But perhaps you should remember, in the midst of your zeal to condemn Mrs. Henderson for what you perceive as her *commonness,* that character has little to do with background. As you have just so clearly demonstrated."

He pivoted to leave, only to turn back. "And one more thing, Marie-Hélène—as my grandmother's friend, your mother is welcome to visit any time she likes. You and your daughter, on the other hand, are no longer welcome here. My mother may have been flighty, but she was never cruel."

He felt the pair of stunned, indignant glares burn through the back of his dinner jacket as he went back inside.

"She claimed she wasn't feeling well," the princess whispered from her perch on the love seat, frowning past Alek in the direction of the trio of husbands and Brigitte Girard, who was fluttering about like a small, frail moth. "What—"

He interrupted her question to tell her what he had overheard.

"Oh, dear God." Ivana lifted worried eyes to him. "That would certainly explain why she was so agitated—"

"Ivana!" Brigitte said brightly, tottering in their direction, her smile as tight as her brunette curls. "Is anything the matter, *chère?*"

"No, no—Alek! Where are you going?"

"To make sure nothing is!" he said, already halfway across the room, noting, when he passed Marie-Hélène and her daughter in the hallway, that they at least had the good sense to shrink against the wall.

With a sigh, Luanne sank into the sofa and leafed through the half dozen or so smaller envelopes inside the big one, mostly notifications of withdrawals from her checking account for utilities bills and the like, her car insurance notice…and a slightly mangled envelope from some attorney's office in Dallas, which had apparently gone by way of China before landing in Sandy Springs.

Puzzled, she opened it. The cover sheet on the attorney's letterhead stated that Mr. Henderson had requested the enclosed be forwarded to her in the event of his death, but that the attorney—Everest Thornton Fitzgerald, Jr., she read at the top of the letterhead—had no knowledge of the contents of said letter, and should she find herself in need of his assistance, to not hesitate to contact him at any of the numbers listed above. She couldn't imagine what on earth this could possibly be, since the will had been all sorted out ages ago—

The note was in Jeff's handwriting, on a piece of plain white photocopy paper. Her throat clogged as she began to read it, the clog strangling her heart as the implications of what she was reading sank in.

Her scream seemed to come from somebody else's throat.

Chapter 12

Alek had barely reached the top of the stairs when he heard Luanne's cry. He rocketed down the hall and through the unlocked door to her suite to find her sitting stiffly on the love seat with one hand clamped over her mouth, staring at a piece of paper in her other hand, which was shaking so badly, both were a blur.

"Luanne! What is it?"

Her head snapped up, her gaze unfocused in a face almost totally devoid of color. His heart knocking painfully against his ribs, he took a cautious step closer. "I heard you scream...."

Color flooded back into her face, even as awareness dawned in her eyes. She struggled to her feet, leaning heavily on the arm of the sofa. "You *knew.*"

Premonition iced his veins. "Knew what, *mila?*"

She hurled the piece of paper in his direction, jerking back her hand as it floated ineffectually to the floor a few feet in front of him. Never letting her out of his sight, Alek crouched to retrieve what he could now see was a photocopy of the letter he had indeed burned, barely a week before.

In silent horror, he picked it up. But how did she get this? And why now?

"When did you get the original, Alek? Right after the accident? Is that why you searched us out?"

His gaze flew to hers. "No!"

"Why you've been so...attentive to me all these weeks? To...to honor a last request?"

"No!" The word bellowed from his lungs. "Damn it, Luanne—" Fury and frustration roared through him as he bit back what he knew would be an extremely ill-timed declaration of his true feelings. "I had no idea he'd send a duplicate to you! I knew if you found out, it would devastate you." He stopped, his heart cracking at the hopelessness—and mistrust—in her tear-filled eyes. He lifted his hand to touch her cheek, but she slapped it away.

"How *dare* you, Alek! How dare you keep something like this from me!"

"I couldn't bear the thought of your being hurt, Luanne! Not more than you already were. And the last thing I wanted to do was to tarnish the memory of the man I thought you loved!" He sucked in a deep breath. "A man who at least had the guts to take on a responsibility that should have been mine."

Luanne shook her head, then awkwardly reached behind her before dropping back onto the sofa. Alex hesitated, then sat beside her, reining in a desire to hold her that was so intense, he burned with it.

"Why is it," she said softly, not looking at him, "that every single thing I do...?" Instead of finishing her sentence, she only shook her head, yanking her hands up by her shoulders when he reached out. "Don't...don't touch me." Then she got up, lurching toward her bedroom.

"Where are you going?"

"To pack."

Alek bolted after her, stopping just inside the bedroom doorway. "And where, exactly, do you think you're going in your condition?"

"I don't know. I don't care." She pushed past him, lumbering over to the dresser, where she yanked open the top drawer, started hauling things out of it. "I just know I can't stay here.... What're you doing?" she said when he grabbed her clothes and shoved them back into the drawer.

"Preventing you from doing something stupid."

She glared at him, but her anger was pockmarked with pain. "It's too late for that." Once again she shoved him out of the way, tugged open the drawer.

"Luanne, you're not being reasonable—"

"My reasonable days are now officially over!" She slammed shut the drawer with enough force to knock over the small vase of dried flowers on its top. "All my life I have just about twisted myself up in knots trying to be logical and practical, and for what? And I did everything in my power to make that marriage work! I did!" She crumbled into helpless sobs. "I...did..."

Anger knifed through him: how could any man do this to a woman he purported to love? And why? With a groan, Alek gathered the sobbing woman to him, finding it ironic that after finally falling in love himself, fate would dump him in a situation where he didn't dare say the words.

Show her, his grandmother had said. *Show her you love her.* "This isn't your fault," he said fiercely into her hair. "You must believe that."

Shaking her head, Luanne pushed away, sinking onto the edge of the bed with her arms wrapped around her middle. "All those years," she whispered, staring blankly in front of her, "I never told a living soul what was in my heart. For Jeff's sake. For Chase's." She swiped at her cheek. "M-maybe even for mine. Maybe I couldn't love Jeff as much as he loved me, but I wouldn't've hurt him for the world...oh, *damn* it! If it hadn't've been for those photos, if he hadn't seen the resemblance between you and Chase, he would've never realized you were Chase's father—"

"Mama?"

Alek whipped around to find Chase standing just inside the room, Tomas right behind him. The boy's face contorted in confusion as his eyes darted from Alek to his mother and back to Alek before he spun around, shoving Tomas out of his way in his rush to escape.

"Chase!" Luanne cried, pushing herself up off the bed, her heel getting caught in the hem of her dress as she tried to round the footboard. "Chase, come back!"

Yelling to Tomas to go after the child, Alek grabbed for Luanne before she went down, catching her clumsily in his arms. She let out a sharp gasp of surprise, then gripped his arm as a warm torrent drenched the bottom of one of Alek's pants legs.

Two short hours after her world had once again been turned inside out, Luanne lay on her side, staring at the perfect little creature beside her who, such a short time before, had been squirming around inside her and probably wondering what on earth his mama was goin' on so about.

Forget even trying to get to the hospital. Just like with Chase, the minute her water broke, she'd gone from zero to sixty in about ten minutes. Dr. Palachek had gotten there just in time to say, "Anytime you want to start pushing is fine with me," and it seemed like no more that a couple minutes passed before the baby popped right out, squalling his little red-faced head off.

And looking so much like his daddy, it just about broke Luanne's heart.

She reached over to stroke a finger down a plump, soft cheek, blinking back tears. Wasn't fair, this moment of joy and wonder getting so balled up with all these troubles. Somewhere around here, she had another son who probably hated her, who she knew she should be talking to but couldn't, not with her barely dulled grief being ripped wide open all over again like this.

The baby trembled and stretched, his tiny mouth forming a perfect O when he yawned. "Why'd you do it, Jeff?" she whispered through a blur of tears. "Why'd you give up on the baby we'd tried so long to have?"

Her heart twisted inside her. What if she'd never be able to look at this child and not think about what his father had done?

Was she doomed to lug around yet another secret inside her for the rest of her life? When this child—this still-nameless little boy who'd grabbed her heart the instant Dr. Palachek had laid him on her chest—asked her what happened to his daddy, would she simply say he'd died in a car crash, implying it was an accident? Or would she someday find the courage to tell Jeff's son the truth—that his father had killed himself because, no matter how hard Luanne had tried, she hadn't been able to hide her love for her first child's father?

"…and you know me, Alek," Jeff had written in his letter. "I never could stand coming in second…."

And then Jeff had bequeathed Alek with the responsibility for his new child "…since I took care of yours all these years…"

She curled herself around both her new baby and the knot of guilt throbbing inside her, drawing the just-washed infant closer so she could watch all the funny little faces he made as he slept, so she could nuzzle the fine, red hair that lay like strands of silk over his gently pulsating soft spot, so she could give to him what she'd never been able to fully give to his father.

Tapping on her door frame made her look up. "Hey, there," Alek said softly. He'd changed into jeans and an oatmeal-colored sweater, she noticed. And didn't he look the picture of a man who'd just coached a woman through birth, with his hair all rumpled and the bottom half of his face all beard-hazed like that? "Am I allowed in now?"

The poor man had been banished while Anka and Elena set things to rights after the birth. But even in Luanne's addled state, she caught the double meaning behind Alek's question. And the answer was, how could she allow Alek Vlastos into her heart, her life, now? As impossible as things had been before, now they were five times worse. Anger and disappointment, both, prickled, surprising her.

"Of course you can come in," she said, her heart rate betraying her as he closed the space between them, the corners of his mouth tilting up as he looked down at the baby.

Then his gaze shifted to her. "How are you feeling?"

She didn't want to look at him, couldn't keep herself from doing just that, couldn't help the fresh bout of tears that threatened upon seeing all that goodness and worry and sense of responsibility in his eyes.

He'd never left her side, not for an instant, had never panicked even when it looked like he might have to deliver the baby himself. He'd been strong, he'd been *there,* he'd been everything she'd always known, deep down, he was. And when she saw him swallow back tears when the baby came, when he turned and gave her a wobbly smile that pretty much summed up all the emotions attending this birth, pain shot through her far worse than the cramps of afterbirth, that this moment had only come about because Alek was simply following Jeff's posthumous directive.

For the first time in her life, there was no answer, logical or otherwise. Wrong or right, her love for Alek had been a precious thing, even if it wasn't something she could exactly put on public display. Or so she'd thought. *Had* she given herself away every time she looked at Chase, as Jeff had told Alek in the letter? Had it really been that easy for Jeff to see inside her heart?

Had she really driven a man to take his own life...?

...and another one to take on an obligation he would never have done on his own?

"Where's Chase?" she asked, dodging both Alek's original question and the wayward path of her thoughts.

"With my grandmother. In the sitting room."

"He want to see me?"

Alek tenderly swept back a curl off her cheek. She might've screamed, if she'd had the strength. "You, yes. Me, probably never again." Then, "Will *you* ever forgive me?"

And she thought she'd been weary *before.* "Oh, Alek...please. Not now. Everything's just too scrambled up inside my head...."

He leaned over; she braced herself against the sensation of his lips brushing her temple, about how it felt so real when she knew it wasn't. Except he skimmed one finger over the baby's cheek with a tenderness she knew he couldn't possibly have faked, and she got confused all over again. "He's beautiful." And when he looked at her, tears hovered on his lower lashes. "I'll get Chase," he said as he straightened, then turned to leave.

"Alek?"

He turned back, brows raised.

"Dr. Palachek says if I feel up to it, I should be able to go home in about three weeks."

She saw a muscle in his jaw tighten, like he was fighting to keep from saying something he knew he shouldn't. "Whatever you wish."

Now why should she feel…deflated? After all, he was willing to let her go without giving her a hard time. Which was a good thing, right?

Shaking her head, as if that might settle down her thoughts, Luanne pulled herself upright against a mound of pillows, taking the baby in her arms just as she saw Chase set foot inside her room. "Hey, sugar…come on over here and see your new baby brother."

His hands shoved in his pockets, a crease wedged between his brows, he hesitated, then cautiously made his way over to the bed.

He wouldn't look at her.

Luanne swallowed past the lump in her throat and shifted the baby so Chase could get a better look. "What d'you think?"

The child swiped a hand under his nose, shrugged. "He's okay, I guess."

"You wanna hold him?"

He shook his head, still not looking at her, although she noticed his gaze was riveted to the baby.

"Honey? I know you're real ticked off with me right now, but try not to take it out on your brother."

"I'm not mad at…what's his name, anyways?"

"I haven't decided yet. Maybe you can help me pick out something—"

"Why didn't you tell me? About Alek?"

Just then Luanne noticed Alek standing at the door, ready to run interference, she imagined, should that prove necessary. For a moment she resented his intrusion, until it dawned on her that this was every bit as much Alek's concern as it was hers and Chase's. "Because we couldn't figure out how—"

"I don't mean now. I mean a long time ago."

"When you were little, you mean?"

He nodded.

She looked away. "Because I didn't want to hurt your fa— to hurt Jeff."

"Except he figured it out, didn't he? That's what y'all were fightin' about that day, wasn't it?"

"We weren't fight—"

"I *heard* you!" Tears streamed down his cheeks now. Luanne saw Alek make his way over to the bed. "When I came home from school, I heard you and Daddy in the kitchen, only Daddy was yellin' an' I knew it must be bad because I never heard him yell at you before!"

"Chase," Alek said gently, laying a hand on the child's shoulder, "this isn't—"

Chase shrugged off Alek's hand, stumbling in an effort to get away. "Get away from me!"

"Alek, no, it's all right—"

"No," said another voice as Dr. Palachek briskly entered the room. "It is definitely *not* all right, Luanne. You need more stress right now like you need an enema. Alek, please take Chase into the other room."

"You can't make me!"

"Then I will take your mama and your new brother away to the hospital for a few days where maybe she can get some peace and quiet."

Chase shot Luanne a horrified look, but she was suddenly too blamed wiped out to even care. She reached for his hand, thinking about how fragile it felt, that he was still just a little boy and not prepared to deal with any of this. Which, considering how ill equipped *she* felt to deal with any of this, made her ache for him all the more. "Baby, I know this is a mess, and I promise it'll get all sorted out, somehow, but I just can't fix it right now. I'm sorry."

Betrayal shot from his eyes before he took off.

Alek caught up to Chase and grabbed him by the arm, which was not unlike trying to wrestle a pissed-off octopus. A pissed-off octopus wearing cowboy boots. "Cut it out, Chase," he said, dodging the flailing feet for the second time since they'd met. "Come on. You and I are going to talk."

"I don't wanna—"

"I'm well aware of that. Tough." Keeping his grip just tight enough to prevent the child's wriggling free, Alek steered him toward the stairs. "Your mother's just had a baby and she's exhausted and just as upset as you are, so, like it or not, I'm your only option."

The kid came to a dead halt, nearly putting Alek's shoulder out of joint.

Frowning, Alek turned, met the frightened gaze.

"Mama's gonna be all right, isn't she?"

Empathy careened through him. "Of course she is," he said gently. "The doctor said it was one of the easiest births she'd ever seen. That doesn't mean your mother's ready to deal with any more stress right now." He tugged on Chase's arm again. "So let's go."

"Where?"

"Outside. Where no one can hear us. Where you can call me a million names if you like and no one can hear you. Or stop you."

That bought a few seconds of silence, during which Alek prayed mightily to know what the hell to say to this kid who had every right to both his anger and confusion. The man he thought of as his father was dead; and now his mother was out of his reach, as well, leaving him with some man he still didn't know. In the kid's shoes, he'd be ready to spit nails.

A minute later they were out on the terrace where they'd had lunch that first day. The night had begun to cool off, finally, though not enough to raise goose bumps. Alek crossed to the balustrade, hoisting himself up onto it.

"Okay," he said, brushing grit off his hands. "Do your worst."

That got a skeptical look. "I can really say anything I want?"

"Anything at all."

Naturally, the kid went completely silent, shoving his hands into his pockets and glaring off into space.

"All right," Alek said. "I'll go first." He angled his head at his son. "You're mad as hell, aren't you?"

The kid looked around, then slumped into a wrought-iron chair, his long, slender fingers curled around the ends of the arms. After several more seconds, he nodded.

"And that scares you."

Wide eyes greeted that. "I'm not—"

"Yes, you are."

Two or three beats passed. Then: "Why'd y'all lie to me?"

Alek squinted into the darkness, then back at the frail-looking form sprawled in the chair. "We...opted not to tell you everything until we felt you'd be more prepared to deal with it. Until we'd worked out a few things."

Accusation slashed the space between them. "You're *still* not telling me everything, are you?"

The rough stone bit into Alek's palms. "What do you mean?"

"Why was Mama crying earlier? Before the baby came?"

His heart tripped. Oh, God—how much did he dare tell him, even now? Especially without Luanne's consent, or even her knowledge? Alek wanted to protect the child just as much as he was sure his mother would. Just as he'd wanted to protect Luanne. Except, that had certainly backfired, hadn't it? Now he had no idea if he could ever regain her trust, a thought which made him sick to his stomach. But if he pulled his punches now, would he jeopardize Chase's trust in him?

Or would telling the truth be even worse?

Alek looked over at the boy, noticed he was sitting stock-still. His attention was riveted to Alek, his expression—or what Alek could see of it, at least—now more one of apprehension than animosity. He willed his heart to quit knocking quite so painfully against his ribs, then said, as evenly as he could, "How strong are you, Chase? Inside, I mean?"

Even in the dim light, he saw the child's face go pale. "Why?"

"Because I've got something to tell you, something about Jeff. About…his death—"

"No!" The boy bolted from the chair, his fists raised as he lunged toward Alek. "It was an accident! It was! He wouldn't've left Mama an' me, an' you can't make me believe he did!"

Alek's blood went to ice as he neatly captured the pummeling wrists, then clasped the sobbing child to his chest, so Chase wouldn't send both of them over the balustrade. "Dear God," he whispered into his son's hair. "You *knew?*"

One small, potent fist rammed into Alek's upper arm, then grabbed his sweater, hanging on for dear life. "It ain't true! It ain't true…."

Alek squeezed shut his eyes against the stab of déjà vu, remembering all too clearly how he'd railed at his grandmother when she'd told him about his parents, screaming his denial, that she must have heard wrong, that there had been a mistake….

"I'm so sorry, Chase," came out in a tortured, ragged whisper. "But it is."

His son yanked out of his embrace, taking a wild swing, which made contact, not with Alek, but with a clay flowerpot of hardy geraniums sitting a few feet away. Alek grabbed for the pot, which teetered for a second before falling over the side to crash spectacularly on the flagstone landing below. Chase's hands flew to his ears to muffle the sound of the crash, his body heaving with sobs.

For a full minute, maybe longer, the distraught child stomped in large circles around the table and chairs, swearing and sobbing and occasionally kicking out at whatever was handy. And it nearly killed Alek to simply stand there, watching, but the next move was Chase's. Which they both knew. Questions and explanations could wait.

Finally the boy's crying jag ceased just long enough for him to spew out, "I *hate* him!" He looked at Alek, his body still jerking spasmodically even as it bristled with rage, his hands fisted at his sides. Still, truth had won out, leaving the child's earlier denial little more than a limp, lifeless thing at his feet.

Whether Chase would ever be able to forgive Jeff for what he'd done, Alek had no idea, but Alek had no doubt whatsoever what he'd do to Jeff Henderson if he ever met up with him again in another life. Alek took a single step closer, managing not to react when the boy clumsily backed away.

"Chase, listen to me. I know you don't know me very well, so you really have no reason to believe me or trust me. And I understand that. But one thing you don't know about me is that while I don't make a lot of promises, the ones I do make, I keep. Without fail." He took another step, breathing an inward sigh of relief when the child stayed put. "So I'm making a promise to you, right now, that I want you to tuck away in your heart until such time as you feel like taking it out and examining it more closely."

Now near enough to touch his son, Alek did just that, laying a hand on his shoulder. "I'll admit, I'm rather at a loss when it comes to being a parent. And I think it's a fairly safe assumption that I'm going to screw up from time to time. In fact, count on it," he added with a rueful grin, which actually got the merest twitch of a smile in response. Encouraged, Alek leaned over to capture his son's watery, wary gaze in his. "But from the moment I found out about you, I knew two things— that I wanted nothing more than to see you happy, and that I would never abandon you." He gently shook Chase's shoulder. "*Never.*"

I will not do what Jeff did to you....

The unspoken declaration shimmered between them for what seemed like an eternity. Then Chase slipped from Alek's grasp and walked away. But just a few feet. And his fists were no longer clenched.

"Mama just found out tonight, didn't she? That Daddy...?"

Alek's breath left his lungs in a rush. "Yes."

Chase turned, an old, painfully gained wisdom settled in his child's eyes. "I didn't want her to find out."

"Neither did I." At the boy's frown, Alek added, "Jeff had sent me a letter, which I got shortly after the crash, in which he not only told me about you, but about...his intentions. I hadn't planned on telling your mother about it. Which, in hindsight, probably wasn't the best decision I could have made, but we don't want to hurt the people we love, do we?" Chase stared at him, hard, then slowly shook his head. "But what I hadn't counted on was her getting a copy of the letter."

Chase swore. Under the circumstances Alek let it go, instead suggesting that Chase tell Luanne he already knew.

"No way."

"I'm not giving you an option. You need to tell her. Tonight. Or she's just going to worry herself to distraction about how to break it to you."

The child looked as though he might be ill. Then, tears shining in his eyes, he nodded.

"Madam! You should not be up so soon after having baby!"

Luanne glanced up at Elena, standing just inside the bedroom, breakfast tray in tow. Dr. Palachek had suggested a live-in nurse for at least the first few days, but Elena had just about had a hissy-fit, declaring that, after six children, she was more than capable of taking care of both mother and baby, thank you, and there would be no more discussion on the subject. She had therefore donned a flannel tent and stayed the night on the sofa bed in the sitting room, fully prepared for whatever came her way. The baby had slept straight through his first night, and Luanne—who hadn't slept much at all after hearing Chase's "confession"—had still felt up to at least getting dressed and running a brush through her sorry-looking hair.

"I'm fine, Elena, really."

But the maid was clearly having none of it. Now in her uniform, she swept across the room, plunked a breakfast tray on the bed, then practically snatched the whimpering baby from Luanne's hands to change him.

"I know how to change a diaper, Elena!"

"Is not matter of knowing how to change diaper. Is matter of Mama must feed herself before she feeds baby. So. I change diaper. You eat."

With a resigned sigh, Luanne picked up the plate of eggs and sausage from the tray, settling into an armchair where she could watch the maid deftly change her new son's diaper, chattering to him in some guttural language Luanne didn't understand at all. "Is Chase awake yet?"

Elena, who, as far as Luanne knew, was still ignorant of the previous night's revelations, shook her head. "And I do not think he will be for some time, not with so much excitement from last night. Oh…" She picked up the baby, splaying the tiny infant across the top of one stupendous bosom. "What a fine boy you are. But so tiny!" The maid turned to Luanne, eyeing her speculatively. "You not have stitches?"

Luanne swallowed a bite of the eggs which seemed to be rapidly disappearing. "No. In fact, I barely feel like I gave birth at all. This one was much smaller than Chase."

"This one? He not yet have name?"

"I keep tryin' out different ones, but none of them seem to fit."

Elena chuckled. "By sixth daughter, it took husband and me whole week to come up with name. The right one will come, you will see."

The baby's whimpering began to gain some momentum. Luanne wiped her mouth and hands on a napkin, set the empty plate on the table next to her, then reached out. "My turn."

With obvious reluctance, Elena gave up her new little charge, who latched on to Luanne's nipple as if he hadn't eaten in a week. She winced, then sighed right along with Elena who said, "The staff, they cannot wait to see him."

Luanne smiled up at her. "Tell them I'll take him on a little tour, maybe later this afternoon."

"Very good. Madam is finished with breakfast?"

Luanne allowed as how she was, so Elena took the tray and left her alone. With a huge sigh of relief, Luanne leaned her head on the back of the chair and let her eyes drift closed, aware of nothing except the baby's tugging at her breast. The shock had worn off some, leaving a heaviness in its place that she figured was going to be part of her for some time to come.

Her own reaction to finding out about Jeff's suicide had paled in comparison to Chase's confession last night, although it had taken her a good few minutes after the initial blow to figure out that Chase hadn't actually *known* that Jeff had taken his life as much as he'd surmised that's what'd happened. Which was partly why he hadn't said anything to her, she'd realized through the haze of disbelief, the other part being he hadn't wanted to cause her any distress. Of course, then there was the little matter of Chase's not wanting to believe it himself, even though, deep down, he couldn't deny it. Not when Jeff had hundreds and hundreds of races under his belt, and had always, always been a fanatic about safety, his refusal to use the HANS device aside. So how much sense, Chase had pointed out, did it make that he'd lose control of his car on a dry track in perfect weather, and it just being him and one other driver besides?

That alone should have alerted her that something was off, she now realized. But she supposed a person tends to see only what they want to.

Or more to the point, deny what they don't.

But there had been more. Before he'd left that last time, Jeff had apparently given Chase a "now, if anything happens to me" speech, which he'd never done before.

And the child had never said one word.

Her heart still bled for what it must've been like for a ten-year-old to shoulder that kind of burden alone for all these months. In some ways she wanted to swat him one for keeping

something like that to himself, for not thinking he could come
to her—

Which made him just like his daddy, didn't it? No, not the
one who had said he would do anything for her, only to get
that concept so fouled up he couldn't figure out there were less
drastic ways to end a marriage that maybe wasn't working out;
but the one who'd stood behind Chase last night with his hands
on his shoulders, giving silent encouragement while his son
came clean.

Except she realized she wanted to swat Alek, too. Chase's
keeping his secret was one thing. After all, he was just a kid.
And besides, he didn't really have any concrete evidence to
back up his suspicions. But Alek had *known*. Irrefutably. Did
he consider her too weak, too emotionally unstable, to just
come right out and tell her the truth? Well, she wasn't sure
when, or if, she'd be able to forgive that. Let alone ever trust
him.

Heck. Right now, she wasn't sure she'd ever be able to trust
any man, ever again. In fact, if somebody came up with a plan
to ship all males over the age of eighteen to Mars? She'd be
first in line to pack a picnic lunch for the trip.

"Hey, Mama."

Chase stood not three feet in front of her, looking like…well,
like he'd just crawled out of bed. When it got cold, he wore
sweats to sleep in, but he must've outgrown the ones he had
on now sometime during the night.

"Hey, baby," she said softly, shifting her new son to her
other breast.

After a yawn or two, Chase planted himself on the edge of
her unmade bed, his toes curled on the bedrail, blinking owl-
ishly at the baby attached to her breast. Not that he could see
much, the way her blouse was, but she didn't figure there was
any point in making a big deal out of something completely
natural.

"You get any sleep?"

He hunched his shoulders, then frowned.

"Mama?"

"Yeah?"

"If Alek's my real daddy…does that make me a prince, too?"

And her heart jolted against her ribs. "Yeah, baby. It sure does."

Chase seemed to think on that for a while. "That mean I have to live here from now on?"

Luanne pretended utter fascination with the baby's little ear. "No, it doesn't. I mean—" After a moment she got up enough gumption to look her son in the eye. "Alek and I haven't had a chance to work any of that out. You'll need to be here some, but what we were thinking was holidays and vacations for now. That you'd still live with me during the school year. Then, when you're older…" The sentence drifted off. "Well, actually, we hadn't gotten that far yet. And that's a long way off, in any case."

At that Chase got up, only to fold himself up at her feet so he could touch the baby's hand. His mouth stretched into a timorous grin when the tiny fingers clamped onto one of his.

"He's so *little*."

"So were you," Luanne said, then tried to smile. "Then you had to go get all these long arms and legs and things and ruin the effect."

Chase kind of giggled, which relieved her some, except she noticed the frown was still in place. Where it would remain for some time, she imagined. Then he ambushed her with, "Do you love Alek? I mean, more than you did Da—than you did Jeff?"

That he'd immediately stripped Jeff of his paternal title was not lost on her. Even as she waited out the twinge of regret, however, she noticed she was not inclined to correct him.

"People love people in different ways," she began, but her far-too-bright child shot her a look that just slashed her attempt at prevarication to shreds. "Oh, Chase—I don't rightly know how to explain any of this to myself, let alone to you or anybody else. Yes, I have feelings for Alek. Strong ones. But just because a person has feelings for someone, or is attracted to them, doesn't necessarily mean those feelings are right. I mean, Alek and I...well, we don't exactly have a lot in common, sugar.''

Chase shifted. "Neither did you and...Jeff. I mean, you liked to read and listen to the classical station on the radio and stuff, and he always gave you grief about it."

She reached out, skimmed his tattered hair off his forehead. "You just made my point."

At that, Chase skootched around, his back against her knees with his own pulled up to his chin like he used to when he was little. "Alek said, now that he knows about me, he'll always be there for me. That he'd *never* leave me."

She caught the implication. "No, honey. I'm sure he wouldn't."

Her oldest looked up at her, backward, his gaze steady and far too mature for someone who'd just turned ten not four months ago. "I think he meant you, too, Mama."

She frowned. "And that doesn't bother you?"

He idly scratched his arm, then shrugged. "A little, maybe. But..." He shrugged again.

Luanne stifled a sigh. "Honey, don't go gettin' *responsibility* confused with *love,* okay? Your daddy—and by that, I mean Alek—takes his responsibilities very seriously." *Or at least he does now,* she silently amended. "He's supposed to take care of you, sugar. You're his son. And in your case he loves you, too. I'm as sure of that as I've ever been about anything in my life. And I guess he feels a sense of responsibility toward me, being as I'm your mother and all. But even if I was ready to go gettin' involved with another man—and with everything that's happened this last little while, believe me, I'm not—I'm not the least bit interested in becomin' another man's responsibility. Even if that man is your birth father. Even if I do have feelings for him. It just wouldn't be fair to any of us."

Chase's brow crumpled again before he twisted away. Luanne lifted a hand to smooth the dozen cowlicks sprouted all over his head. "I'm sorry, baby. I guess it seems like grownups make things awfully complicated sometimes, doesn't it?''

No answer.

Luanne shifted the baby up to her shoulder to work out a burp, then said, ''The doctor says I can probably make the trip back home in three weeks or so. Maybe things'll settle down some once we get back to Texas—''

''I don't want to go.''

Her hand stilled on the baby's back. ''What did you say?''

''I don't want to go back to Texas. I like it here. And I want to stay.''

Luanne took a minute to get her heart beating again, then said quietly, ''You remember when you went to overnight camp the first time when you were seven? And how much you hated it the first couple of weeks? So we said we'd come up and take you home, only by the time we got there a week later, you'd made friends and everything, and then you didn't want to come home? You remember that?''

''This ain't—*isn't* the same thing, Mama.'' He shook his head. ''I can't explain it. It's just this…feelin' inside me. It's like…I've come home or somethin'.''

''Chase, honey, I know you think you mean that, but what with everything that's happened—''

''No. I felt this way before…before last night.''

The baby had fallen asleep. Awkwardly Luanne pushed herself up from the chair to lay the infant back in the bassinet, wondering what on earth she was supposed to say, to *do,* now.

''I can't stay here, Chase,'' she said at last, afraid to look at him. ''I don't belong.'' Now she turned, only to find herself facing her oldest son's profile. ''And if you're thinking something's gonna happen between me and Alek…I'm sorry, but don't even bother goin' down that path. As much as I love you, as much as I'd do almost anything in my power to make you happy, I can't make a life with somebody who doesn't really love me. Now, I've said you can come back, maybe over Christmas, if you want. And for the summer, too. And Alek can come see you anytime he wants to. But we're leavin' in three weeks, Chase. And that's that.'' She rubbed the baby's back for a moment, waiting for the explosion. When it didn't come, she wasn't sure whether to be relieved or not. "Why don't you go get dressed, honey, go on down and get some breakfast?"

After a moment Chase got up, quietly made his way to the door. And she thought, well, maybe he was coming to terms with the fact that sometimes, things just are what they are, and there's no sense getting yourself in a tizzy over what can't be changed. Except then he turned around and said, "You know what Alek told me?"

Luanne shook her head.

"He said he didn't tell you about the letter—the one from Jeff that he got?" She nodded. "He said he didn't tell you about it because he couldn't stand the thought of hurting someone he loved."

It was a good five minutes before Luanne could breathe properly.

Chapter 13

"Will there be anything else, sir?"

"No, I don't think so, Tomas," Alek said as he strode out of his dressing room, yanking a sweater over his head. "No, wait—" He tugged the sweater the rest of the way down his torso. "Do you know what time the florist opens?"

The young man gave what could only be called an indulgent smile. "In your case, sir, I think it's safe to say it's open anytime you call."

Alek skimmed a broad brush over his wayward hair. "True. But you know I don't like to impose like that."

"I doubt the Lattiaks would consider it an imposition, Your Highness."

Probably not, Alek mused as he slipped on his watch, frowning at his reflection in the mirror over his bureau. "I don't suppose you have their—"

"The number's already on your desk, sir."

Alek grinned. "Good man."

"Thank you, sir," Tomas said, then softly cleared his throat.

"Is there a problem, Tomas?"

"I might ask the same of you, sir. Since things seemed to be…if you don't mind my saying so…a bit chaotic last night?"

"Chaotic, hell. Try *crazy*."

"If you say so, sir."

After a moment Alek said, "Chase is my son, Tomas."

A slight smile flirted with the aide's mouth. "Yes, sir. I was there when—"

"Oh, right. Yes, yes, of course you were."

"But—" The young man glanced down, tugging at the hem of his cardigan.

"But…?"

"It's just…well…" Tomas looked up, his bow tie bobbing. "It was not exactly a surprise, Your Highness." Color flooded his pale face. "Since, um, the resemblance could not be easily dismissed." He cleared his throat. "Sir."

Alek sighed, then walked away a few feet, rubbing his jaw. "In other words, the palace halls have been rife with speculation?"

"Well, it's just that…um, yes, there has been a great deal of talk. And…and while I would not presume to advise Your Highness on…on anything, especially a matter of such a delicate and personal nature…" His hand lifted to adjust his glasses. "I…I would like to point out that…I think…everyone would appreciate your being forthcoming about Chase's…true parentage."

"I see." Alek crossed his arms, then asked, "And…what does *everyone* think about Chase's mother?"

Tomas actually sucked in a little breath. "You have no idea, do you?" Alek shook his head, not sure whether to feel amusement or apprehension when his aide took a step closer, as if what he had to say required the utmost discretion. "Well, Your Highness, many people are saying how much Mrs. Henderson reminds them of your mother. Well, those that remember her."

"My mother?"

"Oh, yes, sir. No, not in the way she talks or dresses, but in her ability to look a person right in the eye when she speaks with them, as if she truly cares about what they have to say. The way she has a smile or kind word for everyone, even when she is troubled herself. She is a very good woman. Just like your mother was. And—''

''And…what, Tomas?'' Alek said, his brows rising at the blush once again stealing across the young man's prominent cheekbones.

''And some say you would be a fool to let her get away. Sir.''

''Oh. Well, in that case, I suppose I'll take your…observations under advisement, shall I?''

The young man nodded. ''Very good, sir.'' He turned to leave, only to pivot back. ''I'm sorry—I forgot to ask if you could do without me this morning for an hour or so?''

''I suppose I'd manage. But why?''

''I met up with Elena in the kitchen earlier, and she mentioned that Mrs. Henderson needs some supplies—for the baby and such—from a few of the shops in the village. But Elena cannot get away, so she asked if I might be able to run the errands.''

''No, Tomas,'' Alek said slowly, grabbing his leather jacket from where he'd tossed it over a chair some days before. ''I'll go. And I'll make a swing by the florist's while I'm there.''

''Oh! Yes…that would be—'' the young man rummaged, almost frantically, first in one baggy pants pocket, then the other ''—an excellent idea. Here's what she needs,'' he said, proffering a neatly scripted list to Alek and hastening from the room before Alek could—he glanced at the list and felt a blush steal across *his* cheeks—realize he'd been suckered.

The village was just beginning to stir by the time Alek parked the Jag alongside the narrow sidewalk fronting the chemist's. Edgy, early-autumn sunlight winked from between the tiny shops, few of them more than two stories tall, clotted together in the center of town. A few shops down, the greengrocer, his breath clouding his face, had begun to put out some of his hardier offerings, while next door the bookseller and his wife argued amiably about where to best place a bin of secondhand books. The scent of strong, freshly brewed coffee and

just-baked bread filtered across the street from the baker's, min-
gling with the aroma of sausage from a nearby café.

And something like…excitement trickled through Alek's
chest as he pushed open the heavy wooden door to the chemist's, setting off an old-fashioned bell overhead. Alek doubted
the shop had changed much since before the war, although Otto
and Gerta Duprok had taken over for Otto's parents—as Otto's
father had for his and on back through God knew how many
generations—sometime in the early seventies. Nor had many
of the products, Alek surmised as, list in hand, he began a
systematic sweep of the cramped aisles, his loafers scraping the
discolored, uneven planks of the wooden floor. Within five
minutes, he had found the Pampers, baby powder and some
ointment called Desitin, but some of the other items were proving more elusive. Then he heard a mouselike scuffling, and a
round, cheerful face popped into view. "Is there anything I can
help you with—oh! Your Highness!"

Alek grinned down into Gerta Duprok's slightly startled blue
eyes. The poor woman seemed undecided whether to curtsy or
faint. "Yes, actually you can. Mrs. Henderson had her baby
last night," he said, which got a delighted "Oooh!" and many
congratulations which might well have spawned any number
of questions had Alek not gently redirected the effusive
woman's attention to the list. "I seem to be having trouble
finding…these."

Gerta grabbed for her glasses, dangling from a chain round
her neck, becoming even more flustered when she read the item
in question.

"Oh! Well, they're right around here…" She bustled around
to the next aisle. Alek followed. "We have two brands, actually." A chubby finger pointed first to one box. "These are
more absorbent—" then another "—but these, um, conform
better to her, uh…" Gerta gestured vaguely in the area of her
rather generous chest.

A quandary indeed. "Hmm," Alek said, doing his level best
to retain his dignity. "Best give me two of each." There was
a pause. "Is there a problem?"

"Well, no, Your Highness. I mean, it's just…" The woman

went beet red, then peered around the aisle, as if to make sure they wouldn't be overhead, only to state in a stage whisper, "If a woman, ah, leaks, two boxes won't last a week."

"I see," Alek said, feeling a trifle on the warm side himself. "Then I suppose…a half dozen boxes? To start?"

"Very good. I have plenty in the back. But…might I recommend…?"

She picked up a box of some other ointment, dropped it into his basket as if it were hot.

Alek picked it up, peered at it. "What's this for?"

"To prevent cracked nipples, Your Highness," the poor woman choked out, then skittered to the back to get the rest of his order.

Having survived that—and the debacle in the women's clothing shop that followed: well, of *course* Luanne only knew her American bra size, for the love of God, which unfortunately made picking out the right nursing bras a mite tricky—Alek felt positively…buoyant. And as giddy as Scrooge on Christmas morning. Within an hour he'd paid visits to the bookshop, the toy store, the clothing shop—again—and at last, the florist, where he eschewed white roses for a mixed bouquet of flowers that reminded him of those he'd seen growing wild along the Texas highways when he'd been there. And along the way, he'd caught up on news of weddings and gall bladder operations and job promotions and a hundred other details that made up the lives of the people he would one day rule.

Not to mention a multitude of congratulations on the birth of the baby, just as if he'd been the father. Of course, by the time he loaded up the Jag with all the bags and boxes, he pretty much felt that way himself.

He felt as though a storm, long dreaded and much feared, had passed. Granted, there was a lot of debris to clear away, still, but the worst was over.

He had three weeks, he realized on the short drive back up the hill to the palace, three weeks in which to convince Luanne that they could build a life together, for their son's sake as well as their own. However, if at the end of those three weeks,

Luanne still wished to leave, Alek would do nothing to stop her. He would not trap her the way she'd been trapped before. But damned if he wasn't going to do everything in his power to show this woman how much he wanted—needed—her courage and generosity in his life. Forever.

The challenge exhilarated him even as it frightened the very life out of him. He knew how much it hurt to lose someone you loved, how much risk was involved. And the timing was still awkward, to say the least. But as his grandmother said, if he wanted Luanne, he'd have to fight for her.

And that's exactly what he intended to do.

"Wait—there's more!"

The snoozing baby snuggled to her chest, Luanne could only stand there, flummoxed, as Alek carted in bag after bag of heaven-knew-what, dumping them in an ever-growing pile in the center of her sitting room. She exchanged a puzzled glance with Elena, who only shrugged as she arranged the flowers in a crystal vase on the end table next to the love seat, her own expression as baffled as Luanne's. And about a hundred times more amused.

Damage control is what this was, she thought as she watched Alek's to-ing and fro-ing. Only she snatched that thought as it scampered past and examined it a bit more thoroughly, her breath catching in her throat. When had she become so cynical? She'd always taken human goodness at face value. Now, suddenly, she saw ulterior motives lurking in every act of kindness.

She did not think this signified an improvement to her character.

Chase was just about beside himself with excitement, however, nearly as wound up as the gift bearer himself. Who, when he'd at last finished hauling in the goodies, stood in the center of the room, hands on hips, the biggest dang grin she'd ever seen spread across his face. And those silver eyes of his glittered with all sorts of things that just made her heart do this big old flip-flop inside her chest, even though the rest of her knew better.

Weak-kneed, Luanne sank onto the love seat, clinging to the

baby like he was her last link to reason. Was it just her, or was all this festivity just a little...weird after the events of last night?

"Mama?" Her gaze sort of drifted to her son, who was wearing a pretty big grin himself. And she realized, as painful as the double whammy had been for him, the half-truths festering just below the surface had been far worse. "C'n I open some of them?"

"Wait—" Alek lunged toward the pile, picking through the bags until he retrieved a few which he then handed to Elena. "These should, um, probably go straight to Luanne's room."

Elena glanced inside, gave a startled laugh. "Yes, Your Highness, I think you are right," she said, then hustled them way.

"Okay, kiddo," Alek said. "Go for it."

It wasn't like the gifts were extravagant or anything. A chemistry set, a pair of inexpensive binoculars and a boxed set of classic science-fiction books for Chase; for Luanne, the flowers—which had just about brought tears to her eyes—a few paperback novels and a couple of very practical tops she could wear for nursing; and for little what's-his-name, an adorable sweater and leggings set, complete with a bunny-ear hat that just about cracked her up, a few stuffed animals, a squishy toy Alek said the toy shop owner had told him was very popular, and a set of tiny booties with clowns on the toes that would rattle whenever the baby kicked, which Alek insisted on putting on him immediately.

Kneeling on the carpet at her knees, Alek frowned. "He isn't kicking."

Luanne had to laugh, even though her heart was twisted near to inside out. "He's asleep, doofus. Trust me—he'll get to kicking soon enough." Only then she realized that she—and the baby—wouldn't be around when that happened, most likely. And that made her a lot sadder than she would have thought even ten minutes ago. So she directed her gaze to Chase, who had ripped open the chemistry set and was carefully inspecting every single bottle and vial and gizmo in it.

"Thank you," she said softly, then got up the nerve to look

into those sweet, silver eyes. "I know I told you not to spoil him—"

Alek briefly squeezed one of her knees. "If anything, I was spoiling myself. I haven't had that much fun since…well, I can't remember when. I could get used to this, *mila.*"

So could Luanne, which was a definite problem. She glanced again at Chase, who was sitting with his chin resting on his knee, frowning in concentration as he devoured the instruction booklet splayed on the carpet in front of him. "He needed the diversion. And since I'm a little preoccupied right now…."

Alek levered himself onto the love seat beside her, where he unabashedly looped one arm around her shoulders and gently drew her against him. Resting his cheek on the top of her head, he reached out to play with the baby's hand. Through the open door to her bedroom, Luanne heard Elena singing as she went about doing whatever it was she did.

"The worst is over, *mila,*" Alek whispered. "*Over,* do you hear me?" he added with a brief squeeze, and she thought, *Not hardly.* "Now we begin to repair the damage."

She shut her eyes against the stab of pain his reiteration of her earlier thought provoked. Some damage, she realized, is irreparable. And no amount of gifts or promises or gentle touches was going to change that. Still, it felt good, snuggled up against him like this, watching him play with her baby. Safe. Sweet. Almost like…magic.

"So…have you thought of a name yet?" he asked.

Grateful for the change of subject, she shook her head. "Afraid not."

"Hmm. I'd suggest one of the Vlastos family names, but they're truly horrible. I mean, there's Heinrick and Dieter and Imrick, to name a few. Or then, on my father's side, we have Lloyd, about a dozen Johns and, for reasons no one has yet to fathom, an Alphonse."

"Alphonse?"

"Mmm. Some distant cousin from my father's mother's side of the family. He ended up being a cleric in some small, bleak town in Northern England where it rains something like three hundred days out of the year. I saw a picture of him once, when I went to visit my father's parents one summer.'' He shuddered, which made her smile.

His hand was idly stroking her upper arm, she noticed. Chase and Elena were both pretending not to notice, she noticed. And his touch was stirring things that by rights should not be stirring at all this soon after giving birth.

This was a dream. A very nice dream, to be sure, but a dream all the same. And even a fool knew you woke up from dreams, sooner or later.

She shifted out of the loose embrace, citing the need to get her shower while the baby was still asleep. Only, she hadn't counted on Alek's sending Elena and Chase off to get lunch, after which the maid was to take the rest of the afternoon off, he said. He then stood and calmly extricated the infant from Luanne's arms, settling him into his own with a sweet possessiveness that was doing nothing to ease the tension threatening to strangle her.

''Go,'' he said to Luanne, actually shooing her away with one hand, the other clamped protectively against the baby's back. ''And don't hurry. We'll be fine.'' He craned his neck to peer down into the baby's face, chuckling at his scrunched-up little face. ''Won't we, Mr. Baby Man?''

But either perverseness or survival instinct, she couldn't quite tell, rooted her to the spot. ''Alek?''

He looked up, and oh, dear Lord above, there was something so…potent and arousing about the sight of those strong, gentle hands nestling her tiny son against that solid chest. Her mouth went so dry she had to swallow three times before she could speak.

''I appreciate everything you're doing, I really do. And part of me wishes…'' She stopped, waited for the knot in her chest to move over enough for her to get out what she had to say. ''Part of me wishes things were different. But as nice as they are, a few gifts aren't going to change…anything. Or make me change my mind about leavin'. I don't belong here, Alek—''

''Luanne, give it a rest.''

She blinked. ''Excuse me?''

He let out a mighty sigh, then quelled her with a look that

was equal parts desperation and exasperation. "Damn it, I know it's too soon and you're bound to think I haven't a grain of sense in my head...oh, for the love of God, woman—haven't you figured it out yet? I'm head over heels in love with you."

She went rigid with shock.

Alek watched as Luanne simply stood there, mouth open, gawking at him as if he'd just shown her his Martian driver's license. Which meant, if his hunch was correct, this was the first time in history anyone had succeeded in rendering Luanne Evans Henderson speechless. Since, however, she also looked absolutely terrified—or appalled, he wasn't sure which—Alek took little pleasure in the accomplishment.

Bracing the baby securely against his chest with one hand, he lifted the other to cradle her jaw, his thumb wiping away the tear that had tracked down her cheek. Her eyes were wide—with apprehension? distrust?—kindling reciprocal spasms of terror in his gut. That he might fail in this, the first and only thing he'd ever truly given a damn about...

"Oh, Luanne...am I ever going to be able to get through that lovely, thick skull of yours that I'm not trying to manipulate you, or buy Chase's affection? All right—perhaps I got a bit carried away with the gifts, but I only did it because that's what people in love do, damn it. And because you deserve a little break from the hell you've been through this past little while. It gives me pleasure to make you happy. If you'll let me," he said, touching his forehead to hers, swallowing hard when he realized she was trembling like a cold, wet kitten. "I swear by all the saints that I love you—"

"Alek—no." She lifted her head. Tears welled up in her eyes, even as she covered his hand with her own. "I can't...it's not right—"

He shushed her, slipping his fingers to the back of her neck and tucking her head underneath his chin. "You can resist all you like, *mila*. You can run back to Texas the instant Dr. Palachek gives you clearance to go. But nothing can alter what I feel for you, or the fact that you and Chase and this child are part of this family now. Part of *me*. I will never, ever abandon you again.''

She stilled in his embrace for several seconds, saying nothing until she finally pulled away, citing the need to go take that shower. And deep inside him, in the old void that was now filled with a love so strong it hurt, alarms went off. On the surface her silence might seem a blessed relief after weeks of protestations, but Alek was not so much of a fool as to think it signified acquiescence.

And what it did signify scared the very devil out of him.

Three weeks later, Luanne had done little to assuage his fears. Nor did it help that Luanne's doctor didn't seem inclined to take his concerns seriously.

''Well, yes...'' Anka set her coffee cup down with a soft clink, her brows pulled together. ''I suppose she did seem a bit more subdued that usual, but—''

''Subdued?'' Alek pushed his plate away, then leaned back in his chair in the sun-washed breakfast room, his own forehead so knotted he was giving himself a headache. ''I haven't heard her laugh, not once, since the baby's birth.''

Anka smiled. ''She's simply exhausted, Alek. Nursing mothers often are, you know. Especially with colicky babies—''

''And what can we do about that, by the way? Surely it's not normal for a baby to cry for hours at a time, is it?''

The doctor gave what sounded suspiciously like an indulgent laugh. ''Spoken like a man who's not been around many babies. Unfortunately, crying jags are perfectly normal for some babies. For this one. I swear to you,'' she said when he opened his mouth to protest, ''the baby is absolutely top-rate, growing just the way he's supposed to. And for a woman who gave birth only a few weeks ago, and who's been through what she has, Luanne is doing quite well.''

''What about that thing that some women get after giving birth? Baby blues?''

Anka leaned her wrists on the table, her brows quirked. ''Alek, I know the signs of postpartum depression. Luanne isn't exhibiting them. Or at least, not enough to concern me.

We had a lovely conversation during the exam, she's obviously in love with her baby, interacting with him just the way she should be—"

"Then why hasn't she named him?"

"Well, this may be a long shot, but perhaps because she's yet to come up with the right name?" At his snort, Anka smiled. "She was even joking about that. Alek…relax. Luanne's all right. She's just *tired.* Which is why I did suggest she not attempt to make the trip back for another week, at least. By that time perhaps the baby's tummy will settle down enough for him to sleep for longer stretches at night. But there's honestly nothing to worry about. Her blood pressure's back to normal, her milk supply is good…I'm sure, once she's begun to get some sleep, she'll be fine. Now—"

The doctor rose from the table, fastening the single button on her boxy tweed blazer, then retrieving her bag from where she'd left it at her feet. "I really must run before my clinic patients decide to try their hands at treating each other!" Alek stood, as well, but just until a servant appeared to show Anka out. Then he dropped back into his chair, knuckling the crease set permanently between his brows.

He didn't care what anyone said—there had to be more going on here than a case of postnatal exhaustion. Yes, despite a chronic lack of sleep, Luanne was functioning exceptionally well—by the third day after the baby's birth, she'd resumed Chase's lessons; she came down for most of her meals; she'd taken his mother's car and gone into the village on her own several times, once even showing off the baby at the Children's Home. Nor was she cold to Alek as much as…careful. True, when he presented her with the occasional small gift, or offered to keep her company, or asked Gizela to prepare some dish that might alleviate some of Luanne's obvious homesickness, she seemed genuinely grateful. But her smile no longer reached her eyes, and that nearly broke his heart. Especially as he could pinpoint the exact moment the fight had gone out of her:

When he'd told her he loved her.

Slowly he banged his fist on the edge of the linen-draped table. How ironic that he would finally find someone to love—

and get up the nerve to actually admit it—only to have her look at him as if he'd cursed her instead.

He'd even cornered her one evening after the children were asleep, asked her point-blank, Was it the timing? Was it that she still didn't trust him? Was she still angry with him for not telling her what he'd known about Jeff's death?

Had her feelings changed?

She'd only shaken her head in answer to each question, her eyes brimming with tears, leaving him to believe that either he was losing his mind or he hadn't asked the right questions, both of which were distinct possibilities.

Their only actual argument had been over her plans to return to the States. Not the fact of her return—it was clear nothing would dissuade her from that, even though Chase was clearly none too pleased about it—but the logistics. When Luanne had insisted she and the children would make the trip on their own, Alek nearly blew a gasket, declaring there was no way he was allowing a woman who'd just given birth to make a long trip on her own with two children in tow, that either she let him escort her back in the same manner by which they'd arrived, or he wasn't letting her go.

The minute the words had left his mouth, he'd figured he was in for it. Nothing was more likely to get her back up than his pulling some macho number on her, never mind that her blasted stubbornness simply infuriated the life out of him. When, however, she quietly backed down instead of exploding, he found himself strongly tempted to shake her—

"Oh! You're still here."

Startled, he looked up at the sound of her voice. A short cashmere sweater in a soft-rose color and a pair of gray wool slacks accentuated her recently restored figure; a pair of silver combs—ones he'd given her—held her thick hair off her face. She certainly didn't look like a woman in the throes of depression; yet the hesitancy of her stance, the way she still seemed unsure of protocol, even after all these weeks, certainly spoke of her lingering lack of confidence.

He stood. Smiled. Found it damn near impossible not to be

irritated by this ridiculous formality buzzing between them. "I seem to be battling a touch of inertia this morning."

She actually smiled back before making her way to the buffet and pouring herself a glass of orange juice. She picked up a plate, began lifting the tops to the silver chafing dishes one by one.

"I'm afraid most of it's gone cold by now," he said.

"No, actually—" she tossed a quick smile over her shoulder "—everything seems to be fine. The baby's fallen asleep for a bit, so I figured I'd better grab a bite while I had the chance."

"I'm amazed you can even stand up at this point."

The hitch in her movements was subtle, but Alek caught it. "Yeah, well, you do what you have to do. I suppose I could've put the baby on a bottle and let Elena feed him once during the night—heaven knows, she's volunteered often enough—but I just feel better, nursing him. And nobody ever said bein' a mother was easy." The lid to the dish containing what was left of the bacon clattered when she replaced it, as if her hand was shaking. "Has...Chase already gone up for his riding lesson?"

"As far as I know, yes."

"Good—" she put one of Gizela's fresh-baked croissants on her plate, carried her food to the table "—because I need to talk to you without old big ears hangin' around."

Instantly on alert, Alek waited to sit back down until she came to the table, taking the place directly to his right. He poured himself a third cup of coffee, which he drank in nervous anticipation while she delicately shoveled in her breakfast for at least a full minute. Then, almost casually between bites of scrambled egg, she said, "I've decided to let Chase stay."

Alek nearly choked on his coffee. "*What?* Why?"

She took a sip of her juice, then shifted her suddenly earnest gaze to his. "Because it's what *he* wants. Because takin' him away would be like I was tryin' to punish you—and him—when I've got no good reason for doing either. He's happy here. He's blossoming. And he's healing. He wants to go to school here, with Zoltan and some of the other village children he's met. And I finally realized that forcing him to go back with me would only make both of us miserable in the long run.'' She looked away. ''Besides…he's yours, Alek. He's a prince. He belongs here.''

Stunned, Alek reached for Luanne's hand. ''But he's yours, too, *mila*—''

''I've had him for ten years already. Seems to me y'all have a lot of catching up to do.''

Alek let go of her hand to collapse back in his chair. ''And you seem to have forgotten my promise, that I would not take him away from you—''

''And if you'd've tried to,'' she said with a little smile, ''I would've fought you tooth and toenail, and you know it.'' Then she frowned. ''Trust me, Alek—if you'd've been a jerk, we wouldn't be having this conversation. Oh, don't sit there lookin' so shocked, for heaven's sake!'' She got up to pour herself some more juice. ''This is what's best for everyone—''

''Even for you?''

She stilled, her back to him. ''Hangin' on to someone you love is the surest way I know to kill that love. The only way I'm gonna be able to keep Chase is to let him go.''

''But you're still going back?''

After a moment she turned. ''I have to, Alek. I've told you—I don't belong here. Not permanently. That business with Marie-Hélène proved that—''

''You don't mean to tell me you're still upset over a thoughtless remark made by some brainless, social-climbing twit?''

Her smile was sad. ''And you expect me to believe that her attitude is unique? For crying out loud—I couldn't even make the grade with the women in that fancy country club Jeff joined when we moved to Dallas. And, okay, so I'm learnin' how to dress and act and all, but that doesn't change who I am. And no amount of designer clothes or etiquette lessons ever will, because people will always know where I came from. I'd always feel like I was pretending. And I've been that route once, remember?''

He got up, swallowing down his anger as he approached her. ''And the fact that I love you, that I've never loved another woman, means nothing?''

He'd come close enough for her to cradle his cheek in her

palm. "You really are a dumb cluck, aren't you?" she whispered. "Your love means everything to me. But that's one gift I can't accept, no matter how much I want to."

"Luanne—"

"And I'm leavin' tomorrow afternoon. The baby and I, by ourselves, so just shut your mouth and forget whatever it was you were going to say. I've already made all the reservations, so unless you're of a mind to physically prevent my going, there's not a blamed thing you can do."

"But I thought Dr. Palachek said—"

"She advised me to stay another week, I know. But I doubt I'm gonna feel any more rested by then. If anything, I'll just be more stressed out." She slipped her hand out from under his and placed it on his chest. "I love you, Alek, with all my heart and soul. I always have, from the moment I laid eyes on you in Ed's, and I always will. Now, if you love me, you'll let *me* go."

Alek searched Luanne's eyes for even a hint at some chink in her resistance, only to suddenly realize it wasn't simple recalcitrance that was motivating her, no matter how much it would appear so on the surface. The woman was genuinely terrified of staying, even to the point of being willing to leave her firstborn behind.

He folded his fingers around her hand and played his last card. "Then, since you're letting Chase stay, I have little choice but to make an official announcement about his identity."

She went rigid, then jerked her hand away. "That's blackmail."

"No, *mila*—it's a matter of exigency. I'm not trying to force your hand, Luanne, believe me. But I can't put this off much longer. Even Tomas has said there is talk, that people are noticing the resemblance. Every day I wait, the more I run the risk of losing my country's trust. Carpathians have had a lot of experience in forgiving their monarchy's foibles, as long as we're honest. Heaven knows, I would prefer you to be there when I make the announcement. But you know that, since I've made it perfectly clear I want us to be a family. I'm sorry, I truly am…but I'm not the one putting up obstacles."

Hurt flashed in her eyes for a moment or two before she turned sharply and left.

"And you let her walk away."

Alek and his grandmother were in his study, ostensibly discussing his imminent trip to Stolvia the following day to witness—finally—the signing of that long-awaited peace treaty. However, at the moment, Luanne and her dual announcements that morning were vying for Alek's attention far more than politics.

He allowed a rueful grin for the princess. "It seemed the wisest course of action at the time."

"As will be your letting her leave tomorrow, I suppose?"

"Not unless some hitherto unseen brilliant plan comes to me in the middle of the night. Besides, weren't you the one who said I needed to be willing to give Luanne her head in this?"

Seated in one of the wing chairs, Ivana snorted, then let out a sigh. One of the dogs whined softly, laid her head atop the princess's wool-skirted lap. "And what was Chase's reaction to her decision?"

"Mixed, to say the least." His son had come to him, bewildered and upset, after Luanne told him of her plans. Alek had assured the child that he was free to go back with Luanne or stay in Carpathia, whatever he wished, but the boy was clearly torn. Finally it was decided he would stay for a week; if at the end of that time he wanted to be with his mother, Alek would be happy to escort him back to the States....

"Yes, I imagine so," the princess said with a frown, then stood up. "Perhaps I should have a little talk with her—"

"And perhaps you should stay out of it."

Both brows shot up at that. "I just thought—"

"I know what you thought. And I appreciate your concern. But this is between Luanne and me. Or, perhaps it would be better put, between Luanne and Luanne. And if I don't love her enough to give her the freedom to work out whatever this is on her own, then my love is worthless, isn't it?"

Unfortunately, while his head may have come to grips with that sentiment, his emotions had other ideas, which meant the rest of the day was shot as far as getting any actual work done was concerned. And it took him damn near forever to fall asleep, only to be awakened at some ungodly hour—close to 2:00 a.m., if his blurred vision could be believed—by his sister, who had apparently forgotten all about things like time zones in her zeal to share the news that the "flu" she'd thought she'd had was the variety that lasted nine months.

Sophie's glee was almost too much to bear, even though Alek was truly thrilled for her. He knew, before she'd met Steven, she'd just about given up on the idea of ever falling in love, of having children with a man who'd dote on her the way Steven obviously did. But his own cock-up with Luanne rather tainted his ability to feel too rah-rah for his sister. Especially at 2:00 a.m. He hoped, however, his less-than-enthusiastic response hadn't been too obvious, and he breathed a tremendous sigh of relief when she ended the call, citing the need to inform basically half the free world.

So now Alek was awake, edgy—no, that was far too mild a word: ready to climb the bloody walls was far more accurate a description—and mildly hungry. Which prompted him to throw on a robe over his pajama bottoms and strike out for the kitchen, only to be stopped dead in his tracks outside Luanne's door by the sound of the baby screaming his bloody head off.

Chapter 14

Elena had the night off, Alek realized after a moment, helping out her youngest daughter, who was due to give birth herself within the month. And Chase had been moved into another room a bit farther down the hall so the baby's crying wouldn't keep him awake at night. Which meant Luanne was alone.

And probably dead on her feet.

And there was no way Alek could simply go on as if this were none of his concern.

He knocked softly at first, then more insistently, until it finally dawned on him that she couldn't hear it. So he carefully tried the doorknob, found it unlocked and stepped into the room.

Where the howling was ten times louder.

The only light came from a small porcelain lamp on the end table by the love seat. Standing barefoot in a pair of loose flannel pajamas, her hair in a wild tangle around her shoulders, Luanne faced away from him, bouncing and jiggling the shrieking, red-faced infant with a kind of desperateness that clearly betrayed her exhaustion. He knew calling her name was pointless....

She turned, letting out a shriek that even surpassed her son's. "What are you—?"

Alek pointed to the crying baby, then to his ears, before reaching out and attempting to pry the infant from what he quickly discovered was an amazingly strong grasp. She shook her head, shouted, "Go on back to bed. You've got that signing tomorrow. Besides, this isn't your concern."

To which, since only a blind man would have missed the tears hovering on her lower lashes, he shouted back, "Anything that goes on in this palace is my concern. Give him to me." When she opened her mouth to say...whatever, Alek arranged his features into his fiercest expression and said, "Now."

They engaged in a bit of a Mexican standoff for a second or two, but in the end she gave up the baby, as well as the tears, which were accompanied by a garbled explanation about how she'd fed him and changed him and burped him and if Chase'd been like that, she'd've thought a lot harder about ever having another one.

The baby nestled on his shoulder on top of a soft receiving blanket, Alek shooed Luanne off to the bedroom. The minute he heard her bedroom door click shut, he snatched another baby blanket off the arm of the love seat and tucked it around the tiny shoulders.

"All right, Mr. Baby Man—let's say you and I go raid Gizela's pantry, huh?"

An hour later Alek was definitely ready to admit that, as far as fun activities went, this ranked rather low on the list. His ears were ringing, his shoulder was soaked with baby slobber, and his back was killing him from pacing untold miles of palace corridor. A few times the baby had actually gone quiet, deluding Alek into thinking he could, perhaps, sit down for a minute.

Wrong.

So they'd walked.

And walked.

And walked.

And Alek found himself wondering several things near the

end of that hour, not the least of which was how he could be so tired when this tiny person who weighed about as much as a good-sized chicken could still be going strong. For another, he wondered how on earth Luanne thought she was going to manage this on her own, night after night. But the thing he most wondered about was why, instead of feeling irritated or fried or ready to move someplace that outlawed children under the age of six, he should instead feel so damn good. As though everything in his life had been leading up to doing just this.

Except he decided he was far too tired to think about that right—

Wait—had his ears stopped ringing, or had he simply gone deaf?

He craned his neck to peer into the baby's face.

The baby's *sleeping* face. And from what he could tell, the kid was down for the count.

Alek zipped back to Luanne's suite, only to realize the only place to put the baby down was his bassinet, which was in Luanne's bedroom.

He carefully opened the door: she'd neglected to draw the draperies; moonlight spilled through the windows, across the double bed. The comforter pulled up to her shoulders in the chilled room, she lay on the side farthest from the bassinet— but closest to the door, as if she'd only made it that far before she passed out—her hand tucked underneath her cheek, her lips parted slightly. And absolutely dead to the world.

The moonlight was gentle; the barrage of emotions that now assaulted him, anything but. Dear God, Alek thought as he nuzzled the downy head underneath his chin, what this woman had endured at the hands of most of the males in her life: her father, Alek, Jeff…even this latest addition who seemed deter-mined to keep her from ever getting a decent night's sleep. She deserved more than constantly being left with some guy's screw-up to fix.

She deserved to understand that she was worth more than that.

Luanne shifted in her sleep; holding what little breath he had left, Alek quickly laid the baby on his back in the bassinet, as he'd seen Luanne do, covering him with a couple of soft blankets. Then he'd fully intended to leave. He had. He truly hadn't meant to sit on the edge of Luanne's bed, but his legs simply gave out on him. He really hadn't intended to lie down. Or shut his eyes, just for a minute, just until his back quit complaining quite so vigorously....

Alek awoke with a start, his heart thumping against his ribs. Totally disoriented, he stared wildly into the soft darkness until the baby's soft snuffles clued him in as to his whereabouts. The clock on the nightstand glared at him: 3:45. Which meant he'd only dozed off for a half hour or so. But in that half hour, he'd somehow managed to get underneath the covers.

Next to Luanne.

Right next to Luanne.

Who was lying there watching him, her eyes wide and curious, her breathing oddly uneven.

Temptation *whoomphed* through his bloodstream.

But before he could gather enough wits to make his apologies and get the hell out of there, Luanne reached over and traced one finger down his cheek. And the next thing he knew, their mouths were touching and she was touching and *he* was touching and buttons were being undone and pajama tops were being flung, and he knew this was wrong, knew he'd regret it, knew this might be his only shot at swaying the court.

Need flared inside him, so fierce and primitive it sucked him dry. He wanted to possess this woman, mark her as his, mate with her and tuck her away somewhere where he could guard and protect her and prevent anything bad from ever happening to her, ever again.

Nothing like slipping a few thousand rungs down the evolutionary ladder.

Her nursing bra, one he'd bought for her, was strictly utilitarian—white, cotton, full cut. About as unsexy as an undergarment could get. Which of course accounted for the sophomoric groan that rumbled from his throat at the sight of it. Although, to be honest, at this point he'd probably be turned on by a feed sack, as long as Luanne was inside it.

He caught her searching gaze in his, met her halfway for another kiss that set his hormones tripping and sliding and careening totally out of control. Limbs tangled with limbs, tongues with tongues, as their heartbeats collided in an out-of-sync tango. And if this had been only about sex, he would have vaulted from the bed the instant he'd realized he was in it.

And if he knew what this *was* about, he'd feel a lot more secure than he did at the moment. Way, way deep in the furthermost recesses of his brain, the thought niggled that perhaps he should make sure he understood exactly what was going on here, what she expected, what she wanted, what she didn't want—

Like hell.

Through the bra, he cuddled one breast. Something stiff crackled beneath his palm.

"Nursing pad," she whispered against his mouth. He could feel the heat of her blush against his jaw. "I might leak."

He reached around, unhooked the bra, practically ripped it off of her. Her nipples, flattened by the pads, slowly distended like night-blooming flowers. "I'll take that chance," he muttered, drawing her to him to seek out one of those sweet, hard nipples with his mouth. She sighed, groaned, arched…then suddenly yanked away from him with a little cry, grabbing blindly for the tissue box on the night stand. Sitting up, she hunched over, pressing wadded tissues to both breasts. "I think I got you."

Alek slicked moisture from his chest. "At least this won't draw ants. Will it?"

A short, startled laugh bubbled up from her throat, only to quickly peter out. He heard her ball up the damp tissues, toss them into the wastebasket by the bed, then heave a sigh so loud, he half expected the baby to wake up.

"Should I go?" he asked softly.

"Probably." She hitched the covers up over her breasts. "But I don't want you to. And what kind of sense does that make?"

A glimmer of hope elbowed its way through desire so strong, it was making him dizzy. Alek sat up, curved his torso up against her bare, warm back. "You want to make sense?" He swept back her hair, pressed a kiss on her right shoulder. Claimed one breast underneath the covers. It wasn't leaking anymore, but it was still full of milk, hot and heavy in his hands. "Or make love?"

Several moments passed. "It may not exactly be a whole lot of fun for you, you know. You'd have to be…careful."

He skimmed his fingertips down the side of her breast, whispered them across the taut, damp nipple. "Like this?"

She made a little gasping sound that shot straight to his groin.

"A-and the b-baby might wake up."

His heart swelling right along with other things, Alek shifted behind her to give the other breast equal time. "I know that."

Luanne reached up, caught his wrists. "And I'm still leaving tomorrow."

Alek dropped his hands to circle her waist, pull her nearer. "I know that, too."

A twist of her head snapped her gaze to his. "But you're hoping I'll change my mind."

"I won't lie and say I'm not."

"Don't—"

"Sh, sh, sh…" He slowly winnowed the fingers of one hand through her mussed hair, brought his mouth down on hers, his heart cramping at her sweetness, her softness. Then he broke the kiss, tucking her against his chest. "Eleven years ago you asked for one night. Now you can return the favor."

A sudden breeze outside sent a shower of leaves skittering across the windowpanes. "So, do you have any, um…?"

He smiled. "I'll be right back."

He wasn't gone but two minutes, which was more than enough time for a person to come to her senses if she had a mind to. Which apparently Luanne didn't. Well, honestly, you'd've thought she'd've at least made *some* progress during the last decade. Eleven years ago she'd just wanted the one time. Now she just wanted a *last* time. With the same man, no less. Another hour, maybe, of magic, to hold close to her heart, along with the knowledge that she could've been a princess.

Once upon a time.

Alek lay down beside her, scooping her into his arms. And, oh, he was so warm and strong and loving, smelling faintly of his cologne and baby spit…she snuggled as close as she could to his bare chest, as if doing so would somehow squeeze out the cramp in her heart. Oh, Lord, it was going to hurt tomorrow, leaving Alek, leaving Chase, leaving half her heart behind in a country that felt a lot more like home than she dared let on.

But this was not the time for going over her reasons for leaving. Not when the only man she'd ever loved from the depths of her soul was doing everything he could to convince her she should stay.

Three weeks after giving birth was awfully early to be doing what she was about to do. But since, well, she couldn't exactly come right out and ask Dr. Palachek about it, she'd read up some, and decided, if things didn't get too wild, she'd be okay. But this wasn't about having great sex, anyway. It was about something far more precious than that. And she could tell, from the soft fire in Alek's eyes, from his whisper-soft touches, from the way he was taking his time reacquainting himself with a body that had undergone a few changes since he'd last done the things he was now doing, that he felt the same way.

And when, after enough slow, sweet loving to ensure she was as ready as she was ever going to be, Alek carefully entered her, she bit back tears, not from physical pain—although it did hurt, some—but from the blinding realization that only once before had this act felt right.

And that all the times between, with Jeff, had been a lie.

"Luanne, love—" Alek skimmed a knuckle down her cheek, a crease of concern carved between his brows. "I'm hurting you—"

"No, no," she said, shaking her head against the pillow. "I'm fine, I swear—"

"If you're sure—"

"Yes!" *No.*

She clutched his arms as he braced himself above her, shaking with restraint. A single bead of sweat, then another, trickled down his iron-set jaw to land between her tingling breasts. He moved with such exquisite control inside her, she thought she'd die from the sheer pleasure of it, as well as from the bittersweet irony of *still* not being able to fully reciprocate a man's love.

Even though she would love this man, with everything she had in her, until the day she died.

Sensation arced and snapped along her nerve endings, irradiating her emotions until they almost ignited inside her. She wanted to cry and cry out, both, from the agony, the sweetness, the incredible power...the incredible sense of hopelessness. A moan spun from her throat as Alek coaxed her higher, sharper, laving her swollen, oh-so-sensitive breasts...

She tensed...teetered...then fell apart on a long, shuddering sigh that left her feeling completely...empty.

And unbelievably stupid.

A few feet away the baby stirred, whimpered, annihilating what little was left of the afterglow. Almost panicked, Luanne scrambled out from underneath Alek, grabbing for her bra and pajamas, gulping in both oxygen and whatever molecules of reason she could glean from the hormone-charged atmosphere.

"Let me change him—"

"No!" She hadn't meant to bite Alek's head off, but that's what getting battered by your emotions will do to a person. She shoved her ratted hair behind one ear, checked the baby's diaper. He seemed dry enough to get by without changing him until he'd fed—

Her hands were shaking so hard, she could barely get the baby's sleeper snapped back up. Tears bit at her eyes; she wanted Alek gone, wanted to *be* gone, wanted to take back the night and her idiotic, irresponsible actions.

"Luanne?"

She could feel his anger vibrating clear across the room. She whipped around, clinging to the baby, for some reason just now realizing only one of them had reached fulfillment and it hadn't been Alek. Inside her head, her blood pulsed; her mouth felt sand-dry when she tried to swallow. "I'm sorry," she said, heading for the armchair where she usually nursed the baby, who was beginning to fret for real by now. "I didn't mean to leave you in the dust."

The bedside lamp clicked on, making her blink. "If by that you mean I didn't finish...no. You were obviously too tender for that."

Her eyes shot to Alek as she fumbled getting her bra undone, the baby to her breast. Even though he'd known that would be the last time they'd be together, he'd put her need ahead of his own....

He'd pulled on his pajama bottoms and was standing by the bed, his hands braced on his hips. "Damn it, Luanne," he said quietly. "Why the hell do you keep slamming the door in my face?"

The baby let out a squeal. Tears swimming in her eyes, Luanne looked down, readjusted baby and breast.

"Tonight was a mistake—"

"For whom?"

"For both of us."

"The hell it was."

She adjusted the blanket more snugly around the baby's shoulders. "For me, then."

The floor creaked softly under the weight of Alek's footsteps as he covered the few feet between them, crouched down in front of her where she couldn't avoid his eyes. Those lambent, quicksilver eyes, as revealing as moonlight.

"Whatever I have, whatever I am, is yours, *mila.* You know that. But you are, without a doubt, the most stubborn woman I have ever met. Like the Stolvians who'd bought into their opposing mind-sets for so long, they simply couldn't see any other way to look at their problems—"

"It's not the same thing—"

"Isn't it? I think you've spent so many years convincing yourself of all the reasons why it was just as well I walked away that night that you simply cannot conceive of things working out between us. Even though we have a son. Even though I have done everything in my power to show you that

I'm not the man who breezed through Silver Springs eleven years ago, that I am worthy of you—''

Her breath left her lungs in a rush. "Oh, Alek—no, no. This has nothing to do with you."

"Then what, damn it? Because you don't 'fit in'? And just how much did you ever really fit in in Sandy Springs? Did you ever ask yourself why you chose me to be your first lover when, by your own admission, there were any number of local boys more than willing to do the honors? How many people there knew you loved classical music or that you'd read half the books ever written or that you spoke fluent French? *Why* were you so lonely that night, Luanne?"

Except for a slight trembling she could not control, she sat stock-still, simply staring at him.

"Or is it because of Jeff?" Alek now asked, more gently, one hand stroking her wrist as she held on to the baby as if afraid she might drop him. "Because of his...manipulation of events?"

Slowly she shook her head. "It's not because of Jeff, either," she whispered, then sucked in a rattling breath. She shut her eyes, feeling the baby pull at her breast as feelings she couldn't handle just then tugged at her heart. "Alek...from the bottom of my heart, I am sorry for putting you through all this. And I know I'm not making sense, at least not to anyone but me, and I wouldn't be offended if you ended up hating me, but please...I really need you to leave right now."

After what seemed like half a lifetime, Alek rose up enough to kiss her on the forehead, stroke a tear from her cheek. "I'm leaving early in the morning, and I doubt I'll be back before dinnertime. When does your plane leave?"

"At three."

Which meant this was goodbye. After another long moment, Alek stood, letting out a long sigh. "God knows, I may not understand you, *mila*. But I would never hate you. Especially as you seem to be doing a bang-up job of that all by yourself."

Chapter 15

"No, Elena—don't bother packing the maternity clothes."

From the other side of the bed, the maid frowned. Well, frowned harder, since her face had had more folds in it than a Shar-Pei's all morning. "Madam is young, yet. You will have more babies, yes?"

This was one discussion Luanne was avoiding at all costs, especially considering the tattered condition of her heart. But as far as the clothes went, she felt like she'd emerged from some kind of fashion chrysalis; the items she'd brought with her simply no longer "fit," in more ways than one. "Since I don't have a crystal ball, I have no idea. But in any case, I won't be needing those. In fact, do y'all have a charity or something that gives away used clothes?"

"Well, yes, we do, but—"

"Good. Then that's settled." She smacked her hands together, trying to look far more in command—not to mention awake—than she felt. Especially when she caught Chase's accusing expression as he slouched in the armchair across the room, the pup strung across his knees. He'd given up the baggy jeans in favor of more fitted ones, worn with a tailored shirt, a nice V-necked sweater. Still casual, but definitely the clothes of an emerging prince.

"Elena," she said quietly, "would you mind leaving Chase and me alone for a little while?"

"*Da,* madam. Of course."

After the maid left, Luanne sat on the edge of the bed in front of her son, rubbing her palms over her velour-covered knees. The oversize shirt and matching leggings would travel well….

Oh, for pity's sake. Like she cared two hoots about her wardrobe when she'd gone and hurt just about everybody she cared about.

"I still don't understand why you have to leave," Chase said.

And if her heart survived this, it could survive just about anything. "The same reason why you feel you have to stay, sugar."

But her conviction seemed shakier than it had before last night. Before she'd let Alek inside her. Not just physically, although that wasn't helping her ambivalence any, but *really* inside her, where the truth had been cringing in a corner for about a million years. Because of what he'd said? About her not fitting in even in Texas?

He'd hit the nail right square on the head.

And there was something to be said—all right, a lot to be said—for a man who cared enough to see what a person couldn't see for herself, who cared enough to make good-and-sure she did see it.

If she really didn't belong, how come she was already missing it? How come the thought of never tussling with Elena or having another lesson with the princess or driving through the countryside or paying another visit to the Children's Home was making her feel so blamed wretched?

And if she didn't belong with Alek, why was the idea of walking away from him making her ill?

Maybe she did hate herself, like Alek had said. But then, maybe she had a good reason to.

She got up, zipped up her last bag, feeling her son's gaze

burning into her back. "You know, you can come with me. It wouldn't take but a couple minutes to pack—"

"I'm sorry, Mama. I can't."

Pride burst through the sorrow at his quiet conviction, a quality that would come in real handy when Chase became Carpathia's ruler himself one day. Luanne turned, felt her face burn with the effort not to cry. "Then I'll come back with the baby at Christmas, if you want to spend it here. I promise. But I guess we each have to do what's best for us, don't we?"

The glare in Chase's eyes suddenly changed to something that looked suspiciously like pity, before he knocked the pup off his lap in his hurry to leave.

She needed air. Sky. Answers. Her chest feeling like it was about to cave in completely, she yanked open the French doors leading from her bedroom, practically hurtling herself out onto the balcony and into the blindingly brilliant fall day. And there, beyond the pristine orderliness of the browning palace gardens, the lush evergreen forests, the soft-edged smokiness of the mountains, blazed her sky—cloudless, pure, reassuring. A sky that would always be the same, no matter where she was. A frigid breeze bit through her clothes, plucked mercilessly at her hair, as she grasped the ice-cold stone railing and pleaded, begged to be shown what to do....

Only, the answer she got didn't bring her any peace. Not at all.

"Madam?"

She swiped at the tears just cresting on her lower lashes, turned around.

"Yes, Elena?"

"Gregori says to tell you, the limo will be ready in fifteen minutes." The kindly face crumpled into a frown. "Madam is...all right?"

"Yes, Elena. It's just...the cold air in my eyes, is all. Would you mind bringing the baby to me so I can feed him before we leave?"

Tugging his tie loose upon his return to the palace late that afternoon, Alek knocked on the open door to Tomas's small office, adjacent to Alek's study. His aide's head snapped up; a broad smile encompassed his features as he stood, came out from behind his desk.

"Welcome back, sir. All went well, I take it?"

"Very well, thank you, Tomas. I can only trust the treaty holds."

"I'm sure it will, sir." The grin widened. "Your Highness made the news, did you know? The young prince was nearly beside himself."

Alek gave a weary smile. "I gathered as much, considering the number of reporters and news cameras present." He stifled a yawn. "Mrs. Henderson...got off all right, I suppose?"

The young man scooted back behind his desk, busying himself with some papers or other. Although there was nothing one could call blatantly disrespectful about his refusal to look at Alek directly, his pique was unmistakable. "Yes, sir. Right on time."

With that, the last shreds dissolved of what had been a fragile hope, at best. "The decision to leave was completely hers, Tomas."

After a moment Tomas lifted his eyes. "Yes, sir. Of course."

Alek tugged his tie out from his collar, unfastened his top shirt button. "And...my son? Do you know where he is?"

"In the media room, I believe. Would you like me to send him up to see you on my way out?"

"Yes, thank you, Tomas. I would like that. I'll be in my study."

"Very good, sir." The young man reached into a closet to retrieve a winter jacket, slipped it on. "I'll just be going, then, if that's all right?"

"Of course. Good night, Tomas."

"Good night, sir."

On a gale of a sigh, Alek wandered into his study, shrugging out of his suit jacket, then tossing it over the back of his desk chair before sinking into it. His head propped in his hand, he swiveled around to his great-grandfather's portrait.

"Now why is it," he asked the portrait, his knuckles grinding into his cheek, "that my first major political accomplishment should leave me feeling so bloody empty?"

As if he didn't know the answer to that. And it wasn't that he felt no pride at all in what he'd brought about in Stolvia. The swarm of Stolvian citizens who'd cheered his arrival this morning was gratifying, to say the least. Not to mention the number of congratulatory faxes awaiting him on his blotter.

But still.

He allowed a rueful chuckle. Any minute now he was going to break into a soulful rendition of "I've Grown Accustomed to Her Face."

And her laugh and her smile and her atrocious Texas twang, and…

He shut his eyes against the stab of loss, just as he heard the door open behind him. Forcing a smile to his face for his son's sake, he swung around.

And froze.

"Aren't…you supposed to be somewhere over England, right about now?" he asked when he finally found his voice.

Her lips tilted in a half smile, Luanne shut the door, leaned against it. "Uh-huh. In fact, I even got all the way to the airport…"

Slowly, so she wouldn't bolt, Alek rose from his chair, started around the desk, fusing her gaze in his. "And…?"

"No, don't…" Tears glimmered in her eyes "Don't come any closer. Not yet."

Alek came to a dead halt, his heart ramming against his ribs. *Just…play along. After all, she came back, didn't she?* "All right."

"Oh, Alek," she whispered, a single tear streaking down her cheek. "I don't want to leave you."

"Then…don't."

Her only reply was a shuddering breath, before finally letting go of the doorknob to walk over to the portrait, her arms knotted over her ribs. He saw her swipe at the stray tear. "I…never got around to asking you who this is."

"My great-grandfather. Prince Hans-Fredrik."

"The one who turned a blind eye to your grandmother's helpin' the Jews?"

"The very same."

She stared at the portrait for several more seconds, then said, "What you said last night, about my not really fittin' in back home? Well, you're right. I might not've ever realized it before, but it's true. That doesn't mean I feel real comfortable about livin' in a palace, or dealing with the Marie-Hélènes of the world, but there really is nothin' for me back there. Especially if Chase is gonna stay here."

She turned, her eyes huge. Hopeful. "And then there's you. The way I love you. I mean, we're talkin' soul-deep, one-and-only kind of love here. And heaven knows, I do want to finish up raising Chase with you. So on the surface, there are a thousand good reasons for taking you up on your offer of marriage. Solid, practical reasons, besides all these emotional ones. But..."

Her gaze snapped back to the portrait, as frustration lanced her words. "But, *every...single...time* I thought I'd made what seemed like the most practical decision, it's ended up backfiring on me somehow. I mean, I certainly thought I was doing the right thing by marrying Jeff, and look what happened. So I can't help but think, what if I make another mistake? What if I've been deluding myself all these years, that there *aren't* any real answers? Or maybe I just don't know how to listen. What if I end up hurting even more people along the way, just like I've always done?"

Alek's heart nearly stopped beating, even as the last pieces fell into place like the tumblers in a combination lock. "Don't tell me you still believe you caused Jeff's death?"

"I never should've married him, that's for sure."

Alek managed, just barely, to tamp down his anger. "So you're saying...you're *afraid* to marry me? Because you might screw up again?"

After a long moment, she nodded.

"And if you walk away," he said quietly to her back, "Jeff wins."

Her eyes flashed to his. "What?"

"I don't know why it took me so long to figure this out," he muttered to himself, then said to Luanne on a frantic, crazed half-laugh, "Don't you see? Jeff never intended for us to get together. He counted on exactly what's happening—that one or the other of us wouldn't be able to get past the guilt."

"Oh, Alek...don't be ridiculous—"

"Jeff Henderson was a driven man, Luanne. Which is what made him so formidable on the track, but... Bloody hell—I saw it in his eyes, that night at Ed's...Luanne!" He closed the distance between them in two strides, clasping her shoulders hard enough to shake her, to shake loose the last remnants of her resistance. "Listen to me—that promise that Jeff had extracted from you, as a condition of the marriage, that the real father of the child never be involved? That was his method of *controlling* you. Of getting the one thing he wanted more than anything in the world—you, *mila.* Yes, it was," he said when she shook her head, her mouth open in protest. "When you'd turned up pregnant, he saw an opportunity he wasn't about to let slip through his fingers. Except, even though you kept your part of the bargain, once Jeff discovered I was Chase's father, he felt that control slipping away. So he decided to...remove himself. An almost noble gesture, in a macabre sort of way. Except there's the matter of that letter. Which, had he just sent on to me, might have still smacked of unselfishness. But that wasn't enough, was it? Oh, no, he has to send one to you, as well. Dear God, Luanne...even from the grave, he didn't want to let you go. Granted, he took a risk, but he correctly surmised your discovery would drive a wedge between us. Only he didn't count on one very important thing."

Luanne had kept her gaze steady throughout Alek's tirade, even though her voice was now anything but. "And wh-what was that?"

"That I'm more driven than he is."

Then Alek waited, breath held, for her reaction. For the longest time there didn't seem to be one. And eventually she turned back to the portrait.

But she leaned against him, laying her hands on top of his arms when he encircled her waist from behind.

Which is when he noticed she'd removed her wedding rings.

"You've never made a mistake," he said gently, his breath stirring her hair. "If anyone's culpable here, it's I. I was the one who walked out on you, because I was so afraid. I threw the stone into the pond that caused the ripples. Not you."

Still nothing. So he went on. "And, yes, I'll admit my initial reasons for contacting you had more to do with responsibility and guilt than love, both because I assumed you'd been in love with Jeff and because I was still afraid. Of loving. Of losing. Of making a bloody fool of myself. Then I woke up and realized I was about to throw away a second precious chance. And *that* would have haunted me to my grave." He enfolded her, possessed her, whispered, "Marry me, *mila*. Let me spend my life proving to you that our love isn't, and never was, a mistake."

An eternity passed before Luanne finally turned, silently snuggling into his arms. And Alek simply held her, rocked her, planting kisses in her hair until she murmured against his chest, "It really wasn't my fault, was it?"

"No, *mila*. It wasn't. Jeff's suicide had nothing to do with you."

She lifted her face to his then, sighing softly when Alek kissed her. Then she pulled away, crossing to his desk, one arm around her middle. She picked up one of the faxes, smiled at it, then laid it carefully back on the pile.

"But I still have to go back to Texas."

Alek thought he might explode from frustration. "Haven't you heard a single bloody word I said?"

But she'd twisted back around, smiling. "To pack, you ninny. Sell off my furniture. I'll be back in two weeks. I swear."

It took a second or two for her words to register; then he held out his hand.

And with a smile she crossed to him and took it.

"A week," he said.

"Ten days."

"That seems like forever."

"But then we'll *have* forever, won't we?"

"Is that a *yes*?"

Her smile was soft. Precious. "Any other answer just wouldn't make sense, now would it, sugar?"

Alek bent to kiss her again, but she pressed her hands to his chest, letting out a little gasp. "I just thought of a name for the baby! How about...Skye?"

"Hmm..." Alek said with a teasing frown. "I don't know...do we really want a kid who thinks he has all the answers?" He laughed when she swatted him, only to capture her smile in a slow, sweet kiss. "Welcome home, Princess Luanne."

She looped her hands around his neck and grinned. "You know, I think I could get real used to that."

Epilogue

"Mama! How do I look?"

Luanne handed Skye to Elena, who whisked him off to the nursery until after the telecast, then grinned down at her antsy son. No suit, Alek had insisted. "My countrymen will want to know their future monarch is more like one of them...." Which meant schoolboy duds—a navy sweater over a white shirt, tan cords. And Alek's own barber had tamed—somewhat—Chase's wild hair. But nothing could tame the combined sparks of excitement and apprehension in the boy's bright-blue eyes.

"You look so handsome, I can hardly stand it," Luanne said, just managing not to muss up his hair all over again. Not to mention blubber like a fool.

"Chase?" They both turned as Alek strode into the room, still adjusting his tie as he dodged the maze of cables and TV lights and what all to reach them. He laid a hand on his son's shoulder, his expression concerned. "Are you really ready for this? I mean, if you're not—"

"I'm fine, Pop. I swear."

Luanne's heart swelled at the way Alek's expression went all soft and mushy. They'd debated, all three of them, about what Chase would call Alek, since "Daddy" didn't cut it in this part of the world. Finally it was Elena who suggested he simply call his father "Papa," like most children did over here. Chase compromised with "Pop."

She'd put off going back to Texas, partly because Alek wanted to get this announcement out of the way first and partly because, well, she couldn't bring herself to leave just yet. Of course, Odella—who'd just about bust a gut when Luanne called her with the news—said, y'know, it really was no big deal to call someone to pack up the books and send them on to Luanne…or maybe she could just donate all the stuff to the Sandy Springs library, the furniture to the local Women's and Children's shelter….

Luanne allowed as how maybe she just might do that.

"And you?" Alek now asked softly. "Are you ready?"

She reached up, ostensibly to flick something off his Italian-suited shoulder, but mainly because she just wanted to touch him. "No more secrets," she said with a smile, which earned her a quick kiss. Then, his arm protectively bracketing his son's shoulders, Alek guided Chase over to the director for last-minute directions before the camera started rolling. And Luanne stood there, her arms clamped over her middle, her eyes burning, hardly daring to believe that so much goodness could possibly happen to one person in a single lifetime.

Had all their problems vanished, just like that? Not by a long shot. Alek and Chase were getting along great, true, but that didn't mean they didn't all still have a lot to deal with concerning Jeff's death. And Luanne didn't fool herself for a minute that her agreeing to marry Alek didn't mean everybody was gonna accept her as a princess.

But she also had no doubt in the least that she'd made the right decision. Not necessarily the *practical* one—there was nothin' practical about a country girl becomin' a princess—but the *right* one. All she had to do was catch the look in Alek's eyes—just like he was doing right now—and a good nine-tenths of the fear flew right on out the window. And the other tenth…well, she figured she had the next sixty years or so to work on that.

The director asked Alek to take his seat behind his desk so they could adjust the light settings. In less than ten minutes her little boy was gonna be introduced to Carpathia as their heir apparent.

Luanne covered her mouth with her hand as she gawked at her handsome prince, a man with the courage to tell the world he made a mistake…and then the courage to stick around and rectify it.

A man who understood the difference between loving someone and wanting to control them.

"Okay, everybody," the director shouted. "We're ready in five…four…three…two…and—"

The elder princess linked her arm through Luanne's just as she caught Alek's wink, a split second before he smiled into the camera. "Good evening, my fellow Carpathians. It is with the greatest humility and joy, both, that I come before you tonight…"

Luanne smiled, as well. After all, who needed magic when reality was this dang wonderful?

* * * * *